NEW 04/16

TRACKING THE BEAST

A STEVE MARTINEZ MYSTERY

TRACKING THE BEAST

HENRY KISOR

FIVE STAR
A part of Gale, Cengage Learning

GALE
CENGAGE Learning®

Farmington Hills, Mich • San Francisco • New York • Waterville, Maine
Meriden, Conn • Mason, Ohio • Chicago

LIBRARY OF CONGRESS CATALOGING-IN-PUBLICATION DATA

Kisor, Henry.
  Tracking the beast / by Henry Kisor. — First edition.
    pages ; cm. — (A Steve Martinez mystery)
    ISBN 978-1-4328-3115-8 (hardcover) — ISBN 1-4328-3115-1 (hardcover) — ISBN 978-1-4328-3110-3 (ebook) — ISBN 1-4328-3110-0 (ebook)
    1. Sheriffs—Michigan—Upper Peninsula—Fiction. 2. Police—Michigan—Upper Peninsula—Fiction. 3. Cold cases (Criminal investigation)—Fiction. 4. Serial murder investigation—Fiction.
  I. Title.
PS3611.I87T73 2016
813'.6—dc23   2015025236

First Edition. First Printing: March 2016
Find us on Facebook– https://www.facebook.com/FiveStarCengage
Visit our website– http://www.gale.cengage.com/fivestar/
Contact Five Star™ Publishing at FiveStar@cengage.com

For Tina,
with grateful thanks for your wisdom and friendship

PROLOGUE

Diego groaned under the night sky as he muscled the bundle across the roof of the railroad car and dragged it to an open hatch. Climbing up the vertical steel ladder with the package strapped to his back had strained his legs and wearied his arms and hands.

For an hour he had suspected what was in the reeking package, wrapped in newspapers and bound with clothesline, but he didn't really want to know. All he was sure of was that the thing weighed less than a hundred pounds and that he was being paid ten times that in dollars for a simple job.

When the *jefe* needed Diego, he would phone, and Diego would drive his ancient Corolla up the interstate highway from Detroit four hours north to the Mackinac Bridge, then west on a two-lane road into the pine and hemlock forest for four and a half hours more. At the end of the journey he would meet the *jefe* after nightfall at a rutted dirt road that crossed a rusty railroad track in the forest. The *jefe* always spoke in a quiet voice, almost a whisper, although there seemed to be no need for silence in the lonely deep woods of western Upper Michigan.

Each time Diego would lift a bundle from the *jefe*'s van and carry it down a rocky trail on one side of the tracks past scores and scores of railroad cars. Then he'd hump it up the ladder of an empty hopper car the *jefe* had chosen and finally dump it through a hatch. Diego had done the job three times before and had been paid immediately in cash, together with a soft warning

7

not to tell anyone what he had done or where he had been.

Today's job was the last, Diego had told the *jefe*. Nothing personal, he said. He was just tired of working in the cold north country and wanted to move back to Chihuahua where it was warm all year. The truth was that Diego was nervous. For months he had been able to tell himself he didn't care about what he was doing, but now the implications of his acts were slowly corroding his conscience. Maybe the police would never know, but God would. As soon as this job was over, Diego would make his confession to the priest, do his penance, and go home to Mexico.

"No problem," the *jefe* had said in a surprisingly kind voice, patting him on the back. "You've done a good job for me and there'll be a bonus."

Just a couple of years ago he had met the *jefe*—medium height, thick-set, and balding, unlike his own tall, lean, muscular, and black-haired frame—at a day labor shape-up just outside a Home Depot near Ann Arbor. In the parking lot dozens of poorly clad workers, almost all of them undocumented Latinos like Diego, gathered in the chill early each morning, hoping contractors would hire them for a few dollars an hour under the table.

Immediately Diego had agreed to the *jefe*'s proposal. Easy money. Two or three times a year there'd be a thousand dollars for a day's drive, then fifteen minutes' labor humping a package on his back down a short path, then up the side of a rail car and finally dropping it into the car. If it worked out there might be other jobs like it, the *jefe* said.

"What's in the package?" Diego had asked the first time.

"Nothing you need to know," the *jefe* said. "Better you don't. We could get busted and it would go easier for you if you can say you didn't know."

Drugs, Diego thought. Of course. After the first job he had

decided that old railroad cars in the woods are a peculiar way to hide and move dope, but for that kind of money he wasn't going to push the question. There wasn't much risk of discovery, anyway. The job site was so deep in the wilderness that few if any police would be around. Maybe the *jefe* knew what he was doing. It was all the same to Diego.

Each time Diego and the *jefe* had met far from Ann Arbor just outside the same deserted and rusty railroad track where the van was parked on an access road screened by trees from the highway nearby. The man had instructed Diego to drive his Corolla through the moonlight the last couple of miles with his headlights out and brake lamps disconnected.

Though night had fallen, there was no need for lanterns. Those would have tipped off night watchers to the intruders' presence. Not that there were any curious eyes about. The *jefe* had said everything had been checked out and no railroad bulls prowled the rails. Starshine through the cloudless sky softly outlined the tree-shrouded tracks and the cars that sat upon them like a line of shadowy dominoes. Soon the moon would rise and the view would be nearly as clear as day, but with deep shadows to hide within. The boss carried a small penlight with a red lens, pointing it down the trail by the tracks. The path was brushy and stony and difficult to negotiate on foot. For a while Diego wished he had a wheelbarrow to carry the bundle, but soon realized that the trail was too rough for that.

Each time, at the *jefe*'s instruction Diego had reached into the back of the van and hauled out the bundle, grasping it by the clothesline. As before, it smelled strangely sweet and cloying, as if it had been soaked in cheap women's perfume, the kind sold door to door by traveling saleswomen trying to augment their husbands' wages.

"That'll throw off the dogs," the man had said. No doubt the eye-watering scent would confuse drug-sniffing hounds, Diego thought. As before, he'd need a long shower to wash off the stink.

He shouldered the shapeless bundle over his back and followed the *jefe* down the long line of parked hopper cars, a few minutes later stopping at the fourth car from the end of a coupled cut of nine. Wordlessly the man handed him a worn pair of cheap cotton work gloves with nubbled rubber palms, as he had done on the previous occasions. That was smart, Diego thought. They wouldn't leave prints. Narcs wouldn't be able to prove their presence unless they caught them in the act.

"This car," the man said. "Go on up and I'll follow you."

There was enough light for Diego to read the lettering on the car. "UNION PACIFIC," it said. This was a different one. The others in the previous jobs had been emblazoned "BURLINGTON NORTHERN" or "WISCONSIN CENTRAL" in faded letters partly covered by murals of graffiti. Enough rust stained the edges of the car to tell him it was not new, and the legend "BLT 8-87" confirmed that impression. Fine gray powder stuck to the steel here and there. The car had last been used to haul cement.

Climbing the first few rungs of the tall vertical steel ladder wasn't so hard, but the dead weight on his shoulder had Diego, a strong man, panting the last three feet. On previous jobs he had used a block and tackle strapped around a hatch to hoist packages weighing more than a hundred pounds, and he wished the boss had brought that equipment along. He stopped to rest after pulling the bundle onto the roof. The *jefe* clambered up after him.

"Okay, open that hatch," the man said, handing Diego a battered three-foot length of two-by-four. With the wooden baulk the Mexican hammered open the steel dogs that fastened the heavy hatch. The noise was loud enough so that for a few minutes the two men waited quietly, listening intently and searching through the night for sudden beams from flashlights. There was no response.

The *jefe* nodded. "Okay, Diego. Do it."

Diego dragged the bundle to the lip of the hatch and with a firm shove dropped it into the void. A short but sharp clang rose from the steel of the hopper bottom twelve feet below.

That's not dope, Diego thought. That would have been a thud. That's something else. And I think I know what it is.

"That did sound funny," the man said, as if echoing Diego's dismay. "Better take a look down there and make sure everything's okay."

The *jefe* handed Diego the penlight. "Go on, have a look."

Reluctantly Diego took the penlight and pointed it into the dusty interior of the car, leaning into the open hatch to see better.

"Don't see nothing," he said. "Wait a minute. Paper broke open. Something leak."

As cold metal suddenly pressed into the back of his neck, Diego realized the truth, and with that epiphany his world exploded in a flash of brilliant white.

CHAPTER ONE

"Got a weird one, Steve," the caller began, as always without preamble. Alex Kolehmainen is a Michigan State Police detective sergeant as celebrated for his brusque telephone manners as he is for his investigative chops.

"What now?" I said.

"Dead body."

I sat silent, waiting for Alex to proceed. It was the first of April, a day to be especially wary of his antic sense of humor.

"Aren't you interested?" he said after a few beats. "Don't you want the particulars?"

"Whether or not I do," I said, "you are going to give them to me, as you always do. Why else did you call?"

"To see if you were on the ball today."

"Why shouldn't I be?" I said with a deep sigh.

Having succeeded in slipping a burr under my collar, a mission Alex always delights in just because he can, the detective chuckled.

So did Ginny Fitzgerald, my freckled, red-headed lady love at the breakfast table in her sprawling log house on the lake. She is constantly amused by the unfortunately one-sided telephone repartee—I think of it as intramural police brutality—the state cop merrily inflicts upon everyone, the sheriff of Porcupine County in particular. You'd never suspect Alex and I are actually good friends.

"You said something about a dead body, Alex?"

"Yup."

"Where?" As usual, Alex was going to make me work for my answers. Getting them was like pulling teeth from a lion.

"Omaha."

"As in Nebraska?"

"Yup."

"Bit out of our jurisdictions."

"Indeed."

"All right, spill it."

"A few days ago a car cleaner in the Union Pacific freight yard at Omaha opened a discharge outlet under an empty covered hopper car and a bunch of bones and old newspapers fell out onto the tracks. The bones belonged to a girl who was about ten years old. So says the medical examiner there."

"And this has to do with us how?" I asked, quickly realizing I already knew the answer.

"Three weeks ago that car was taken out of storage near Rockville and sent to Omaha for cleaning and refurbishing."

At Rockville in the middle of Porcupine County—my jurisdiction—the little Keweenaw and Brule River Railway stores surplus cars from the Union Pacific and other big Class A railroads on a two-mile-long double siding on a rusty secondary line almost hidden from sight in some of the deepest woods of Upper Michigan.

In the past the siding has been an occasional headache for law enforcement. From time to time homeless people force open the doors of empty boxcars and take up residence within, especially during the hard winters. Sometimes they are pushed out by drug entrepreneurs looking for places to set up impromptu meth labs. The railroad doesn't have the resources to send someone out to give the line a cursory onceover more than a few times a year, and neither does the Porcupine County Sheriff's Department. The state cops, equally pinched by their dwindling budget, don't bother to keep an eye on it, either. Only once in my recall has a trooper visited the place, and that was almost a decade ago, when Alex led a bust of a meth lab set up inside an old Santa Fe refrigerator car that somehow had eluded the scrap yards.

"How long had that Omaha car been at Rockville?" I asked.

"Four years." The K & BR, I knew, kept careful records of the cars in storage. On a map the short line, once part of the mighty transcontinental Milwaukee Road from Chicago to Seattle, looks like a scraggly T with its arms in the air. The trunk runs more than two hundred miles south from Rockville to Green Bay in Wisconsin. From Rockville there had been two branches, one running to the northwest and the other to the northeast. The eastern branch runs forty miles east to Baraga, where it joins a Canadian National line to Marquette. The northwestern branch, fifteen bumpy miles from Rockville to Porcupine City, once had been an economic lifeline to the seat of my jurisdiction. When the paper mill at Porcupine City was closed and demolished early in the twenty-first century, the tracks of that branch had been torn up for scrap. Only the roadbed remained, and it was likely to survive only as a trail for all-terrain vehicles and snowmobiles, both major tourist pastimes in the Upper Peninsula.

In today's hard times the K & BR makes more money storing cars on its branches and sidings than it does by hauling meager carloads of pulpwood, paper products, and scrap metal from the western Upper Peninsula to Green Bay. It has only two functioning locomotives on the roster, and both are more than forty years old. Other locomotives sit idle in the company's tiny yard at Green Bay, but they are being cannibalized for parts.

"How old are those Omaha bones?" I asked.

"Nebraska state forensics is still testing," Alex said, "but their best guess so far is three to five years."

15

"Cause of death?"

"None so far that they can tell, and none likely anyway."

"No tissue left?"

"Some cartilage and dried blood, the prelim report says," Alex said. "Barely enough to try a tox screen and the lab doesn't hold out much hope for decent results. Not that a child of that age would have been experimenting with bad shit. But they can do a DNA test."

"How'd those bones get in there?" I asked, just to get things on the table. "Kids fooling around?"

I doubted the surmise. Once in a long while local teenagers would hike in through brush and brambles to explore the hundreds of cars stored on the rails, but they were invariably empty, the contents they once hauled picked over long ago, and that adventure grew old fast.

"Not likely," Alex said.

"Especially not in a hopper car," I said. Few ten-year-old girls, we both knew, would have the upper body strength to climb up the vertical ladder of a two-story-high car and even fewer would have the muscle to lift a heavy steel hatch to peer inside and fall twelve feet to the bottom.

"Nope."

"So she was probably put inside. Maybe alive, probably dead."

"By whom?"

"Some bastard."

I had dealt with my share of human fatalities, as had Alex, but the death of a child always touched us to the core. My stomach churned. I hoped the little girl had not starved to death inside that car, unable to claw her way out.

"Did those old newspapers have a date? A name?" I asked.

"The Omaha cops say the papers were three to five years old, all pages from the *New York Times*, the *Wall Street Journal*, and

USA Today. Nothing local. They could have been printed any-where."

"Forensic tests of ink and newsprint might be able to tell exactly where," I said. "But those newspapers could have been brought in from several cities just to confuse matters."

"Sounds like the bastard could be a smart one," Alex said. "The Nebraska LEOs are declaring the bones a homicide."

"Does sound like it," I said. "We'd better go over to Rockville and have a look at those cars."

"Your vehicle or mine?"

Our budgets had gotten so tight that to save on fuel, Upper Peninsula troopers and local lawmen often shared rides to remote crime sites. For more than half a century since the lumber and mining industries collapsed, the human population of Upper Michigan had been dwindling and the remaining financial resources were being spread ever thinner.

"Want to leave your cruiser at the sheriff's department and we'll take my Explorer out to Rockville?" I said.

"Naw," Alex said "That would be the long way around."

He was right. Porcupine City was about thirty minutes out of Alex's way from the state police post at Wakefield. From Wake-field directly to Rockville the drive takes more than an hour. That's typical of distances in the Upper Peninsula of Michigan. Things are few and far between, and the inhabitants practically live in their cars and pickups. They think nothing of driving two hours for a decent restaurant meal or an afternoon of shopping at a Walmart.

Nor do law enforcement officers. But now the state police bosses were getting so demanding about every drop of gas and millimeter of wear and tear that they'd limited the daily miles of routine patrol the troopers could drive. Speeders were going unarrested and some of the troopers were complaining that they'd have to chase offenders with bicycles.

For the same reason, understaffed sheriff's departments, particularly in the Upper Peninsula, had reduced their road patrols and concentrated on process serving and other county law enforcement tasks closer to headquarters. Overtime was not being paid in cash but instead banked for the future, and LEOs of all kinds had been spending long hours on extra work.

"See you there in an hour or so," I said, and hung up.

Before heading out the door I kissed Ginny goodbye while giving her butt a friendly squeeze. She squeezed mine back. As I opened the door of the department's Explorer I fist-bumped with Tommy Standing Bear, her eighteen-year-old foster son from the reservation at Baraga. Tommy had overcome the poverty of his origins to become an excellent student. He had outgrown the limited offerings of the Porcupine City Area High School, whose student body had shrunk to a little over a hundred, thanks to the rapidly dwindling population, and was spending his senior year driving an hour each way, each day, with two friends to a bigger and more challenging high school in Houghton, fifty miles from Porcupine City. He had been offered an academic scholarship to Michigan State in the fall, and Ginny and I knew that if Tommy was to make the huge leap from rural educational standards to those of a major university, he would have to master vastly more rigorous intellectual habits.

Like me, Tommy is Indian-born but white-raised, Ojibwa to my Lakota. He is small and wiry where I am tall and rangy, and quicker than I ever could have been as the pivot man at second base. He's an excellent ballplayer, and during the winter several Midwestern university athletic directors tried to recruit him.

"Can't go with, can I?" said Tommy. Half the time he wants to become an activist with the American Indian Movement, and the other half he wants to be a cop, never missing a chance to soak up the fine points of law enforcement, even those of a country sheriff. He, Ginny, and I occasionally talk at the dinner table about the very few but always interesting major criminal cases that land on my desk at the sheriff's department, and Tommy sometimes comes up with surprising insights. He often hangs out at the department, pumping deputies for stories and begging ride-alongs with them. They will let him go along on routine missions, such as delivering subpoenas and other county paperwork.

"No," I said as sternly as I could but failing to muster much indignation. "You've still got two months of school. Off you go."

I spoke in a fatherly tone, though I'm not the boy's father, just his foster mother's paramour, or "longtime live-in boy-friend," as Alex puts it. I always demur, pointing out that I have my own cabin on the lake and live there at least half the time. "Steve Two Toothbrushes Martinez," Alex calls me. My proper name is Stephen Two Crow Martinez, all I have left of my birth parents and their culture. I was adopted as an infant by white missionaries and raised in upstate New York.

With only a perfunctory protest Tommy got into the rusty old Ford pickup he had earned doing odd jobs. Hogan, his aging Lab–pitbull mix, trotted hopefully behind him, wanting to go along, but Tommy pointed back to the house and the dog sat obediently. Tommy would not be able to take him to college in the fall, and Ginny and I were already bickering over who would get to give the dog room and board while the boy was gone. I thought I was winning.

I turned back and called to Ginny, who was standing in the door.

"Won't be back for lunch," I said, putting down a hand to prevent Hogan from going along with me, a mission he always demands whenever Tommy makes him stay home. Often I give in and take the dog to work, where he sleeps on the floor beside my desk, his tail thumping in greeting whenever a deputy comes in. Sometimes he rides shotgun beside me when I go out on a call, but not this time.

"I have a feeling today is going to be interesting," I called as I slammed the car door.

CHAPTER TWO

Alex had already arrived in his muddy state police Crown Vic when I pulled up in my equally scruffy departmental Explorer. He stood leaning against his vehicle at a dirt road rail crossing in the woods just a hop, skip, and jump from Rockville, an old logging and sawmill town whose population, like that of every other community in Porcupine County, had dropped drastically over the last fifty years. Once nearly a thousand people had lived in Rockville, but now only three hundred called it home.

During World War II the town's population had almost doubled because of a prisoner-of-war camp nearby. There the U.S. Army had hosted some two hundred and fifty young Wehrmacht enlisted soldiers considered negligible escape risks. They lived in a dozen wooden barracks inside a ten-foot barbed-wire fence in the woods, and during the days worked under perfunctory guard harvesting timber and laboring in sawmills. Two prisoners had attempted to flee, but were quickly caught and sent elsewhere. The others found the work pleasant and the camp conditions cushy compared to those in wartime Germany.

After the war a few of the repatriated POWs emigrated from Germany to the Upper Peninsula, set down roots, and raised families. Except for a couple of tumbledown shacks still standing in the deep woods, most of the old camp buildings had been torn down long ago, but their concrete foundations still stood near the tracks, concealed in bushes and tall grass.

Decades before the war, much of the Upper Peninsula's virgin

21

forest of white pine, hemlock, and birch had been cut over and destumped for farming. Most crops, however, failed to thrive in the cold climate, and now, in the middle of the second decade of the twenty-first century, second-growth forest was looming increasingly tall and lordly, broken only by a few patches of scrub and meadows where farmers raised winter-hardy strains of beef cattle.

White pine, hemlock, birch, and aspen towered over the rails, forming a long green tunnel that in many places hid the tracks from the air. I had flown marijuana-hunting missions over the area several times with the sheriff's Cessna when we still had an airplane, and in spots could not discern the rails through the greenery below. From the highway any railroad cars were invisible behind a long screen of trees. The line had truly become an almost forgotten railroad.

The hulks of two boxcars loomed through the brush a hundred feet or so from the crossing. An access path on one side of the rails had once existed for trackmen but was now largely overgrown with brush and strewn with rocks. It was a narrow and rocky lane, shaded by the high cars and just wide enough for a small all-terrain vehicle. "It'll take a four-wheeler to get in there," I said.

"Already called the tribals," Alex said. "Camilo's sending a pickup with an ATV and a couple of officers. Be here in half an hour or so."

The headquarters of the tribal police at the Ojibwa reservation on Lac Vieux Desert lay three-quarters of an hour south at Watersmeet in Gogebic County. The tribals often lent assistance to neighboring sheriffs and troopers. Camilo Hernandez, the police chief, is one of my closest friends, not because he is a fellow Indian, an Apache from Texas, but because, like me, he is one of many outsiders who washed up in the Upper Peninsula and set down roots. Just one of his present eight officers is Native American. The rest are whites and a Latino or two. He does call frequently on three or four retired Ojibwa tribal officers for part-time work, such as stakeouts and tracking in the deep woods.

"What about the railroad?" I asked.

"Perlman is driving up from Green Bay," said Alex, who had already been in touch with Mike Perlman, the K & BR president, who'd quickly assented to a search of the railroad property. "It'll take him a few hours to get here."

"Let's have a gander with Google Maps," I said, pulling out my iPhone. Earlier in the year the sheriff's department had obtained half a dozen of the smartphones with a federal grant.

"iPhone, eh?" said Alex. "I thought you still had outhouses at the Porcupine County Jail."

I ignored him. "Have a look," I said, zooming in on Rockville. The satellite view of the area clearly showed a bird's-eye view of the line. For two miles it was almost choked with long strings of railroad cars, broken only at crossroads.

"Holy shit," Alex said quietly.

"How many cars are stored here?" I asked.

"Three or four hundred, maybe more, Perlman said. He wasn't sure. Said he'd have to ask the office."

"Jeez. Are they all coupled together?"

"No. Most are in separate cuts, or groups, of a dozen or so."

"Oldest in first, newest last?"

"Basically, yes, Perlman said. But cuts of several similar cars—boxcars or hoppers or bulkhead flatcars—are often switched in together and placed so that the cars the railroad thinks will be wanted sooner rather than later are spotted close to this end where they can be gotten at quickly."

Even so, I thought, every single car would have to be searched. The open cars—gondolas, flatcars, pulpwood racks, and the like—would be easily disposed of. Boxcars would take a little longer, because their doors would have to be slid open and flashlights shined into every cranny. Covered hoppers would take the longest, because each car is divided into two or three internal bays, each with its own hatch on top and dumping doors at the bottom. If we were going to find anything, it would most likely be in one of the hoppers.

Searching the area around the tracks would be highly unlikely to turn up any clues because of the passage of time. Footprints would have been eradicated, fingerprints weathered away.

"Your case, Alex," I said. "What do you want to do?"

Alex was technically in charge of the investigation because he had fielded the initial call from Omaha. On paper the state police outranked all other law enforcement agencies except for the FBI, which would be called in only for violations of federal law. In practice, the Feebs from Detroit let us local yokels do all the shoe-leather work in federal cases such as felonies in national forests or on Indian reservations, often taking over and bringing charges only after arrests had been made, and naturally hogging all the credit.

Traditionally the Michigan state police investigated major non-federal Class One felonies such as homicides, because they had a bigger budget and more manpower than the locals. But the troopers' resources were sliding down by ours on the county and reservation totem pole, and so we were sharing responsibilities, rather than blindly following a hierarchical chart, so that we could stretch our resources to the utmost. More and more, we were relying on each other.

"Think the air force would help?" Alex said, echoing an idea that had been forming in my mind ever since we arrived on scene.

Until two years before, the Porcupine County Sheriff Department's aviation division had constituted a single thirty-year-old

Cessna four-seater, the fruits of a federal grant for police equipment promoted by Gil O'Brien, my highly capable undersheriff. Having learned to fly in the army, I was the sole pilot. For a number of years the old airplane and I had flown occasional search-and-rescue missions for lost hikers over the nearby Wolverine Mountains Wilderness State Park and for missing boaters on Lake Superior. With the troopers and the DEA, we had hunted marijuana patches hidden in hayfields and along the verges of county roads.

The trouble with the federal grant was that although it had bought the airplane, it provided no funds for fuel and maintenance. Keeping an old airplane flying ate up so much of the department's ever-shrinking budget—each annual inspection required by the Federal Aviation Administration cost nearly five digits—that the county commissioners regretfully but firmly ordered me to sell her and turn her hangar at the county airport into a shelter for snowplow trucks.

Soon, however, we replaced our old eyes in the sky with a newer and much more modern device, one far cheaper to buy and operate than even an old single-engine Cessna: an unmanned aerial vehicle, as the catalog officially called it, or a drone, as everybody else says.

It was Gil's idea. One day when we were even more short-handed than usual, he had sent himself out of the office on a complaint from a wealthy matron who owned a large house on the lakefront. She had said that her neighbor was watching her from a "nasty spy device" as she sunbathed on the beach in front of her house. The neighbor turned out to be a model aircraft enthusiast with a radio-controlled helicopter, little more than a toy, who had been flying it up and down the beach.

Gil figured—rightly—that the airspace above the shoreline included right-of-way privileges, and told the woman so. The hobbyist also volunteered to let Gil watch the five-minute video the helicopter's little camera had taken that day, and "all it turned out to be was miles and miles of sand and water."

After persuading the matron with some difficulty that her neighbor meant neither harm nor offense, Gil was driving back to the department when the notion lodged in his head that a similar device might help make up for the loss of the Cessna. Over the next weeks he plunged into research and persuaded the county board that the cost of owning a genuine law enforcement UAV would be negligible. Several counties, mostly out West in the wide open spaces, already included drones among their equipment and had reported success in a variety of tasks. Soon a grant came through from the federal government, followed by a large box delivered by a UPS truck.

Inside was an octocopter, a drone a little larger than a garbage can lid, powered by eight propellers driven by small but strong electric motors that were fueled by rechargeable batteries. The craft carried a GPS receiver and a camera on a gimbal that could be pointed fore, aft, or to either side from afar, and turned on or off at will. The camera's still pictures and video were transmitted by wi-fi to a laptop computer whose control buttons made the copter go up, down, forward, back, and to the sides as well as pointing the camera in the proper direction.

The drone had a transmitter range of about two miles and an endurance of about twenty minutes before the batteries petered out. Best of all, its clever little on-board computer knew when the battery charge was low and would automatically tell the GPS software to return the craft to the exact spot where it had been launched.

Three times in the span of a year we had used it to find lost hikers in the deep woods of the Wolverines, and twice we had been successful. The drone was the perfect vehicle for low and slow searches over a square mile or so and far, far cheaper to own and operate than a grown-up helicopter. Like choppers, drones can hover for long moments, allowing pilots to examine the terrain closely, and can even plunge down below the treetops into tiny clearings for better looks. On the second occasion, we'd spotted a hiker with a broken leg sheltering under the canopy of trees, almost hidden from above. He'd waved his red jacket to catch our eye as the drone dipped down into a tiny open space.

On the third occasion, the lost camper walked out of the woods on her own, but we didn't mind the time and effort we'd put into the aerial search. It was good brush-up training.

Not all Porcupine Countians approved of the UAV. To the extreme left-wingers, they were junior editions of the Predators that the Air Force used to assassinate alleged Al Qaeda in "surgical" strikes with Hellfire missiles that caused many collateral civilian casualties. Right-wingers thought the little drones nothing more than miniature black helicopters that swept the countryside looking for guns to confiscate. More sensible citizens worried about the ethics and legality of aerial searches. We were careful to obtain warrants before we took our drone to the air over private lands, just as we did when we went in on foot.

Because Gil had done all the heavy lifting to acquire the drone, I asked him if he'd like to be the chief pilot, and he had not said no. He practiced every chance he got, and soon became expert. Only once had he flown the drone into a tree, and the broken propeller was easily replaced with one of half a dozen spares that came with the machine. That made the county commissioners extraordinarily happy with the sheriff's department, but not so happy that I would allow any of them to fly the thing. I was saving that for when the department really, really needed an infusion of cash from the tight-fisted commissioners. I doubted that would ever happen.

★　★　★　★　★

"I'll get Gil in here right away," I told Alex at the scene.

While we waited, three of my deputies and two more troopers arrived, along with four tribal policemen, including Camilo. So much for conserving gasoline. But this was not routine patrol.

"Couldn't stay away, could ya, Camilo?" said Chad Garrow, my most valuable deputy. Chad is the size of a small silo and loves to play the dumb rube he looks like, especially with smart-ass speeders up from Chicago. He is actually a crackerjack investigator and, like me, a favorite prospect of state police recruiters. But both of us like our shared wilderness bailiwick too much to want to start over as troopers downstate.

"Not too many homicides in our neighborhood," said Camilo, as short and wiry as Chad is tall and barrel-shaped. The Apache was right. Lots of Yoopers died in accidents or booze-fueled fights, but few were dispatched by means of premeditated murder. In the semi-wilderness there's very little to kill for, except sex and revenge and sometimes drugs. The few murder cases I had handled mostly involved highly unbalanced personalities. Alex sometimes called me a magnet for psychopaths.

"We don't know if the girl was killed and dumped in that car here or elsewhere," I said. "We'll have to ask the K & BR and Union Pacific to track where that car had been before it was stored here. I'm sure the Omaha cops have already done that."

Camilo nodded. "But if the deed went down here, there might have been others," he said. "We just gotta look."

"Before you start," I said, "take a look at the kind of hopper cars out there. There are all kinds. Some have tiny round hatches on top, no more than a foot wide, and most of those are emptied from the bottom with air pressure through hoses. They're generally big and round-sided and carry plastic pellets and flour and other lightweight stuff. We can save those for last and instead focus on the cars with big round hatches or long rectangular ones, hatches that somebody could shove a body through. They have gravity outlet gates at the bottom that dump the loads directly downward into bins below the tracks."

"You seem to know a lot about that railroad stuff," Camilo said.

"Picked it up here and there," I said. Alex chuckled.

"Your guys could start with that first cut of hoppers," he said. A string of almost new Burlington Northern Santa Fe grain cars stood before us, unsullied by graffiti and clearly the most recent addition to the siding. Immediately Camilo and his quartet of tribal cops clambered up the ladders of the hopper cars and opened their long, skinny hatches, examining the interiors with powerful Maglites.

"Still some old grain in the bottoms," Camilo called. "We'll have to open the gates."

A trooper walked along the cut of cars, leaning in under their bottoms and pulling the levers that opened the gates. A few gallons of dried-out grain, twigs, and clouds of dust poured out, but no bones.

I clambered up the ladder of one of the newer cars and peered along its top. In only a few months a grimy film of blown sand, dust, and leaf particles had formed on the light gray paint of the roof—and the tribal cops' footprints showed clearly.

By then the undersheriff had arrived with his equipage.

"Come on up here, Gil," I called. He did.

"See these marks in the dirt on the roofs?" I said. "If you fly the drone slowly along the tops of these cars, you'll probably be able to spot disturbed areas around their hatches."

"Very good, boss," Gil said. "I'll give it a go."

In less than five minutes Gil had his aviator's "cockpit"—a Macbook Air and a battered lawn chair—set up next to his departmental pickup, and with a loud whir the drone lifted off from the bed of the truck. Alex and I leaned over Gil's shoulder, watching the laptop screen.

"Better fly her about eight feet or so to one side of the cars," I said, "so the downdraft from the rotors doesn't blow off all the dust and wreck our crime scene."

"Ahead of you," Gil said. "It'll be easier to see marks on the cars from an angle instead of directly overhead. I'll fly alongside a dozen cars in both directions, then along another dozen, and so on. Okay, boss?"

"You're pilot in command," I said. "The rest of us are just observers."

"It's almost noon," Gil said. "The marks won't show up all that well in direct overhead sunlight. It'll be better in the late afternoon when the sun's low and shadows will be clearer. We could do a preliminary search now, then about four o'clock do another one."

"Works for me, too," Alex said.

For thirty minutes at a time Gil slowly guided the octocopter down and back over about a quarter of a mile of stored cars before landing the craft to load a pack of fresh batteries while the used ones recharged. Between landings and launchings, he drove his pickup and its equipment down the rail line, parking at dirt-road crossings so that he could keep the drone more or less within line of sight as well as wi-fi range.

Two hours went by while Gil searched, finding nothing except the carcass of an owl. The rest of us sweated and swore as the sun rose higher through clouds of blackflies and the temperature climbed into the humid eighties. Snowbanks still hid in the shadows, but were melting rapidly in the unseasonable heat. April is like that in the Upper Peninsula, mostly cool during the days and often below freezing at night, but with occasional freakishly warm episodes when strong southerly winds blow up from the Gulf of Mexico. As the hunt continued, Camilo dispatched a policeman to a roadside market in Bruce Crossing for sandwiches and iced tea.

At noon there was a sudden flurry of activity when on the laptop screen Gil spotted a man aiming a scoped rifle at the drone from a small clearing half a mile downtrack. "Whoops!" he shouted, violently yanking the drone into a steep climb and jink backward from its flight path down the line of cars. "We've got a hostile!"

There was no sound of a shot, but Alex and Chad and I crowded around the laptop. Gingerly Gil returned the drone and its camera to the clearing, ready to pull it out of harm's way. We watched on the screen as the camera traversed the clearing and stopped at a deer hanging by the antlers from a branch of a stout oak. The camera zoomed in on the deer's belly, freshly slit open by a knife. It was being dressed.

"Poacher," Gil said.

"Ray!" I yelled. Ray Glasson, the Michigan DNR conservation officer for Porcupine County, came running. "Gil, can you play back the video?"

Quickly Gil tapped several keys on the laptop, returning to the first scene in the clearing. Ray peered closely.

"That's Herbie Hokkanen," he said. "Busted him half a dozen times for poaching. He's just looking at the drone through the rifle scope. Bet he never heard of them."

Hokkanen had been an occasional guest in my lockup, twice for poaching and at least once for Saturday-night disturbing of the peace.

"Go bust him again," said Alex. "See if he knows anything about this case. Shake him up with a charge of threatening a police officer."

"Is a drone a police officer?" I asked.

"It's official police equipment anyway," Alex said. "You'll think of something, Ray."

As Ray sped off in his pickup, a four-wheeler in its bed, Alex and I both shrugged. We knew Herbie Hokkanen. Though he scratched out an illegal living selling deer hide and antlers, he was a couple of carrots short of a goulash and highly unlikely to be a master criminal.

Shortly after one in the afternoon Gil shouted, "Got something!" and hovered the drone near the roof of a covered fertilizer hopper a mile and a half from Rockville. We crowded around the laptop screen and peered. The scuffs and tracks on the roof were nearly invisible in the harsh sunlight, but they were there.

Stumbling down the rocky path alongside the cars, Chad and I mounted the ladder of an old Wisconsin Central three-bay fertilizer car and clambered over its rusty and dusty steel roof to the first hatch. Quickly Chad undid the dogs and pried open the hatch cover. We both looked in, playing our Maglites around the interior. Deep in the central hopper, surrounded by old fertilizer pellets, lay a bundle of old newspaper in shreds. From one corner jutted a yellowed bone. It looked heartbreakingly small.

CHAPTER THREE

"This whole two miles of tracks is now a crime scene," Alex declared.

"We'll never get enough tape to cover it all," I said. Two miles of railroad would need twice that of yellow "POLICE DO NOT CROSS" crime-scene tape, and all we ever carried in the trunks of our cruisers were rolls of a hundred feet or so.

It was obvious to us, however, that the thick bush that surrounded the place made a natural crowd barrier. To control the inevitable gaggle of rubberneckers and reporters, we'd just need to tape off the end of the track where the gravel road from the highway crossed the railroad line, and send a couple of officers down the line to seal the next crossing and watch for trespassers curious—or stupid—enough to brave the brambles, blackflies, and mosquitoes between the roads. An early batch of stable flies had hatched that morning, and though they'd add to our torment in the heat, they'd also deter snooping civilians.

"I'm calling Lansing," Alex said. "We'll need more forensics before we can go into that car." Alex was trained in forensics, but is not as well equipped or specialized as those at state police headquarters. After a few minutes on his cell he said, "They're sending a squad right away. They'll fly into Porcupine County Airport by three this afternoon. Let's set up a generator and lights so they can do their thing all night if necessary."

"I'll call and get ours," I said. My department maintains a remote crime-scene kit that includes several floodlamps on tripods and a noisy gasoline-driven generator. The sole deputy at the jail, Joe Koski, our corrections officer, would borrow a mechanic from the county highway garage and send him out with the kit. Meanwhile, the state police post at Wakefield would dispatch a Suburban to collect the forensics squad at the airport and chauffeur it to Rockville.

"That's two bodies so far connected to this place," I said, voicing what everyone thought. "There may be more. We'll have to keep searching."

As the afternoon wore on, as Gil flew combat air patrol with the UAV and as reinforcements trickled in, we continued to clamber over cars, swat mosquitoes and blackflies, and peer inside, examining their meager contents even more thoroughly. Although Gil was pinpointing the likeliest hiding places from the air with the help of Mike Perlman, the railroad president, we still needed to examine and eliminate every possibility, and that meant searching every single car parked on the railroad. There was a flurry of excitement when a deputy unearthed a pile of bones inside an open gondola car, but we quickly dismissed them as the remains of a coyote that had sought shelter against harsh weather. Nevertheless, we bagged them carefully in a plastic sack. Anything and everything was evidence until forensics declared it wasn't.

Car after car slowly passed under our scrutiny down the line as if we were traversing a horizontal cliff on a knotted rope pulled from hand to hand. At about four o'clock we discovered still another set of human bones, jumbled at the bottom of a grain hopper car like pick-up sticks among shreds of old newspaper and rotted clothesline. Again the skeleton appeared to be that of a child, and cracks began to appear in the dispassionate professionalism we cops tried to maintain while doing our jobs. For good reasons we are trained to withhold emotion during investigations, but we are human and sometimes our feelings get out of hand. Still we tried to keep them in check to avoid carelessly contaminating the scene or the chain of custody of evidence.

Just before dusk we made our third discovery of human remains in a cement hopper car near the end of one of the tracks. This time, as Chad levered open its farthest hatch, he was greeted by an invisible but overwhelming cloud of decay, and he vomited over the side of the car before he could issue a shout. Wiping his mouth on his sleeve, he quickly recovered his composure and called, "Bring the hazmat masks! We got a fresh one!"

Alex was first to peer inside, illuminating the interior of the hopper with a powerful 360-degree electric lantern. He winced at the stench, so strong it punched through the air filter of his mask, but kept on examining the scene.

"Looks like two bodies," he said as I scrabbled over the car top to the hatch, myself blindsided by the sickly odor rising from inside. "One's the same as the others, a small bundle covered by newspapers and clothesline, and the other is a grown man. Most of his head looks blown away by a gunshot. The bodies can't be more than a couple, three weeks old."

"Jesus," I said, echoing what everyone else felt.

Alex and I swung down from the ground and assessed the situation. A dozen deputies, troopers, and tribals gathered close by. The forensics guys were still working on the first car and their sergeant said they thought they'd have to wait until morning to address the second.

"It might be another day before they can get to this one," Alex said. "I'll see if Lansing can spare another team." He fished out his cell phone and called his superiors.

None of us needed to be told to start searching for a weapon, and the officers began shining their flashlights on the gravel roadbed under the cars as well as inside and atop them all.

"We're going to need a lot more help," I told Camilo at my elbow. "The reporters and rubberneckers have already begun to arrive." It hadn't taken long for townspeople in Rockville to notice the steady stream of cops through town on their way to the sidings, and they had kept the wires humming on the Upper Michigan jungle telegraph. The word was out and spreading rapidly.

Two tribal cops kept a small clutch of civilians at bay behind the crime-scene tape at the road crossing, arguing with a news camera team from Marquette. I could almost hear one of the tribals threatening to throw their interfering asses out, but he knew the journalists were just trying to do their jobs.

I'd been at crime-scene circuses before. Ours was the biggest criminal story the Upper Peninsula had seen in years, and despite the remoteness of Rockville it would draw newspeople in the dozens and onlookers in the hundreds by the time we'd finished, and that might take days.

"I'll call Gogebic and Houghton counties and get some more deputies," Camilo said.

"While you're at it, see if you can get some more COs," I said. Conservation officers—game wardens—are also sworn, trained, and armed lawmen, and their knowledge of these woods might come in handy, as Ray Glasson's had with Herbie Hokkanen.

"It's going to be a long night," Camilo observed unnecessarily.

I nodded, looking about. Chad was already stringing yellow tape in a wide arc around the reeking hopper car, creating a smaller crime scene within the big one, as we had done with the other two cars where bones had been discovered. He saw me watching and shook his head sadly.

"Merle's is sending down supper and breakfast," Gil called. Despite the smell, I was beginning to get hungry. Merle's,

Porcupine City's premier downtown cafe, catered not only all jail meals but also held the contract for provisions for LEOs at remote crime scenes within the county.

Gil had called it a night with the drone, hefted his gun belt, and gazed balefully at the screen of trees on one side of the tracks. Anyone who broke through our first line of defense at the road crossing was going to feel the wrath of this former marine drill sergeant with the brass-knuckled voice, and I was confident in its deterrent powers. Long ago, as a lowly fledgling deputy fresh out of army military police in Desert Storm, I had experienced it.

Things are awful, I mused as night began to fall and the second squad of forensic technicians, freshly arrived from the airport, flicked on their crime-scene lights. But at least they're under control.

CHAPTER FOUR

Two weeks later we were no closer to catching the killer than we had been at Rockville.

"So what do we know?" Alex said at the war council, as Camilo liked to call our official gatherings that the trooper had organized at the Wakefield state police post. The day before, Lansing forensics had issued its preliminary reports. "Some, but not a hell of a lot."

"Let's lay out what we do know," I said, handing out a pile of stapled papers summarizing the meager facts we had as Alex, Camilo, and Dan Roane, sheriff of Gogebic County, where Wakefield is located, pulled up chairs around a table. Dan was there not as an official investigator but because he was interested in the case. It was the biggest one to hit western Upper Michigan in years. The last had been a string of muzzle-loader murders, one of them of a retired congressman.

We were joined by Lieutenant Susan Hemb, a criminal profiler for the Michigan state police, who had driven up from Lansing to consult in the case and enjoy a little rest and recreation with Alex, her longtime squeeze. As a sergeant Alex was technically her subordinate, but having passed the lieutenant's exam a few years before and immediately declining promotion, he considered himself her equal. So did everyone else.

"The bones of three young girls have been identified," Alex said. "The first is Sheila McWilliams from Holland, Michigan, ten years old. She was white, and her skeleton was discovered in the Union Pacific yards at Omaha four years and three months after she disappeared while walking home from school. The identification was made with DNA samples taken from her parents and brother. Date of death, approximately the middle of 2008. Cause of death, undetermined. The car her bones were found in had been moved from a grain processing plant at Muscatine, Iowa, to the siding at Rockville in March of that year. There's no indication when or where the homicide was committed, or when or where the bones were put in the car.

"Almost the same with the second victim, the first set of bones we found at Rockville. DNA shows her to be Latonya Harris from Fremont, also in lower Michigan, sixty miles from Holland. African American, eleven years old. Last seen in midafternoon after school leaving a playground near her house. Date of death, early 2009. Cause of death, undetermined. Place of death, unknown. The car had been on the Rockville siding since late 2008. That suggests the body was put into the car there.

"The third set of bones, the second one we found, has not been identified, but forensics says they belong to a Caucasian female between nine and eleven years old. Date of death, last quarter of 2010. Cause of death, probably strangulation. Place of death, unknown. Her hyoid bone was broken, forensics said, in a manner consistent with a stricture applied to the throat. The car she was found in was brought to Rockville in November of 2010. The body could have been put in it before or after the car arrived.

"The postmortems on the fourth and fifth bodies," I continued, "yielded more results because a large amount of soft tissue was present, however deteriorated. The fourth body was quickly identified as Andrea Lacoste, ten years and three months of age, of Newaygo, Michigan, near Fremont. She had also disappeared while walking home from school. She had definitely been strangled about three weeks before her body was found; her hyoid was broken and petechiae were found in the remnants of her eyeballs. Her hymen was torn, and her vaginal tissues were bruised and abraded. Semen was present. Her body was found with the legs drawn up in a fetal position and the arms bound in front, making a squarish package covered by recent newspapers and bound in cotton clothesline. The hopper car she was found in had been moved to Rockville in July of 2011, two years before the murder. We can therefore conclude that the body was stashed in the car on that site, although we don't know where she was killed.

"As for the adult male with her, no identification was found, but DNA and tissue analysis indicates he was of Latino origin, approximately thirty-two years old, six feet two inches tall and muscular.

"An aluminum penlight with a broken red lens was found underneath the body. The batteries had been completely depleted, suggesting that the man had been using the penlight when he entered the car and it wasn't turned off when he was shot.

"Two letters found in his shirt pocket were addressed to Diego Guzman at a YMCA in Ann Arbor. They were from a young woman living in Juarez across the border from El Paso. Juarez police said Guzman had no criminal record in Mexico, and when they contacted the girl, she said she had not heard from Guzman, her fiance, in a month. She said he was a farm laborer and construction worker and had gone over to the U.S. illegally several times to pick fruit and haul building materials, and had regularly sent money home to her. She said she was worried because she heard from him almost twice a week, but the letters suddenly stopped coming.

"She identified a photograph of a wristwatch taken from the body as his, but she was not shown a picture of his face, because there was no face. Guzman had been shot in the back of the head with a .32 revolver at point-blank range. A heavy deposit of burned smokeless powder ringed the wound. Of course, that was the cause of death. A .32 slug was recovered at the site and matched to the gun. Five unfired rounds were found in the cylinder. The gun was found on top of the body. No prints.

"The gun is a Saturday night special, serial number filed off. Thousands like it on the bootleg market. Untraceable."

"Suicide?" Alex said, quickly answering his own question. "Unlikely. It would be just possible for someone to shoot himself in the back of the head, but that's almost unheard of. Suicides aim for the temple or the mouth. In any case, gloves were found under the body, one of them on Guzman's right hand, and no trace of smokeless powder was found on either glove. That's strong evidence he didn't fire the fatal shot. Most important of all, the semen wasn't his."

"Just for the argument," Camilo said, "suppose the guy was the perp and wanted to end it all, but didn't want to be remembered as a rapist and killer? Maybe he wanted to be thought of as a victim himself?"

"Doubt it," Sue said. "Serial murderers who commit suicide are almost never concerned with moral legacies. If anything, they want to be celebrated for the heinousness of their crimes. And there's that semen. It doesn't match. Guzman did not sexually assault that girl."

"And so we can be pretty sure that Diego Guzman was himself a victim," I said.

"Indeed," Sue said.

"But what was Guzman doing in that hopper car?" Alex said. "We know he was killed there because we found the slug that killed him in the same place, right under his body. Could he have killed the girl and then been killed afterward by a third party?"

"Maybe that third party raped and killed the girl," I said, "and that Guzman was working for the person who killed him," I said. "He was a pretty big and strong guy. It's not easy for the average person to climb a vertical ladder sixteen feet up a freight car, and it would take a lot of muscle to hump even a small body that far."

"Couldn't he have just pulled the body up with a rope?" Camilo said.

"Yeah," Alex said, "but no rope was found except for cotton clothesline with the old newspapers. Clothesline's too thin and weak for hoisting much weight, and besides, the forensics guys didn't find any scuff marks in the paint at the edge of the roof of the hopper car that could have been made by rope of any kind."

"What about that newspaper?" Camilo asked. "Why was it used instead of something else? It must have been awkward and clumsy to wrap the bodies in those small sheets of paper."

"Quick deterioration," Alex said. "The paper would crumble to small shreds within a few months if it were soaked in the products of decomposition, like the clothesline. In two or three years there wouldn't be much to fall out of the bottom of the car when it was opened for cleaning. Nobody pays much attention to that routine in the yards. They just yank open the doors, stick a hose into the car to wash out the debris, and walk away. This guy knew what he was doing."

"As for Guzman," I said. "There's nothing from the Mexican police report that suggests he was a sexual predator or any other kind of criminal. Maybe he was just a guy trying to make a living. He may have been hired to dispose of those wrapped packages. Maybe he thought he was just moving contraband, like a drug mule. When his usefulness was over, he was himself disposed of."

"A reasonable scenario," Sue said. "Why would he have been

hired in the first place? Because he was big and strong. That suggests the rapist and killer wasn't, and had to pay someone else to get rid of the bodies of his victims. I think we can conclude we're looking for someone of relatively slight stature, maybe a small person. Probably not a female, though. The presence of semen belies that idea."

"Could we be looking for two main subjects?" I asked. "A male rapist, a female killer? A really, really depraved and murderous couple? There might be a hired hand, but he wouldn't be one of the brain trust."

"It's a possibility," Sue said. "It has happened. But I think that absent other evidence, that's unlikely. Serial killers who are also rapists almost always operate alone."

"Kill alone, perhaps," I said. "Afterward, maybe not."

"Yeah," Alex said. "I think if we find the person the semen belongs to, we'll find the killer."

"Okay," I said. "But why secrete the victims in hopper cars? That's a very strange MO. Look, Upper Michigan is full of good locations to hide bodies—old mines, remote forests, places where nobody goes for years. Rivers and lakes, too. Unless our guy is a squirt or wimp, there would be no need to hire someone else to get rid of the bodies and risk his squealing."

"I'm thinking railroad cars, maybe just railroads, are an important component of the killer's sexual history," Sue said. "Let me go out on a limb here and suggest that maybe the killer himself or herself was sexually assaulted as a child in a railroad car, a boxcar perhaps, or even in a structure on a railroad, such as an old handcar shack. Such victims sometimes deal with their victimization by repeating the event."

"Makes sense," Alex said. "I think we've got a working hypothesis to start with. We're looking for a small or weakish man or possibly a woman who knows something about railroads and railroading."

"Size doesn't always matter," Sue said. "The killer could be tall but very thin or perhaps ill or terribly out of shape."

"Maybe a foamer," I said.

"Foamer?" Sue said.

"Rail buff, railfan, a hobbyist who lives and breathes railroads. Real railroaders contemptuously call them foamers because they supposedly froth at the mouth when discussing their favorite hobby. Foamers can be very odd birds. Some of them appear to have Asperger's syndrome, but most are quite harmless."

"Asperger's?" said Camilo. "How so?"

"Obsession with schedules and train orders and bills of lading and locomotives and freight cars," I said. "Railroading is a business of precise and orderly numbers, which appeals to minds that follow rigid channels. Asperger's lies on the autism spectrum."

"Where does a country sheriff learn that kind of shrink stuff?" Camilo asked. "I thought Sue was Alex's girlfriend."

Before she could retort, Alex said, "Steve's a rail buff. He likes to ride trains and read about them. You should see the piles of train magazines at his cabin."

"I travel by train when I can," I said loftily. "More civilized than flying."

It's true. In the past, when I took a rare vacation, Ginny, Tommy, and I drove south into Wisconsin and caught the Empire Builder, Amtrak's train from Chicago to Seattle. Two days later we were skiing in Whitefish, Montana, after many pleasant hours of conversation with other passengers, reading and watching America go by outside the window. I'm not exactly a foamer, but you might call me a modest train lover.

Camilo suddenly brought us back to earth. "Sometimes a cigar is just a cigar and a hopper car is just a hopper car," he said. "Convenient place to stash a stiff. Moves around a lot, and also sits in one place a long time. Confuses things. I think we ought to keep looking at those, and old boxcars and cabooses, too. Anything on flanged wheels that can be closed up from outside."

The phone rang. Alex picked it up and listened, saying nothing but grunting now and then, as he always does when he is being nattered at. Finally, he nodded, belched into the mouthpiece, said "Sure, bye," and hung up.

"That was Jack Adamson," he said.

"Surprise," I said. Adamson was the FBI special agent in charge in Detroit.

"FBI's taking over," Alex said.

"Surprise," I said again. From the beginning we had known that the FBI would step in because murders of children often mean kidnapping, and the FBI always leads those investigations. That first night in Rockville we'd called the Detroit office of the FBI, but the agent on duty asked us to keep on digging until a huge sting operation the agency was leading could be finished. He wouldn't tell us what it was.

"Of course the Feebs want us to continue investigating until they can get their ducks in a row," Alex said. This is not at all unusual. The FBI is always busy, especially in cases involving national security, and often depends on local law enforcement to do the initial spadework before the G-men start tramping around crime scenes. The federal bigfeet, however, often piss off local LEOs with their arrogant assumption that big-city boys know more about local scenes than do the cops who have worked there all their lives.

Jack Adamson looks like a cookie-cutter product of the School of J. Edgar Hoover, tall and ramrod-straight in suit and tie, his hair neatly cut, his white shirts pressed, with a sober and no-nonsense mien. But he is one of the rare special agents I have encountered who treats locals with respect. He had been a young state trooper in California before going to Stanford Law School and graduating with honors, then applying to the FBI.

He had enjoyed a long and successful career in Washington, cracking several high-profile cases and rising high in the hierarchy. We never found out what exactly happened, but the scuttlebutt was that he had trod on one exalted toe too many and was punished by banishment—not to a desolate wilderness posting like Brownsville, Texas, as rogue agents often are, but to a more important one, a major American city with a long record of crime and corruption. He had arrived in Detroit at age fifty-five and now was two years away from retirement.

Jack was hardly buddy-buddy with sheriffs and troopers, although he always treated us with as much candor and openness as he dared without besmirching his loyalty to the Bureau. He knew who signed his paycheck and wasn't about to let anything threaten his pension.

"So let's get started," I said.

"But where?" Alex said.

"Your guess is as good as mine."

CHAPTER FIVE

Ten more days passed before anything new happened, and it threw a monkey wrench into our ideas.

Skeletal remains belonging not to a young girl but a middle-aged male turned up in a grain hopper car being prepared for the fall harvest at a BNSF yard in Bismarck, North Dakota. At the FBI's request, railroad carmen around the country were carefully checking the interiors of empty hoppers before returning them to service. Sure enough, records showed that the car had been stored at Rockville for two years and a month before being moved to Bismarck. And the coroner there said that pending the full postmortem, it was likely that death had occurred no more than three years before. The investigation was continuing, but the Bismarck cops had little hope of identifying the corpse. There was no wallet and no watch. There were teeth that had been worked on, but nobody knew who the dentist was. In fact, there were no clothes. Only tattered and faded shreds of newspaper and clothesline bore any similarity to the evidence found at Rockville. There also was no visible cause of death, no evidence of a gunshot, no broken bones.

"Who was this guy?" Alex said over coffee at Merle's, keeping his voice low so that the locals breakfasting at neighboring tables couldn't overhear him. "Where was he from? Could he have been another Diego Guzman, an expendable to be eliminated once his usefulness was over?"

47

"Maybe. But there's damn little evidence to suggest that," I reminded Alex.

"Looks like the killer used cars at Rockville to stash all his victims," Alex said. "But where did he commit the assaults and the murders?"

"Or she," I reminded him.

"Or she."

"What's the FBI think?" I said.

"They're not sharing much with us."

"So what do we actually know?" Alex said. "Three of the four child victims, we know, were kids from downstate Michigan. Were they raped and killed there, then transported up over the Mackinac Bridge and driven west to Rockville? That's around five hundred miles."

"The killer would have run the risk of being stopped for speeding or a broken taillight or something like that," I said. "A conscientious cop might check the back seat or ask the driver to pop the trunk if the driver seemed suspicious. How would you behave if you were transporting a body or a trussed-up living child and got stopped by the police? To a cop, a nervous re-action would be probable cause. He'd ask the driver to open up, and if he refused, detain him until a warrant arrived."

"There's that," Alex said. "Maybe the killer brought them up, dead or alive, to the U.P. by boat across Lake Michigan, say from Grand Haven to Escanaba, then drove them the rest of the way? There are damnably few cops on the road up here, even us troopers, let alone you guys."

"There are damnably few cops on the road down there, too," I said. "I guess we just have to accept the idea that the killer used a vehicle to transport his victims."

Alex and I sat silently, gazing out the storefront window of Merle's at the passersby on River Street, Porcupine City's main drag. I don't know what Alex was thinking, but with a pang an old memory of a bunch of little girls walking home from school along River Street struggled to the surface. Giggling and carefree, they spun by one arm around lampposts and linked hands as they ducked around passersby. That sight was growing rarer and rarer as the population dropped in the Upper Peninsula.

People on the street had been growing older and older and fewer and fewer. From time to time high school kids drove by noisily in their old pickups, but their numbers also were dwindling. School districts all over the U.P. were consolidating as student bodies shrank. Their parents—folks in their twenties and thirties—were also disappearing. With the closing and demolition of the paper mill, jobs had nearly dried up in Porcupine City, and families had picked up and moved elsewhere. Many of the county's young men had either joined the military or left for the oil fields of North Dakota.

The exodus had left behind hundreds of empty dwellings in town and out in the woods. So many "For Sale" signs had gone up all over the Upper Peninsula and especially Porcupine County that real estate agents only half-heartedly advertised them locally, concentrating instead on publicizing recreational properties attractive to out-of-staters looking for cheap vacation homes. But even once valuable houses and land along the shore of Lake Superior had become hard to sell at decent prices.

Unable to pay their mortgages and property taxes, many Porkies just abandoned their old homes to the banks or county. Their dwellings were often ancient wooden cottages or double-wide trailers on small lots, some of them little more than rustic deer camps. Teenagers sometimes broke in to smoke dope and party, but fewer and fewer young people remained for that, and we weren't getting many trespassing calls. For a couple of years now, no one had set foot in many of these forlorn dwellings. No one was watching out for them. No one cared.

"Alex," I said. "I've got an idea."

"You do?" the trooper said, mock skepticism in his voice. "Shall we inform the FBI of that?"

"Asshole," I said amiably.

"Shoot."

"All these old abandoned houses and shacks and camps in the U.P. One of them could be the perfect place for a creep to hide a child and commit assault and murder. We ought to mount a house-to-house search in the Rockville area."

"You've got something there, Steve." Alex straightened up in his seat.

"But this would be needle-in-a-haystack stuff," I said.

"Still worth doing," Alex said. "What else can we do?"

"Let's get cracking."

The first thing I did after Alex left was call Jack Adamson at his FBI office in Detroit and tell him what we planned. Jack was affable, possibly, I thought, because the FBI was basking in the glory of the massive and successful drug raid it had led the previous day. The Bureau had coordinated with the Drug Enforcement Agency, the Bureau of Alcohol, Tobacco and Firearms, the Detroit police, and the Michigan state police in a huge drug sweep against ethnic gangs of all kinds. Hundreds of gangbangers had been arrested. Every agent in Detroit and imported feds from half a dozen cities had been involved. Only that morning did we learn the details of what Jack wouldn't tell us ten days ago. I didn't blame him. The fewer who knew about such a scheme, the better.

"Go right ahead," Jack said. "Keep us posted."

"As always," I said, for he was the boss, as the FBI inevitably is. The irony evidently eluded him, for he hung up after a cheery "Keep your nose clean up there."

★ ★ ★ ★ ★

By the next morning we had enlisted a dozen troopers from western Upper Michigan, the same number of deputies from three counties, ten tribal policemen from two Indian reservations, and a double handful of conservation officers, Forest Service rangers, and their Michigan State Parks counterparts— all of them sworn law enforcement officers.

We also temporarily deputized sixteen members of the Porcupine County Search and Rescue squad, most of them military veterans and all experienced woodsmen and women, attaching a deputy to the squad to make legal law enforcement decisions if necessary.

We figured that the hunt would take two days, possibly three. Our search area, with its geographic center the sidings at Rockville, would encompass all of Porcupine County and large portions of adjoining Gogebic and Houghton counties. We divided the area into mile-square quadrants, mapping the dwellings within each quadrant with the help of charts from the county tax assessor's office.

Shortly after dawn our small army fanned out over the countryside, moving from house to house like combat infantrymen mopping up the enemy. A pair of officers would stop at each inhabited house or trailer or cabin and ask the residents if they had seen anything suspicious or unusual in the last few weeks. Nearly all the derelict structures we encountered had been left open to the elements and had become apartments for wild animals of all kinds. We were especially careful not to rile skunks that had taken up residence within.

Some of the country folks said they had seen suspicious goings-on, but they were almost all irrelevant. "There aren't as many crows this year," one said. "They're all dying off in these parts." Others complained about a boom in marauding wolves and demanded that we do something about them. We referred them all to the Department of Natural Resources. The over-whelmed DNR receptionist later called us and asked why we were shaking all those crabapples out of the trees.

Early in the afternoon on the first day, less than a quarter of a mile from the Rockville siding, an old woman told the two tribal cops in her doorway that from time to time in the last couple of years she had seen mysterious red flashlight beams passing through the brush in the night near an old shack over by the railroad. There were two of the lights, she said.

"They looked like the eyes of the Beast," she said. "I know they belonged to the Devil himself."

"Why didn't you tell us before?" said the tribal cop who was interviewing her.

"You didn't ask," she said. That was hardly surprising. Up here in the deep backwoods, many people mistrust the government, so much so that they refuse to go out of their way to volunteer information to law enforcement. They prefer to let things alone so that they will be let alone. They often refuse to file income tax returns and have eluded the IRS only because their income is so meager that the taxmen, as beleaguered by pinched budgets as we are, simply don't consider them worth going after. Yet. If Congress ever increases the IRS's funding, these poor wretches could be scooped up and squeezed of every nickel.

Some of them subscribe to the tenets of white supremacy. The backwoods have always been fertile ground for neo-Nazis, but so far the would-be stormtroopers have been so inept and inefficient that all they seem to manage is a get-together in the woods a few times a year for target shooting and drunken strutting around in swastikas and jackboots. In my bailiwick and its vicinity, they have been more annoying than dangerous. But I worry. Hard times and controversies over gun control and immigration always kindle their anger, and in many places the election of a black President of the United States has provided fuel for the kind of blind hate that often results in violent irrationality.

"Well, we're asking now!" said the tribal cop with considerable asperity.

Within half an hour Camilo and his crew found the old shack the woman had mentioned. It was an abandoned and completely forgotten one-room sentry post, eight feet by ten feet and crudely built of pine two-by-sixes, at the old prisoner-of-war camp half a mile from the tracks and completely hidden in thick brush far from human habitation. We should have found it during our initial investigation weeks ago, but the undergrowth screening the building from the tracks was so thick that the searchers missed it.

Someone had repaired the shack's rotted roof with scraps of tarpaper and replaced broken panes in two windows with plywood patches. Plastic water jugs and empty cans of hash and baked beans ringed a single stained mattress in the center of the room. In one corner lay a small, forlorn pile of rags. On its side by the mattress was an old tin wastebasket stamped "U.S. Army." At the bottom of the wastebasket, hidden in shreds of facial tissues, lay half a dozen used condoms, dried semen still in their reservoirs.

"If our subject is the one that old lady called the Beast and is also the one who fixed up that shack, he's not as smart as he thinks he is," said Alex that evening after all the searchers had returned to base, leaving a state police forensics team from Wakefield to collect and chart the new evidence. They had bagged the condoms and sent the package by courier express to the FBI in Detroit. The staties knew the feds would want them right away.

"But is this really our guy?" I asked. "Couldn't those condoms have been left behind by teenagers rather than a killer?" That shack, we all knew, would have made a perfect love nest for mindless and horny youth.

"If the DNA in those rubbers matches that found in the fourth girl at Rockville," Chad said with feeling, "we've got the Beast hammered to the wall like a butterfly nailed to particle board."

"Nailed?" I said. "Particle board?" I said. Chad often takes metaphorical flight in his remarks as well as reports, but sometimes his similes need work. All the same, his fervent use of the first-person plural emphasized the growing determination of all law enforcement in the Upper Peninsula: We will not let up until we catch this killer. Ordinary homicides dismay us— they upset the increasingly delicate balance between the human population and nature in these parts—but murders of small children are an absolute moral outrage.

"The FBI will go to town with that evidence," I said, "but I don't think they'll hit pay dirt. Sure, the killer could have used the shack, but the woman didn't actually see him going in there. She only saw him in the vicinity. I'm betting it was teenagers who fixed up the place."

But we quickly adopted "the Beast" as a working name for our perpetrator. It was both more specific and more heartfelt than "the Unsub," as the FBI and other law enforcement agencies like to call an unidentified subject. The person we were looking for had committed beastly crimes.

CHAPTER SIX

Chad in particular quickly took the case to heart.

"Done me some digging," he announced in the squad room two days later. He had spent hours on the phone, a manner of investigation I encouraged because it was cheap—our contract with AT&T gave us unlimited minutes—and because Chad was good at it.

"Those victims we know about weren't really profiled in the medical examiners' reports, you know," he said. "So I made some calls and found out more stuff about them, from local cops mostly, but also Jack Adamson. It might help."

Adamson actually was sharing. That was noteworthy. But was he being generous with information because he believed in interagency cooperation, or because the FBI was stuck at a dead end and didn't want to admit it?

"Tell us," I said, sliding back my chair and lifting my feet onto the desk. Gil, the starchy old marine, hates that, and bristles every time I do it. Deputies don't dare. They know he'll rip them a new one. I get away with it because I'm the boss. Besides, the relaxed gesture is subtle encouragement to my people—most of them, anyway—to open up and speak their minds. Gil, however, needs no encouragement. He always tells me directly what he thinks I need to know, whether or not I want to know it. In the marines he had been not only a drill sergeant but also a company first sergeant, used to telling lieutenants and captains how to run their commands. He's as often right as he is wrong.

"Sheila McWilliams from Holland," Chad said, looking at his notes. "That's on Lake Michigan 180 miles, or about three hours, due west of Detroit. Neighbors told the cops that she's— was—an ace student, all A's, a Girl Scout with a bunch of merit badges, and a promising ballerina. She took classes three times a week with a ninety-three-year-old teacher, a former prima ballerina with the Paris Opera, who said Sheila was the best prospect she'd seen in many years. In fact, Sheila was grabbed up on her way home from school to get her ballet stuff and go to class. They say she was cute, with blond hair and piercing blue eyes, and a very sunny personality. Everybody liked her. The Holland detective investigating the case almost broke down when he told me about her. Said she reminded him of his own daughter."

" 'Scuse me," said Chad, blowing his nose noisily and wiping the corners of his eyes as he shuffled his notes. "Musta got a cold coming on."

"Lashonda Harris from Fremont. Another gem of a little girl. Mixed race. Daughter of a decorated black army sergeant about to be rotated home from Helmand province in Afghanistan. Mother white, an elementary school teacher. Another child popular in her hometown. A good student, a competent athlete often chosen first for playground teams. Did a lot of church work with her two older brothers, helping shut-ins. The detective said church was her whole life and she wanted to become either a missionary or a coast guard rescue swimmer. One way or the other she wanted to save people. When she disappeared from that playground she was on her way to her church to help prepare Meals on Wheels."

The squadroom fell still and quiet as Chad spoke. Even Gil put down his accounts and charts, folded his hands on his desk, and listened.

"Andrea Lacoste wasn't exactly a saint," Chad said. The Newaygo County sheriff said she was a troubled little girl, constantly getting into jams of all kinds. She was picked up a couple of times for shoplifting and once for throwing a rock through the living room window of an old lady who had yelled at her. Of course that juvenile record had been suppressed, but the sheriff knew all about her. She had a long record of truancy. Her neighbors said she smoked reefer in the garage. She was an only child. Her dad is an alcoholic and regularly beat her mother, who just about had given up trying to hold the family together and has moved out to a battered women's home. Now, of course, the sheriff said, there's nothing left to hold together."

For a long moment we remained silent.

Then Joe Koski spoke up. "Fremont and Newaygo are only eleven miles apart," he said. "They're good-sized small towns, not like Holland, which is a small city. Holland is only sixty or so miles from either town. Think our subject is from around there?"

"Maybe, but not necessarily," Chad said. "The FBI said there have been only two unsolved cases of young girls missing in Newaygo County in the last ten years, and Sheila and Lashonda were both of them. Andrea was one of about half a dozen girls between the ages of nine and fifteen who disappeared in Holland over the same time. Two were abducted by their birth fathers."

"The MO similar in all the cases involving the girls?" I asked. We all knew the answer, but it helped to hear it again.

"All three victims were apparently taken while walking home from school or a playground," Chad said. "That's a bit unusual in itself. These days most parents pick their kids up from school or otherwise keep an eye on them. Too many bad guys around."

"That's true in the cases of Sheila and Lashonda," Chad said. "But they lived in small towns. They had to walk only a block or two between their homes and schools, and the neigborhoods were both made up of single-family houses. Lashonda's church was also only a few hundred yards from the playground where she disappeared. Andrea, on the other hand, lived on the far side of town from the school she attended, when she bothered to attend it. She had been suspended from her own neighborhood school once too often."

"I think we'll see the same pattern with the fourth girl when she's identified," I said. "If she is. The Beast apparently haunts schoolyards and playgrounds, and may prefer small towns because their people are more trusting."

"Kids are at their most vulnerable after school," Gil observed. "They're in class all day, feeling safe, and then they go outside, carrying that feeling with them. They're happy to be sprung and don't think about the bad people their parents warned them about."

"Nobody saw anything at those schools?" I asked Chad.

"Nope. No witnesses at all. Not one said they saw a snatching. The Feebs have interviewed everybody there is to interview. Adamson told me that when parents pick up their kids at school, their attention is entirely on the kids. They're not looking around for strangers or people who look like they don't belong. Same with the teachers of really small kids, preschoolers through first or second graders. They're looking to make sure their pupils are released in the charge of their parents or grandmas or nannies, people they know. Only the older teenagers are thought to be mature enough to be allowed to go off on their own."

"Surely the older kids are savvy about strangers with candy and stuff like that," I said.

"Yes," said Chad. "That's why the FBI thinks the Beast is a snatch-and-grab artist. Drives slowly along behind a kid walking alone, then speeds up and stops, jumps out and grabs the kid unawares, throws her into his car, and speeds off. Maybe knocks her out with chloroform or something, trusses her up with tape, and throws her into the back seat. If he's fast enough and lucky enough, nobody sees anything."

"That would be hard to do in a car," Gil said. "But not in a van or RV with big sliding side doors."

The undersheriff spoke in a tone surprisingly angry even for him. He echoed what we were all feeling. Up to now we had tried to look at things professionally and dispassionately, as we always should and usually do, but now the case had gotten personal. These were our little girls who were being kidnapped and murdered.

Other jurisdictions were feeling the pressure. Everywhere, especially in the Midwest, parents now were phoning the police in a panic when their children didn't come home at the appointed hour or otherwise had flown the coop to parts unknown, as youngsters often do. When the kid showed up at suppertime Mommy and Daddy often didn't let the police know, forcing the cops to phone them so the matter could be closed.

A few children truly did disappear, as they do every day all over the country, especially in the big cities. If they are poor and black or Latino, the press doesn't care. Old bigotries still rule at many levels of our supposedly enlightened country. It's only when kids are white and blond, and their mothers are the same, happen to be camera-pretty, and live in the right neighborhoods, does the media take notice—especially the vultures of so-called cable television news.

"No other girls from that area are missing, are they?" Alex asked.

"None," Chad said.

"I'd be surprised if any more of them turn up," I said. "I hope not, anyway."

"But what about that skeleton at Bismarck?" Gil said. "He doesn't really fit with the girls, so far as we know, or with Diego

Guzman. Adamson said bone measurements and DNA tests showed the Bismarck bones belonged to a smallish guy, fifty-some years old, who was probably half Irish and half Italian. He had been sick with diabetes. Probably not big and strong enough to be a mule for our killer. If he was murdered, it probably wasn't with a gun."

"Right," I said. "Frankly, I doubt very much that we're done finding new corpses."

"Why?" Gil said.

"That Bismarck guy."

"So?"

"His presence in that hopper car could be completely unrelated to the little girls," I said. "Maybe the Beast doesn't just go after children but also kills adults. Maybe there's more than one bastard and the existence of the same MO is just a co-incidence. What we've found may only be the tip of the iceberg. There could be a lot more bodies out there in freight cars that were disposed of by a lot of bastards over the years. And there may be bodies that we'll never find, because the cars they were stashed in were cleaned without anybody noticing what was in them. It was just happenstance that that car cleaner in Omaha saw what fell out."

"So what now?" Alex said, voicing the question in all our minds.

"Time to throw a neighborhood party," I said.

CHAPTER SEVEN

By "neighborhood party" we meant an official town meeting, little more than a press conference with coffee and doughnuts to which everybody is invited, an event ostensibly designed to reassure nervous Nellies that the cops are on the case and that it soon will be solved. We'd set up chairs in a church hall or other public place and invite the neighbors as well as the press to come hear what law enforcement had so far found out.

Cops hold these events all the time everywhere. Some worries are soothed and some PR is done. But those are not the real reasons for the gatherings. Perpetrators like to revisit the scenes of their crimes, partly to revel in the social upheaval they have caused and partly to find out what the cops really know and how close they are to catching the bad guys. Naturally law enforcement is greatly interested in who attends and where they come from. With luck someone will stick out like a sunflower in a daisy patch and with even more luck that someone will be the subject they're looking for.

And so we planned our neighborhood party with an eye to spreading our limited resources as efficiently as possible. Ideally, we needed a two-story structure in the middle of a large yard, preferably a meadow, surrounded on all sides by thick wood and brush, and easily accessible only by a single road. We'd hide troopers and deputies behind the windows of the second floor to watch all approach points and photograph everyone who came. Tribal cops in plain clothes would sit in cars where the road met the highway and photograph the license plates of every car that drove in. Nobody could get in or out without being noticed and, we hoped, identified either on the spot or later. That way we hoped to narrow down our search for the killer.

The beautiful old Lutheran Church of the Woods just outside Rockville, a quarter of a mile down a gravel road from U.S. 45 through thick forest, was the perfect place, and the pastor and church fathers agreed to our plan so long as we promised to repair any damage to the buildings or grounds the visitors might cause. How we would come up with cash for that I had no idea at all. But I thought we would be able to get people to behave and, if they didn't, to "volunteer" to paint scratches and fix ruts in the lawn. We'd done that with Saturday-night drunks who agreed to a few hours of community service on county properties in lieu of a fine for disorderly conduct. In the boonies, plea bargaining is a wonderful thing. Everybody wins.

For three days we called every radio and television station and newspaper in the Upper Peninsula to inform them of the town meeting. Chad even phoned a reporter he knew at the *Detroit Free Press*. If we were lucky, we reasoned, a hundred or so folks might attend—a number we felt comfortable in handling. Maybe, just maybe, we'd scratch out a clue or two, enough to keep investigating.

To our great surprise nearly five hundred people came from all over the Upper Peninsula, northern lower Michigan, and Wisconsin. Two Duluth television stations sent crews, as did a Marquette outlet. An Associated Press reporter was one of the first on the scene, and so was Harold Wright, the weekly *Porcupine County Herald*'s sole reporter and a stringer for the *Milwaukee Journal Sentinel,* where he had worked as a police reporter before he retired. Like the other members of the media, Harold had been to enough "town meetings" in Milwaukee to know why they were really held, but he was too much the professional to let on. Besides, he likes me and I like him. In the past I have given him exclusives in return for his silence about our strategies in celebrated cases. He is smart and experienced enough to figure them out on the basis of a few public clues.

Ordinarily at solemn public gatherings I wear my formal uniform—blue slacks, white shirt with epaulets and gold stars, gold shield, and gold braid-encrusted garrison cap. This glittering ensemble, typical of sheriffs all over Michigan, causes citizens and deputies alike to call us "The Target," because it makes us stand out so much that we might attract snipers. This time I decided to dress as I always do, in jeans, blue chambray work shirt, and ball cap with a sheriff's star and the embroidered words "PORCUPINE COUNTY SHERIFF DEPT." I figured that would signal to the audience that I was laboring hard on the case rather than preening like a rooster in official finery.

As people filed into the church's meeting room, we asked them to jot their names, addresses, and phone numbers onto a clipboard "just so we can get in touch if we need to. You never know." They didn't know it, but as they signed the clipboard, they were giving us handwriting samples while Joe Koski, shrouded by a potted plant, was photographing their faces with a long lens. A few declined to identify themselves, but Joe captured their images anyway. Not signing didn't mean anyone was guilty of anything—they may just have valued their privacy—but we noted their reticence. We'd check out every one of them as part of the long process of elimination of suspects.

Most of the faces in the throng were strangers to me. The townspeople were familiar, including the dozen middle-aged-to-elderly ladies who had arrived early and taken up most of the first row in front of the lectern. They were the sewing club that packs Wilhelmina's tiny coffee shop in Porcupine City every

Wednesday morning to discuss stitches and exchange mildly salacious gossip. Ginny is a member of the club and nearly every week comes home with an item of intelligence that is occasionally valuable to law enforcement but usually is just good for a laugh at the dinner table.

Just behind them sat all nine of the county commissioners. I felt certain that they just wanted to make sure I behaved myself and didn't embarrass Porcupine County. I had never disappointed them, so far as I knew, but that didn't mean there wouldn't be a first time. They were flanked by most of the pastors of the county's churches, who to a man (and woman) believed in keeping an eye on politicians, the worst kind of sinners.

At the end of one row sat Jack Haygood, one of Upper Michigan's leading authors, a mystery novelist and true-crime writer. He was armed with both a notebook and a digital recorder, and it was obvious a new book was in the offing. He had not yet approached me, but I knew that at some point he would, and I hoped it would be after the case was closed so he wouldn't get in the way and I wouldn't have to lie to him.

In a corner I spotted Mike Perlman, the tall, skinny, and cashmere-sweatered president of the Keweenaw & Lake Superior who had come up from Green Bay in the early hours of our search for bodies at Rockville to help us sort out the likeliest cars to examine. On one side of him sat his chief financial officer, Howard Lehtinen, a soft and pear-shaped bookkeeper in a wrinkled blue suit. On the other side lounged two engineer-conductors, Billy Travers and Jim Braithwaite, both small, skinny, bearded, and bedenimed fellows, familiar to me from the cabs of the locomotives they had brought into Porcupine City when the paper mill was still running and the rails to town had not yet been torn up.

Every folding chair was occupied, and standing-room

overflow choked the perimeter of the room. Scattered through-
out the standees were several troopers and most of my deputies,
including Gil and Chad. I wanted them to be visible in and to
the audience so that the Beast—if he (or she) was present—
wouldn't suspect that other law enforcement was busy outside
taking attendance, photographing license plates as well as faces
from concealed spots in the woods and the back seats of cars
scattered among the dozens and dozens parked alongside the
access road. We had assigned tribal cops and several conservation officers as well as deputies from Houghton and Gogebic
Counties to this task. They were all in plain clothes, and their
faces weren't well known in my bailiwick.

Nor were the three tall and broad-shouldered men in almost
identical dark gray suits, well tailored but not in-your-face
expensive. Two were dark and saturnine and the third blond
and Aryan-handsome. If he were a Hollywood actor, I thought,
he would make a very good Nazi *SS-Hauptsturmfuehrer* in a
World War II movie. He seemed to be in charge.

"They arrived in a black government Suburban," Gil had
whispered. "The three blind mice." Gil detests FBI agents,
except for Jack, with whom he maintains a polite but distant
relationship. That's as buddy-buddy as Gil ever gets with
anyone, and says a lot for Jack's reputation among Upper
Peninsula law enforcement.

"These guys gotta be from D.C.," Gil added. "Hope they're
not pushing Jack around."

"I'm afraid they are," I whispered back. "That's what they do
for a living."

"They look like somebody stepped on their dicks," Gil said.

The agents' sour expressions suggested to me that something
had happened in Washington, something unpleasant, and that
their bosses had put them on the spot. "Produce or else" is a
management tactic sure to demoralize those upon whom it is

imposed. For a fleeting moment I began to feel sorry for the agents, but my compassion quickly evaporated. Shit flows downhill, and I did not want my guys to be the ones at the bottom.

I stepped to the lectern and tapped the mike in welcome. "My name is Steve Martinez. I am the sheriff of Porcupine County. And this gentleman is Detective Sergeant Alex Kolehmainen of the Michigan State Police. Over here is Jack Adamson, who is the Federal Bureau of Investigation special agent in charge at Detroit. Agent Adamson is the leader of the overall investigation into this case, and Sergeant Kolehmainen and I are assisting him in this part of Michigan."

I also mentioned that the sheriffs of Gogebic, Houghton, and Baraga counties were involved, but didn't say that they and their deputies lurked outside in the shadows with the tribal cops, helping keep watch on everyone who came into the building.

I took a deep sigh, hoping I didn't overdo it. "We all know the basic facts of this case, but Agent Adamson will go over the details for you in a few minutes. Meanwhile, I want to assure all of you in Porcupine County that law enforcement thinks that you and your children are in no danger—no danger at all. Medical examiners believe that the child victims we found in freight cars linked to the Keweenaw & Brule River Railroad all died elsewhere and their bodies were transferred to the cars some time after death."

I carefully avoided using the word "dumped," partly because I wanted to sound somber and official, and partly out of respect to the little girls and their families. I also did not mention the discovery of the corpse of Diego Guzman. We had not yet publicized that detail, holding it in reserve in case the guilty party—if we ever caught him or her—inadvertently referred to it during interrogation. It would also help us winnow out the troubled people who liked to confess to notorious crimes just to win attention.

Nor did Jack mention Guzman when he stepped to the lectern and outlined the case on a screen with a digital projector and laser pointer, focusing on videos, photographs, and diagrams of the cars in which the skeletons had been found. His was a typically slick and utterly professional presentation designed to wow the audience with the FBI's technical brilliance. It certainly impressed me, and I felt a touch of jealousy at the federal agents' seemingly limitless resources.

I was not surprised when Jack ended his presentation with a grace note rarely heard from FBI agents. "The FBI can't do everything," he said. "We are grateful to local law enforcement for their initial and continuing work in this investigation. It has been excellent."

I stole a glance at the three agents from D.C. in the audience. They stared ahead stonily. One leaned his head to the agent on his right and whispered. The other agent, the one who reminded me of a big blond Nazi, nodded almost imperceptibly. He still looked unhappy.

"If any of you has heard anything or seen anything," Jack said, "please get in touch with either Sheriff Martinez or Sergeant Kolehmainen. Or with me, for that matter." His laser pointer danced under the three telephone numbers carefully printed on a whiteboard next to the screen. "Now I'll give the mike back to the sheriff."

He stood aside and nodded to me. As a bigfoot FBI agent, Jack walked with a remarkably soft tread.

In turn I handed the mike to Alex, as we had planned. "Okay," he said. "Now we'll be happy to take questions from the audience and from the press."

Hands shot up. Alex pointed to Harold Wright, who was invariably the first we acknowledged at events like this, as if he were the dean of the White House press corps.

"Harold Wright," he said. *"Porcupine County Herald.* Do you have a suspect in the case?"

We were ready. "Special Agent Adamson?" Alex said.

Jack stepped back to the lectern. "At this sensitive point in the investigation," he said, "we are unable to address that detail with the public. We can assure you, however, that we are following every possible avenue and that no stone is being left unturned."

He went on like that for two minutes, delivering his official boilerplate in a calm and even tone designed to reassure the public and the press that the investigators had full confidence they were on the right track and that an arrest soon would be made. The public seemed satisfied. The old ladies in the front row nodded approvingly.

The three blind mice gazed ahead, but this time I thought I detected a glint of approval in their hooded eyes.

"Thank you," said Harold, and sat down. He knew, as did the rest of the press, that Jack's reassuring bullshit simply meant one of two things. Either we were about to nab the perpetrator or we hadn't a clue. There was no use in pushing us.

Not all the public got the point. "Who did this? What's his name?" shouted a middle-aged woman notorious for her constant calls to law enforcement complaining about everything, from the county commissioners' failure to plow her driveway to conservation officers ignoring bears at her bird feeders. Her neighbors quickly shushed her.

Another citizen rose and asked, "Why are all those railroad cars stored there? They're a public nuisance. They attract criminals. All sorts of things go on there. It's public property."

"The president of the Keweenaw & Brule River Railroad is with us tonight," Alex said. "Mr. Perlman, would you care to answer that?"

We had tipped Perlman that the question was likely to be asked, and he was prepared.

"First of all," he said as he stepped to the lectern, "the railroad right of way is private property, not public. Anyone who goes on it is trespassing. That in itself is an offense. We are very concerned about what has happened and we are giving the authorities every bit of assistance we can."

More corporate boilerspeak followed, but it included a careful explanation of why the K & BR stored other railroads' cars as well as its own, and Perlman pointed out that since most of them were secreted on sidings hidden from view, they were hardly a public nuisance.

"Despite what recently happened, over the years not much has gone on there," he said. "I think the sheriff would back me up on that. Besides, the railroad is an important part of the economy of this part of Michigan, and I think on balance everyone would agree that it needs to be here and that the county needs it."

Shouts went up. "Then why did you pull up the rails to Porcupine City?" someone yelled. "You've killed our economy!"

The fellow had a point, but Alex quickly took the mike. "We're not here to discuss that issue," he said. "We are here to talk about something else, and I think we should focus on it. Thank you, Mr. Perlman."

The railroad president sat down with a scowl, as if he had been offended by the question. I knew, however, that he had been ready for it and was grateful he hadn't had to answer. Before the meeting I had told him we'd run interference provided he'd keep cooperating with us. And he had. He had also given me the sense that he genuinely hated what had happened on his railroad and that he wanted to find the criminal or criminals as much as we did.

A few more questions followed, some of them from the press

that were designed to elicit gruesome details about the discoveries of the corpses, but we deflected them with more time-honored appeals to the sensitivity of the investigation. They'd all come out eventually—at the trial, we hoped. Not before.

Alex handed the mike back to me and stood aside.

"Thank you all for coming," I said. "We hope this meeting has relieved any concerns you might have had. Good night."

As the spectators filed out, one of the cable news reporters approached me. "There'll be ten grand for an exclusive on-camera interview," he said almost under his breath.

"No," I said. "Legal reasons. Besides, we've already told you all we can." Furthermore, I wasn't going to let myself be pulled into a mess of prejudicial pretrial publicity. But the news guy shrugged. I had given him the answer he expected.

Just then the leader of the three blind mice buttonholed Jack and whispered into his ear. He nodded with a blank expression and strode over to me.

"After your guys gather their data," Jack said, "Washington wants it all. As soon as possible. They'll do the analysis and any necessary follow-up." He was too loyal to his agency to offer an apology for his superiors' high-handedness, but I did not blame him, and he knew that.

"It will be done," I said, in as neutral a tone as I could manage.

A cell phone rang. We all checked ours. It was Alex's.

"They found another one," he said.

CHAPTER EIGHT

The next morning Alex, Jack, and I convened in the kitchen at the sheriff's department—the closest thing it had to a conference room—to discuss the results of the meeting. They were meager, partly because Eeny, Meeny, and Miney, as Gil was now calling the men from Washington, had driven off with all the photographs and data we had gathered, including the attendance sheets—but not before we had a quick chance to examine them.

"All right," said Alex, "who didn't sign in?"

"Only a dozen people," I said. "Eight of them are locals known to us and most of them wouldn't sign their names to stay out of jail."

"So they came just to keep an eye on us crooked cops," Alex said. "And the other four are the railroaders, who probably thought they weren't supposed to check in because they're more or less part of the investigation."

"So we can eliminate those twelve, do you think?" Jack said.

"For now," I said. "None of them seem worth the trouble."

"What did the tribals say?" I asked Alex.

"Nobody seemed to be out of place. Nobody tried to sneak through the woods. Nobody they saw had a rap sheet worse than a couple of drunk and disorderlies."

During the meeting the tribals had done their due diligence by calling in license plate numbers to LEIN, the Law Enforcement Information Network, and checking out their owners.

"None of the license plates was from anywhere except Michigan, Wisconsin, and Minnesota. And the federal government," Alex said, glancing at Jack.

The special agent remained impassive. "If there's anything to be found in that data, our specialists will find it," he said. "They've got the resources."

For Jack that was almost a defensive remark. But he was right, and we knew it. The Feds had a huge budget, and there were no boundaries to our poverty.

"I don't think that last night was a waste of effort," I said. "I can't tell you why, but I have a strong feeling that the Beast was present in the audience."

Neither Jack nor Alex asked why. They knew my track record with wild hunches. Hunches alone, however, wouldn't get us any closer to the truth. A lot of sweat and shoe leather is always needed if they are to pan out.

"Okay," Alex said, "what about the latest body? What do we know?"

"It was found yesterday in a CSX Railway yard at Philadelphia," I said, looking over the report that had been faxed from state police headquarters in Lansing. "The bones of an adult woman. Prelim says she was in her thirties and had been dead twenty years or so. The remains of short shorts and a halter top were found with her. Also rotted shreds of a gunny sack. No underwear. No apparent cause of death."

"The clothes suggest maybe she was a hooker," Alex said. "What was the sack tied with?"

"Sisal twine," I said.

"Not clothesline?"

"No. A minor departure from the MO with the kids."

"What kind of car?"

"Surprise. Covered grain hopper."

"And where had that car been?"

"Not here," I said. "The car had spent seven years on a storage siding outside Cumberland, Maryland. The CSX hauled it out to send to the scrapper and looked inside only because Maryland state police had asked them to, thanks to the FBI's BOLO."

"Not on the K & BR," Alex said, "but hundreds of miles away. That's a *major* departure from the earlier MOs."

"Jack, what's the FBI going to do about this one?" I asked.

"Washington said the Bureau will let the Maryland authorities handle that one, at least until a firm connection—if any—can be established with the homicides of the three kidnapped children."

"Dumping bodies into railroad cars isn't a firm connection?" Alex replied incredulously.

"There's that," Jack said. "But the FBI always looks harder for similarities in motive rather than in opportunity. After all, people have been stuffing bodies in railroad cars for a hundred and fifty or more years. Opportunity isn't necessarily important here. Anybody could have done that Maryland victim for any reason."

"An awful lot of bodies seem to be turning up lately, though," I said. "A mere statistical sport?"

"Maybe not," Alex said. "After all, we're looking for them. That increases the chances a body will turn up. If we're not looking, a body may not be found."

We mused silently for a minute or two, then Alex broke the vacuum. "Jack, will the FBI share its analysis of last night's sweep with us?"

"Washington might not, at least right away," Jack said. "But they will with me, and I will with you."

That surprised me. Jack was indirectly telling us that he wasn't going to let his employer's institutional bullheadedness stunt our knowledge of the case. He was taking a big chance. I now had a better idea of what he must have done to be sent to Siberia.

"So our work is done here?" Alex said.

"Seems so," Jack said.

"Maybe not," I said.

Alex and Jack stared at me. Both knew as well as I do that a law enforcement officer anywhere on the totem pole lower than the FBI could get himself into deep, deep shit with the Feds if he went off on a tangent by himself. "Interfering with a Federal investigation" is what the Bureau calls it. At the least I could lose my job and at the worst do time in a federal prison.

I held up a hand. "I don't intend to step on the FBI's toes," I said. "I'm simply going to offer advice where warranted. That's okay, isn't it, Jack?"

"Sure," he said. "But they're not likely to listen to a county sheriff, even one with a record like yours, when they've made up their mind on the direction of their investigation."

He wasn't being disloyal, just practical. "Where do you think they're going with it, Steve?" he said with a deep sigh. He knew the answer, and he knew Alex and I knew, too.

"They're going to focus entirely on those little girls," I said. "Child abduction and murder is red meat to the FBI. They're going to think that if they catch their killer they've solved the case."

"And why not?" Jack said.

"Because of those adult skeletons," I said. "The one found with the child can be explained without much difficulty, but the others? Psychopaths don't usually go afield like that. Rather, they concentrate on their obsession. Their victims tend to be similar."

"How do you know that?" Alex said. "You're no shrink."

"A tête-à-tête with your girlfriend," I said. That morning I had phoned Lieutenant Sue Hemb in Lansing and told her my doubts. As a state police crime profiler she knew how the FBI's brilliant minds worked—she had attended the same schools they did, hung out at the same seminars, and knew most of the federal profilers. She had agreed that there was a considerable difference in the MO between the child and adult victims, as well as the likely psychological mindsets of the killers, if there were more than one. Whether or not that was true required more time and investigation. That made sense to me.

"You're always carrying on behind my back with Sue," said Alex with a twinkle in his eye. Jack chuckled.

"And well I should," I said. "She's smarter than you."

"No argument," Alex said. "I ought to listen to her instead of to you."

"So what are you going to do, Steve?" Jack said.

"I'll leave the little girls to the FBI, of course. Much as I'd rather not."

"And?"

"We'll see."

A moment of silence after that, then Jack said. "I'm heading back to Detroit now."

"Keep in touch," I said.

Jack turned as he reached the door. "You, too," he said with an ever so slight spin on the "you." That, I knew, was a friendly warning.

Alex stood in the door with me as Jack drove off. "Going to catch you a killer?" he said.

"No."

"No?"

"I think there may be more than one person involved in this case," I said.

"Which one we going after?" That was Alex's way of telling me he had my back.

"Don't know."

"Come again?"

"I'm not certain the guy who dumped those bodies killed any of them."

CHAPTER NINE

"You're pulling my leg!" Alex said.

"Nope."

"What's your theory?"

"All right. Here we have four apparent kidnap-murders of young girls, evidence that they were killed by a deranged sexual offender. One adult male body was found with one of the girls and clearly can't be a suicide, hence must be a homicide. The skeletal remains of another adult male and one adult female have also turned up inside freight cars. They are probably also homicides but we can't be sure of that just yet. It's possible that one or more died naturally, but we can't be sure of that either. It's possible that one or more were simply disposed of in order to save on burial costs—a funeral on the cheap. Maybe they are all unrelated, except for the means of their disposal.

"Most important, every one of these bodies has been found in some kind of covered hopper car. Not an open hopper, gondola, ore car, tank car, boxcar, refrigerator car, abandoned caboose, steam locomotive cab, or any of half a hundred different kinds of rolling stock available anywhere on railroads in the United States. Only covered hopper cars. People like to use familiar tools. This is part of almost every MO."

Alex leaned back in his chair and gazed at me with frank interest, all smart-ass thoughts banished from his brain. "Go on, Steve," he said.

"This suggests to me that these corpses may have met their

end at the hands of more than one killer, but also that one person is doing the dumping of all of them. Someone who knows about covered hopper cars and why they are stored where they are. Someone who knows that it may probably be years before the cars are moved, that they often go straight to the scrappers, and that when they don't and are cleaned, the residue is dumped largely unnoticed into trash pits. It was only by chance that the car cleaners at Omaha found those bones."

Alex sat straight up in his chair. "Someone who knows about railroading," he said.

"Yes. Not an ordinary rail buff, a foamer," I said. "They're unlikely to know the operational details of car storage. I think we're looking for someone in the industry, a real railroader."

"But you don't think he's the killer?" Alex said.

"No. I think he's the undertaker. The guy who rows the ferry carrying the souls of the dead across the Rivers Styx and Acheron for a coin or two. The Charon."

"Your knowledge of classical mythology always astonishes me," Alex said.

"I did go to college," I said. Four years at Cornell, then two in criminal justice at City University of New York before fulfilling my ROTC duty as a military policeman. "Now and then you pick up interesting stuff in the classroom."

I let Alex draw the obvious conclusion. "So our subject may be a railroader with a sideline in getting rid of bodies for money," he said.

"Exactly."

"I like it," Alex said.

"Four of the six bodies were found on the Keweenaw & Brule River," I said. "Maybe that means our guy works for that railroad. Of course, it may mean that the guy works for another railroad but finds the K & BR convenient for disposal of bodies."

"You think he might have been at the party?"

"A very good possibility."

"All this already would have occurred to the FBI, wouldn't it?" Alex said.

"Also a very good possibility. They may be ignorant but they're not dumb."

"So we're going to have to wait till they've done their thing and tell Jack what they've come up with."

"And will Jack tell us?" I said. "He might tell us something, even most of it, but you know the FBI likes to keep lots of things under wraps." For all the latter-day pieties about sharing of information among governmental investigative bodies, old habits die hard, and sometimes warnings go ignored.

"So we wait and hope."

At that moment Joe Koski stuck his head into my office, and the waiting and hoping suddenly were shunted aside for the daily realities of running a sheriff's department. "We've run out of vapes," Joe said. "The guests are getting antsy."

"Oh, shit," I said. "Is there enough money in the kitty for more?"

Vapes—electronic cigarettes whose nicotine vapor helps calm tobacco cravings—are popular in rural jails, public places where smoking is banned but the majority of the inmates tend to be hardcore tobacco addicts. I find it hard to believe that in this day and age anyone could be stupid enough to get hooked on cigarettes, but it happens with dismaying regularity, especially among the young, uneducated, poor, and ignorant in the country as well as in the city. By the time they fall into a life of crime, they also fall into a life of insatiable craving. Their first brush with hell is often with institutional denial of their bodily needs. The only way out is cold turkey.

Inmates get chances for real cigarettes only on outside road gangs or other such labor details off county property. Some jurisdictions, especially those in big cities, ban vapes because they look and act too much like cigarettes and because the medical profession hasn't yet ruled on their safety. County jails in the boonies give them the benefit of the doubt because they help calm restive inmates with tobacco joneses. The keepers of a few lockups sometimes relax the rules and allow smoking outside in the exercise yards, hoping civilians won't notice, but even they are turning more and more to vapor cigarettes. Some sheriffs even augment their meager budgets by buying e-cigarettes cheaply, then reselling them to the inmates at a handsome markup. The inmates don't complain, because they have precious little else to spend their income on and nowhere to do it anyway.

Porcupine County allows its inmates to buy vapes through Joe, who at my insistence provides them at cost, but they are often jobless when they come inside and have no money. Joe dips into our meager operating kitty now and then to resupply the impoverished and addicted. He is careful to buy only the wares of well-known companies and stays away from home-brewed nicotine products whose ingredients are not only highly dubious but may be lethal. Some of the commissioners are outraged that we'd use county money to encourage a foul and possibly unhealthful habit, but others recognize the reality: Vapes are a cheap way of keeping the peace in a potentially violent jail population. At least for now. I wouldn't be surprised if later on vapes went the way of the real thing and became carefully controlled and even banned in many places.

"Spare change, boss?" said Joe in a broad stage imitation of a big-city panhandler. He often hits on his fellow deputies for dimes and quarters and crumpled dollar bills for the vape kitty. Even Gil coughs up, but tempers his acid remarks, because he knows the facts as well as the rest of us.

I dug deep and came up with a tattered five-dollar bill. Joe is a good corrections officer and knows how to keep the peace.

CHAPTER TEN

It turned out to be the peace that passeth all understanding, at least on the part of the Federal Bureau of Investigation.

Two weeks later, Jack Adamson called from Detroit.

"Every one of those people at the town meeting came up clean," he said. "Even the out-of-towners. Three of them said they were writers scouting out the possibility of a true-crime book or TV script. All of them have published books before.

"The locals were just that, curious locals. A few of them had unkind things to say about us."

"Us being you and me?" I asked with a chuckle.

"Us being the Bureau," Jack said without a chuckle. "One of them"—he named an elderly Silverton woman familiar for toothless threats against county and township officials, including me—"said she hoped the entire FBI ended up in the bottoms of hopper cars."

"Sometimes we country cops feel the same way about you," I said.

"True," said Jack, with what I would swear was a tinge of regret in his voice. "By the way, you're clean, too."

"You investigated the LEOs?" I said.

"Even the LEOs. The Bureau is nothing if not thorough."

"I guess Alex isn't the killer, then."

"No." I could almost hear Jack suppressing his mirth. He knows all about the amiably abusive relationship I share with the detective sergeant. "Some of those tribal cops, however, do seem to have led checkered lives in previous places of employment."

"Yes." More than one tribal policeman has restarted his career with the Bureau of Indian Affairs after leaning so hard on a suspect on behalf of a municipal police department that he was fired for going too far. Generally, however, the tribals are not bent cops, crooked policemen, just formerly overenthusiastic ones. Many of them are excellent investigators.

"What about the railroaders?"

"Nothing to tie them to the case, except proximity, and that's perfectly logical."

"What about means and opportunity?" I asked. If I were leading this case, the first people I'd eliminate as suspects would be the railroaders of the Keweenaw & Brule River. Just like eliminating the husband in the murder of a wife.

"You carry a gun," Jack said. "Isn't that means and opportunity?"

"Yes," I said. "But until this case broke, I didn't know anything about those hopper cars, including why they're stored where they are, for how long, and how to open those hatches."

"Rest assured," Jack said, "that the FBI has found absolutely no evidence to link any railroader to these crimes."

"So far," I wanted to retort, but didn't. "Anything else?"

"I'll fax you a copy of the report," Jack said. "This afternoon or tomorrow morning."

It would be heavily redacted, I knew, having seen such reports more than once. The FBI never shared everything it discovered. The Bureau often cited national security. Sometimes it meant to suppress certain derogatory information about citizens, trivialities they thought might lead an overeager local cop to press frivolous charges. Sometimes it just wanted to hoard all the toys in the law enforcement sandbox, despite repeated efforts by various presidents of the United States to get governmental agencies to share information. The problem everywhere is systemic and institutional inertia. Bureaucrats are forever jealous of their power and mistrustful of other bureaucracies. Anything that slips through the barrier of suspicion usually is lubricated by personal friendships and the calling in of favors owed.

"So what's the Bureau gonna do?" I asked.

"We're concentrating on the child abduction and murders," Jack said.

"As we figured," I said. "How may we be of service?"

"Just let our investigation proceed. But it might be helpful if you and Alex could look into the cases of the two adult remains found in North Dakota and Philadelphia and see if there's a connection to the kids."

"You don't think they're connected?"

"Washington doesn't think so. Washington thinks a whole lot of people around the country must have been using railroads as graveyards." That meant Jack himself was keeping an open mind on the question, although he'd never contradict his superiors in the presence of non-FBI law enforcement.

"All right. We'll see what we can do, if we can spare the time and manpower," I said. "We'll call the authorities in Bismarck and Cumberland and see what they know."

"All right then," Jack said. "Now I have some news for you. It's just come in."

"Yes?"

"Another body in a hopper on the CSX," Jack said.

"Where?"

"On that railroad just outside a town called Connellsville in Pennsylvania. It was found in an old World War II–era hopper car that had been on a siding in the woods for about thirty years. One of those with an old-fashioned outside steel frame. Somebody had bought it and was going to restore it for a railroad museum. The local sheriff had just gotten around to looking inside. It was the sixty-second car he and his deputies had checked."

"What did they find?"

"Bones of a woman estimated to be in her late eighties, early nineties," Jack said. "The investigating officers say that even though her bones were very old, maybe two decades, they could tell that her femurs were brittle, almost powdered. One had signs of a fracture. There was obvious evidence of widespread osteoarthritis in the joints."

"Osteoporosis, also?"

"Sounds like it, pending the medical examiner's report."

"What was found with the body?" I said. "Paper, gunny sack, twine, clothesline as with the others?"

"Nothing. No garments of any kind. Probably the body was dropped naked into the hopper."

"Who would want to kill an old lady?" I said.

"Maybe she wasn't killed," Jack said. "It could have been a natural death."

"Then why not the usual disposition, with an undertaker and all?"

"That is the question."

"Alex and I are beginning to think that more than one perpetrator may be involved. A killer and someone else, somebody who gets rid of the bodies for the killer." I didn't mention Charon and the River Styx. One just does not give a FBI agent the notion that one thinks one is smarter and better educated than he is.

"Washington thought of that, too, but decided the idea is too far-fetched," Jack said. Maybe he didn't think it was, but he wasn't going to say so.

"What's local law enforcement out in Pennsylvania doing?"

"Rummaging around in old missing-persons reports. Canvassing the local hospitals and nursing homes to see if a patient took a walk during the last decade or so. If that happened, the local police will see if they can match the DNA with that of relatives, if they can be found."

"Either of those CSX hopper cars have a connection with the K & BR?" I said.

"Not that we know of," Jack said. "The first has been around a lot, and the second, well, it just hasn't moved since probably the Civil War."

"Anything else?" I said.

"That's all I have," Jack said.

"Okay then. Have a good day."

"You too."

We hung up.

I thought for a moment. Many special agents would have told me nothing, expecting me to ferret out the facts with my own labor, but I suspected Jack had told me everything he knew, or everything he felt safe telling me. It felt as if he were subtly telling me to continue with an independent investigation.

I called Alex and told him what Jack had revealed. This time the trooper listened quietly, without being a smart aleck. That told me he had decided to apply his considerable talents to this growing case, even if his efforts, like mine, officially had to be peripheral to the FBI investigation. As a state police detective, however, Alex's bailiwick encompassed all of Michigan. He could get more done than I could, and more quickly. His feet were bigger than mine, although not as big as those of the Feds.

I knew we were going to have to put out of mind, as best as we could, our deep feelings about those little girls if we were going to keep clear heads while looking for someone who may or may not have been their killer. Alex, I knew, was capable of suppressing his emotions, and so was Camilo. I didn't know about Gil and Chad. I wasn't even sure about myself.

CHAPTER ELEVEN

On a Saturday morning three weeks later I sat glumly at Ginny's breakfast table.

"Penny for your thoughts?" she said.

"That would be too expensive."

"Something's bothering you."

"Oh, it's just work."

"You *are* your work, Steve. I've known that for a long time."

I looked up. "I'm sorry. I didn't mean to be neglectful."

She sat down and covered my hand with hers. "What is it?"

Ginny Fitzgerald, my love, my sounding board, my partner. I keep nothing from her but make her privy to the most intimate professional details. Whoever said two minds are better than one didn't know the half of it. More than once, after we have made love in the enormous oaken four-poster in her bedroom upstairs, an insight into a difficult case has emerged from my unconscious, released in a pleasurable gush of endorphins. I wouldn't call it a blinding flash, maybe just a glimmer.

"It's the case." I didn't need to tell her what case. "I keep thinking law enforcement should be looking for two people, not one. Alex thinks so, too. But the FBI doesn't. And they're running the show, of course."

"Yes," Ginny said. "But they're not running you."

"No," I said, "but you know I've got to be careful."

For several minutes I unloaded my frustrations on her, and she listened quietly, nodding now and then and patting my hand. Finally, I was spent and sighed deeply.

Then I remembered that communication is a two-way enterprise. "Now, what about you?" I said. "Anything on your mind lately?"

I half expected her to bring up our relationship and where it was or was not going, and was ready with the usual excuses, excuses that were hardly convincing but glib enough to paper over things temporarily. But she surprised me.

"It's Tommy. I'm worried about him."

Now she had my full attention.

"He doesn't want to go to college this fall."

"Why?"

"He wants to take a year off and work for the AIM."

I knew why. Tommy had often spoken with quiet outrage over the lot of Native Americans in a country whose majority just wished they would go away. On the Baraga reservation he had met American Indian Movement activists who introduced him to the stories of such heroes as Dennis Banks and Russell Means and the 1973 rebellion at Wounded Knee. Young people are strongly susceptible to tales of oppression, human rights, and self-sacrifice, and Tommy was no different. He would come home from a weekend at Baraga and rage at the dinner table over the stories he had heard about the injustices Indians still suffer at the hands of the white man. I was sympathetic. He was talking about the people both he and I had come from, and I knew their tragic history as well as he did.

The difference between us, besides my upbringing in white society, is that I am a generation older and, I hope, wiser. Tommy wanted to confront injustice head-on and immediately, and batter it into submission. I had been something of a firebrand at his age, too, but my target was far smaller, an antediluvian Republican congressman who wanted to return his constituency to the nineteenth century. I went door-to-door hustling votes for the Democratic challenger. She lost—that upstate New York district was just too conservative—but eventually the congressman was caught taking bribes and tossed out of office.

As I matured I still wanted to make a contribution to society, but soon learned that the best way for me to do so was as a lawman. That was much less dramatic and immediate than Tommy's idea of serving justice. I simply had grown up, and he was still in the process. There was a huge chasm in the way he and I appreciated things, and it would probably be years before he and I saw eye to eye.

"There's something else," Ginny said.

"What?"

"He has a girlfriend."

Tommy had dated local girls at Porky High and the high school in Houghton. Nothing serious, mostly dances, no steady girls. He was a late bloomer. I had been one, too. I thought coming to the party a little late, as I had, would benefit an Ojibwa boy who might run into problems with parents who didn't want their daughters dating an Indian. He'd be a little more mature by the time he had to deal with that.

"Who is she?"

"Adela Rogers."

"Adela *Rogers*? The Adela Rogers from the Baraga reservation?" She was a brilliant Ojibwa kid and a Class III girls' basketball all-stater. She was an engineering student at Michigan State and spent her summers working for the AIM. She was a knockout. And she was two years older than Tommy. My stomach dropped. At those ages, she was practically robbing the cradle.

"I'm afraid she's influencing him," Ginny said.

"What has he said about her?"

"Not a lot."

"Are they getting it on, do you think?" I said.

"He's eighteen years old," Ginny said. "I'd be worried if he weren't. In this day and age, they start early."

"You want me to talk to him?" I asked Ginny. "Will it do any good?"

"I don't know. Can't you tell him that if he goes to college and gets an education, he can do his people a much greater good than if he fritters away his talents in small-time activism?"

"To him it's not small-time," I said. "Of course I could talk to him. But logic never trumps passion, does it?"

"I guess not."

"At least he cares about justice," I said. "It could be a lot worse."

Along about lunchtime the screen door banged. Tommy swept in, Hogan on his heels, and dropped his backpack on the hall floor with a clatter. He never makes a quiet entrance. I kid him about that all the time. "Some Indian you are," I say. "You've never heard of stealth."

"Neither have you," he retorts. He's right about that. In the woods I'm quite the opposite of the silent Indian tracker. Despite my best efforts I trip over roots and blunder into bushes. You can hear me coming a mile away.

But as a law enforcement officer for nearly twenty years, I've learned something about dealing with headstrong young people. Lecturing them never works. Enlisting their help in a mission often opens their eyes. I decided to give that a go.

"Tommy, a word?" I said.

He stiffened. He was ready for an argument. I had often lost dinner-table disagreements because the boy knew how to debate both sides of an issue and sometimes took an opposite view just to show me up. I often thought he would make a very good trial lawyer, because his contentions were always well thought out

89

and he was ready to leap upon the slightest inconsistency in an opposing argument. He always shaped his sometimes maddening opinions calmly and quietly, even though the other side might display red-faced, spluttering indignation. Our relationship was hardly one of father and son, but it sure seemed that way sometimes. This time, however, I was not going to be confrontational.

"About what?" he said warily.

"The case I'm working on." He knew most of its details. He read the papers and listened as well as he argued. He not only hung out sometimes at the sheriff's department but also idolized Alex and marveled that Sue Hemb could be at the same time so smart and so good-looking.

"Typical ignorant males," Ginny often says. "You don't quite appreciate that beauty and brains aren't mutually exclusive. Or that the one doesn't necessarily have to do with the other." I was not sure what she meant by that, but if I ever figure it out I think I will have learned how to understand women.

Otherwise Tommy is a very well-informed eighteen-year-old, and I respect his mind as much as I wish he respected mine. Or maybe he does and just doesn't want me to know.

"Go on," Tommy said, all ears.

I told him, in plenty of detail. "And so there seems to be a difference of opinion," I said. "The FBI thinks we should be looking for only one killer—the one who murdered those children—and that except for the one found with that little girl at Rockville, the other bodies, all of which were found elsewhere, are completely unrelated to our case. We've been calling the killer of those girls "the Beast" because a witness saw two red lights in the woods that she said reminded her of the eyes of the Devil, the biblical Beast. But I personally think someone else is involved, and that someone else is not a killer but a kind of undertaker, one who undertakes to get rid of dead bodies for the people who killed them. So there it is. What do you think, Tommy?"

Tommy sat silently for a while. In his expression I could almost see his mind morphing from Indian activist into detective.

"Exactly why do you think it's two guys, Steve?" he said.

"One of them, not the killer, could be a woman. No evidence for one or the other sex. Anyway, there seem to be two MOs involved. One is clearly rape and murder. The other doesn't seem to involve rape at all. There's absolutely no evidence for that. The only thing linking all the cases is the way the bodies were disposed of. The FBI thinks that's just coincidence. I don't."

"Why not?"

"Just a feeling," I said. "But it's a strong one."

"Trusting your gut?" So young for such insight. But so bright. Hunches are the lifeblood of police work when the trail of evidence has petered out.

"Uh-huh."

"I think you're forgetting something," Tommy said.

"What?"

"Could the killer and the undertaker be one and the same?"

"Yes, but it doesn't seem likely. The criminal mind isn't so easily divided."

"What if a split personality is involved?" he said.

"Dr. Jekyll and Mr. Hyde?"

"Yup."

"I understand split personalities are very, very rare," I said. "The shrinks call it dissociative identity disorder. There's a lot of disagreement about what causes it, let alone how to treat it. Besides, if I have this right, each personality doesn't remember what the other one does. Wouldn't you think that if a person kills someone and then gets rid of the body, that's one personality doing both?"

"I don't know," said Tommy, "but maybe you could talk to Lieutenant Hemb about it. If she comes up here to see Alex, maybe I could come, too." I almost laughed at his eager expression. He looked like a hound dog that has just caught a whiff of a ripe haunch of beef. Tommy has a huge crush on Sue. I didn't blame him. Once I almost did, too, but never mind about that.

"It's an idea, though," I said.

"I've got to read up on that," he said. "The library have some books about psychology?"

"I doubt it." Porcupine City's modest township library is heavy on popular fiction and local history. It doesn't have room for much else. "Maybe you can borrow them from Lieutenant Hemb. Or the college library this fall."

For the rest of that Saturday and well into Tuesday night, Tommy didn't mention a word about Indians and reservations and injustice and the Bureau of Indian Affairs. I hoped I had put a bee into his capacious ball cap.

CHAPTER TWELVE

"Are you in or are you not in?" said Alex Kolehmainen from the doorway of my office a week later.

"You're a famous state police detective sergeant," I said. "Gather your own evidence."

The lanky trooper came in and sat in the chair in front of my desk, awkwardly folding his long limbs the way a flamingo tucks in its wings.

"Is the coffee good this morning?" he asked.

It never is—the county budget precludes anything but the cheapest grinds from the supermarket, which has caused more than one jail inmate, as well as the occasional deputy, to complain about cruel and unusual punishment—but the question told me that Alex had something vital and interesting to say this time. He does have occasional rituals of preamble, and this was one of them.

"I was talking with an old buddy in the U.S. Marshals last night," he said, "and we got onto the subject of criminal disposition of bodies. Turns out there's a mob capo in Chicago the marshals are babysitting before he testifies in a federal racketeering trial later this week. Name of Dom Benedetto. They call him Joey Nails because he has a thing for manicurists. Married one, keeps another as a mistress. He's singing like a newborn canary. After the trial the guy goes into witness protection far away on a foreign shore."

"Singing like a newborn canary?" I said. "You sound like a

third-rate Mickey Spillane."

"What would we do without cheap crime writers to give us our colorful police language?"

"You have me there. All right, what about this mobster?"

"He's an old enforcer, a hit man in Detroit."

"Didn't know the mob was still active there."

"Oh, it is, although it's keeping relatively low profile these days, thanks to the Feds sending some of its members up the river for racketeering and drug running. There used to be more than a hundred made men in Detroit, but that number fell to about thirty or so a few years ago. Some of my sources say that number has increased to about forty-five or fifty in the last couple of years, thanks to new blood from New York and Chicago. They're now sharing the stage with Hispanic and African American gangs that have helped make Detroit number one on every magazine's most-dangerous-city-in-America list. Remember that big federal sweep last month that snared hundreds of gangbangers? Some of them were Mafiosi. Now some folks think the Outfit is on its way out. I doubt that. There's never a shortage of replacements to fill the vacuum."

"And?" I said. Alex does have a way of setting his scenes in a leisurely way and with considerable detail, like the British literary crime novelist P.D. James, whose stories are slow to get going but eventually grip the reader by the throat. I love her stuff, and similarly have learned to be patient with Alex's apparent shilly-shallying.

"In his interviews with the Feds—actually the ATF, because the case involves stolen military arms—Benedetto has alluded to the mob disposing of bodies by means of a third and unnamed party."

I sat up straight. "Go on."

"I told my friend in the marshals about our interest in such body-dumping. He'd heard all about our case and agreed with me that Benedetto might be a lead."

"Hadn't the FBI talked to him about it?"

"They had their shot at him, mostly about other things, the marshal said, but didn't bring up this one."

"I am not surprised," I said.

"Nor am I," Alex said. The FBI, like all law enforcement organizations, has its fixations, and one of them is the kidnapping of children. It appeared to us that the Feds couldn't see the forest for the trees, but we could. On the other hand, maybe ours with the Beast was an obsession, too. Obsessions are not always bad. Obsessions can lead to the breaking of cases. Obsessions can also lead to dead-ends and a lot of wasted money. I didn't think ours was headed that way, but we still didn't know where it was going.

"Can we?"

"Can we what?"

"Talk to Joey Nails."

"That's why I'm here," Alex said. "One of us has to go down to Chicago. I can't. Got too much on my plate in Wakefield at the moment. So it'll have to be you." I wasn't surprised. There had been a rash of minor drug cases, mostly raids of meth labs but also busts of cocaine mules, in the area of Ironwood and neighboring Hurley in Wisconsin, and Alex had his hands full sifting the evidence and helping the prosecutors build their cases.

"I'm only a county sheriff," I said. "Would the marshals cooperate with somebody from the far podunks?"

"The marshal I know says he will with you. He's heard of you." A few of our cases have made the Chicago papers, even the national press and cable TV shows. Nothing ever happens in the middle of nowhere until it does, and often that makes good reading for an audience sated on the sameness of urban crime. But while the man in the street might remember Bonnie and

Clyde, few except for fervent crime buffs could tell you the name of the cop—Frank Hamer—who gunned them down. Cops themselves have much longer memories.

"Give me the particulars."

The marshals, Alex said, were holding the mobster in a suburban safehouse whose location was of course secret, but if I showed up at the U.S. Marshals Service office in the Dirksen Federal Building in Chicago, they'd take me to him.

"Here's the number to call," Alex said. "Good luck."

It was only after he left that I realized that he'd forgotten to tell me the name of the marshal I'd be meeting. But I had a bigger problem.

The county commissioners, parsimonious to a fault, would have to sign off on the travel budget for the eight-hour auto trip to Chicago, and I knew they wouldn't at their next weekly meeting six days hence, let alone today. So the trip was going to have to be on my dime and my vehicle, as it has so often been. But my old Jeep is a gas-guzzler and barely capable of highway speeds.

I called Ginny at the historical museum. "Can I borrow your Prius? Got to go to Chicago."

"Oh, sure," she said. "What's up?"

"There may be a break in the railroad case," I said.

"Go, go, go!" she said. My kind of lady. She may be the sort who likes to take all night for dinner—I often tease her with remarks about being president of the Slow Eaters of America—but when speed is of the essence, she is the first off the mark.

And I went.

I don't often visit the big city anymore, except for professional reasons. Even though I spent two productive years in Manhattan learning criminal justice and grew to love the city's cultural assets—the opera, the museums, and the New York Public

Library in particular—I never cared for the high-velocity urban life of getting and spending, the frantic yammer of traffic, the stench of garbage on a hot August day. One gets spoiled by the wilderness of the Upper Peninsula, where heavy traffic consists of half a dozen cars backed up behind a one-lane path around bridge repairs, where you can go into the woods all day without encountering another human being, where the air is so clean you can take deep lungfuls without coughing, where you can lie on your back in a forest clearing and count every star in the Milky Way.

Despite their struggle to make a living, people in these parts take great pride in their surroundings. If a citizen sees a bottle discarded by the side of the road, he'll often stop his vehicle and pick it up. Several times a year folks band together to gather roadside litter, and there's never much of that. I've been to Central American countries where the road verges are always strewn with trash and garbage, a mess the embarrassed governments blame on the consequences of poverty encouraged by greedy Yanquis. Porcupine County is full of people who are just managing to get by, yet for the most part they have never lost their dignity. To them a decent world is a tidy one. To me, too.

From Porcupine City down to Green Bay the traffic was unseasonably light, but as I approached Milwaukee it began to build up, and by the Wisconsin–Illinois border the steady stream of cars and semis began to coalesce into molasses. At the edge of the northern suburbs the flow had dwindled to a thick syrup, and it took almost an hour to get from the junction of the Kennedy and Edens Expressways into the Loop.

Fortunately, I'd arranged a spot as a visiting lawman in the towering Federal Building garage and after parking the Prius, I negotiated security at the entrance. The bored guards at the checkpoint barely glanced at my badge and ordered me wanded even though, quite unarmed, I didn't set off the metal detector.

A few minutes later I presented myself at the U.S. Marshals Service office on the twenty-fourth floor.

The receptionist was cheerful, polite, and respectful to the country lawman, but I suspected she had been instructed to lay on the charm with all visitors. "Marshal Dillon will be with you in a minute," she said.

"Marshal Dillon?" I said, a tinge of incredulity in my voice. Alex had not mentioned that. I am sure he was chuckling to himself.

She laughed sincerely. "Perfect name, isn't it? I never get tired of people's reactions. Speak of the devil."

"Welcome, Sheriff," said a voice behind me. "I'm Fred Dillon."

Marshal Dillon turned out to be a balding man in his fifties, as tall as the eponymous television character but beefier, his shirt-sleeved bulk augmented by a shoulder holster bearing a government-issue Beretta. He wasted no words.

"You're a friend of Alex Kolehmainen. That's good enough for me. Come on, let's go up to the house where we're keeping Joey Nails. Are you going back to Upper Michigan after the interview, or staying down here overnight?"

"Going back," I said. I didn't want to have to pay upward of two hundred bucks for a hotel room in Chicago. I was living out of my own wallet.

Dillon understood. "Budgets," he said ruefully. "We have 'em, too."

That made me relax. This was not a federal agent who held in contempt law enforcement officers far lower on the food chain.

"Okay," he said, donning his jacket and barely getting the front button closed around his midriff. "Let's take your car. You'll save time getting back on the road. I'll come back downtown in a car we keep up there."

On the way up to the safehouse we passed the time talking about good fly-fishing spots in the Upper Peninsula. Marshal Dillon was a sportsman and knew quite a bit about the rivers that empty into Lake Superior. "I've never fished the Big Two-Hearted," he said, "and I've always wanted to, ever since reading Papa as a kid." That river lies five hours east of Porcupine City, but I knew its literary fame and had even read the Hemingway short story in college.

In forty minutes we arrived at a block-long, three-story-high building in northwest Evanston, the suburb adjoining the north side of Chicago. A drive-in ATM and a medical clinic occupied the ground floor. The building looked fairly new, but of typical latter-day suburban condominium architecture, concrete block clad in brick, stone, and false stucco.

"Twenty-four condos in this building," Dillon said. "We're renting two of them. One for the people we have on ice, one for their keepers."

"Don't the condo owners have a beef about that?" I said. I had had experience with persnickety condominium associations in New York.

"No, because the stupendous rent we pay each month lowers their assessments considerably," Dillon said. "Enough so they don't ask questions. They think we're with the State Department and we're putting up minor foreign diplomats, vice consuls, and the like, while they find places to live in the suburbs. Anyway, we'll be here only a year or so, then we'll find another safehouse elsewhere. We're always on the move."

I supposed they kept the current minor foreign diplomat out of sight so that the residents wouldn't wonder about his rich Detroit underworld accent, but I didn't ask.

In the elevator to the third floor Dillon turned to me and said, "Ground rules. I have to be present during the interview, and you're to say nothing about the racketeering case. Got to be sure no defense shark will claim you're trying to queer his testimony."

"Gotcha," I said.

At Unit 305 we encountered a small elderly woman standing with her ear to the door, blocking it from the outside.

"Good afternoon, ma'am," Dillon said with a polite huff in his voice. "May we enter?"

"What are you running in there?" she demanded fiercely. "I've seen strange men and women and children come and go. Are you operating an illegal bed and breakfast?"

"In a manner of speaking, ma'am, but it's quite legal. Our resident diplomats sometimes have house guests. Excuse me."

Dillon knocked, the door was opened, and we stepped inside.

"Maybe we better move out of this place sooner rather than later," he whispered to me. "It's turned into a magnet for busybodies. They talk. Not good for safehouses."

We stood in the condo's spacious living room. In a large leather chair facing the doorway sat a U.S. marshal in shirt sleeves and loaded shoulder holster, shield at his belt. Across the room, watching an Oprah rerun, lounged a leathery old man in shirt and pants too big for him. As Dillon flicked off the television, the man struggled to his feet with the help of a cane. This was Joey Nails? I thought. He once had been a six-footer, but arthritis had arched his upper back into a permanent stoop, plunging his nearly bald head down between bony shoulders and slashing half a foot off his height. I could hardly believe that this wisp of a fellow once had been one of the Detroit Mafia's most feared gunmen.

"I'm Dominic Benedetto," he said in a reedy voice. "You're the sheriff from Upper Michigan, aren't you?"

CHAPTER THIRTEEN

"He told me why you're here," Joey Nails said, nodding toward Dillon. "I'm all right with that."

As he spoke, his voice, at first soft and whispery, slowly grew in strength and volume, giving a suggestion of the man he had once been. His diction was not coarse underworld dese-dem-and-dose, but surprisingly rich, precise, and almost cultivated, like that of a professor in a small Midwestern college. He spoke not in disjointed and unrelated phrases, as so many Americans do, but in shapely sentences and paragraphs. If the Mafia had had a finishing school somewhere, he must have graduated *summa cum laude*. Perhaps the instructors had taught the proper use of napkins and silverware as well as saps and brass knuckles. "Joey Nails" was hardly an appropriate nickname for this mobster.

I nearly disappeared into a huge leather sofa and Joey Nails took a hard straight chair across from me, squirming painfully as he sought a comfortable position. He clearly suffered from a spinal condition.

"Mr. Benedetto," I said, "I'll be as brief as I can. I don't want to cause you any discomfort."

"Call me Dom," he said, extending a hand. I took it. His grip turned out to be surprisingly firm for such a frail old fellow. Suddenly I realized that he probably would be a strong witness for the prosecution. Whether he had had a change of heart about his profession I did not know. Probably an offer of immunity from prosecution for his crimes and relocation under a false name to a warm and sunny place somewhere had persuaded him to tell the Feds what they wanted to know, and to agree to betray his former comrades. Possibly he had discovered that a boss had ordered a hit on him, a loyal employee who had specialized in hits, and he was exacting his revenge. But that information was not important to my mission.

From my shirt pocket I fished a digital recorder. "This is not an official recording," I said. "It's just a convenience for me, to help me take notes. I'm not using your name or mine. I'm just gathering facts in a police case that is completely unrelated to yours. I'm not going to Mirandize you, and this interview will have absolutely no legal standing against you. It can never be used in court, nor can anything it might lead to, so far as *you* are concerned. Are we agreed?"

Benedetto nodded. If he knew that facts brought out in the interview might be evidence against others, he didn't say. Nor did I.

At the same time I had pulled out my recorder, Dillon took out one of his own and flicked it on. The marshal was sitting in a soft occasional chair on the other side of the mobster.

"Just keeping the sheriff honest," he told Benedetto with a small smile. I wasn't surprised. Every government organization has watchbirds that watch the watchbirds. Dillon was covering his ass.

I sat back and began. "I'm told you have knowledge of people who have specialized in the criminal removal and disposal of human bodies," I said. "Do you?"

Benedetto nodded.

"Who are they?"

"I don't know," he said, utterly without guile.

I shot a glance at Fred Dillon. He offered a soft nod, almost imperceptible but clearly affirmative. Benedetto was not playing games with the rube sheriff.

"What can you tell me?"

"We never saw these people, basically," Benedetto said. "Whenever someone had somebody to get rid of, he'd call a number and make arrangements with the person on the other end. That was twenty-five or thirty years ago, when phones were more secure. In the last few years the doer would send an email to an address so disguised and encrypted the National Security Agency would need years to break it. That's the way it still works."

I now understood why the Feds considered Benedetto so valuable. He may have been an old-timer, but he had kept up with modern technology. He was no unlettered thug with an itchy trigger finger. Except for his choice of specialty, he was as savvy as any white-collar criminal on Wall Street. Except they never go to prison while his kind still does.

"Did you make use of them?" I asked.

"I can't answer that," Benedetto said neutrally, looking me in the eye.

I glanced at Dillon. He shook his head slightly. *Fifth Amendment territory,* his eyes seemed to say. *Stay out of it.*

"But you knew people who did?"

"Of course."

"Who were the bodies that were disposed of—and why?"

This time Benedetto looked over at Dillon. The marshal nodded. *It's okay to answer.*

"Double-crossers," the old mobster said. "Squealers. Guys who got too big for their britches. Guys who knew too much. People who made promises but failed to keep them." He was careful not to name names, and I didn't ask for them.

"Anyone outside the outfit?" I said.

"Some," Benedetto said. "I heard of a Bloomfield Hills tavern owner who wouldn't pay his vigorish and tried to get other barkeeps in the Detroit area to rebel against us. Bunch of union types. Commies."

It was clear how the mobster felt about collective bargaining. "Jimmy Hoffa? Any connection?" I asked.

Joey Nails threw his head back and cackled at the mention of the crooked Teamster union president who had last been seen at an affluent Bloomfield Hills restaurant in 1975. He had been declared legally dead in 1982 and had become the subject of hundreds of articles and books theorizing about his disappearance and usually blaming the Mafia. His body had never been found.

"We have no idea," Benedetto said. "We'd love to know about it. The punk needed wasting, but it wasn't us who wasted him."

You can dress a mobster in white tie and tuxedo, but you can't disguise his black-hearted essence. When Benedetto was moved by emotion, his language degenerated into gangster talk.

"Anyone else you know who worked for the Outfit and whose body was disposed of by a person or persons who were not part of the family?" I asked. That was an oblique way of asking again if the Mob had assassinated Hoffa. It wasn't my business, but I couldn't help asking.

This time Dillon leaned forward. "Don't answer that," he said softly, winking at me. "Don't dig yourself a hole, Dom."

I understood. The federal prosecutors didn't want to have to say they knew all about their star witness' crimes before he stood up for their side in court. The defense would try to destroy Benedetto's credibility, but I thought he would be a tough nut to crack. Afterward the feds could try to squeeze everything remaining out of him before they gave him a new identity somewhere far away and out of sight.

"Did you ever hear rumors about other people whose bodies were disappeared by this unknown party? Civilians, so to speak?"

"Oh yes," Benedetto said. "Wives getting rid of their

husbands, husbands getting rid of their wives, stuff like that. That was just a guess, though, just idle gossip over a plate of spaghetti carbonara. Except for one or two cases, we didn't really know."

"So how did it all work?" I asked. "What was the procedure?"

Benedetto smiled. "You remember what it was like when you were a young man and knocked up your girl. Somebody always knew somebody who could take care of it. Maybe you asked your local pharmacist, who gave you a shady doctor's phone number. Getting rid of a body worked much the same way. You'd ask a bartender who maybe was paying protection to a guy in the Outfit who had a phone number and later an email address.

"When there was a stiff to be disposed of, the party who wanted to do the disposing would send an email to the address we—he—had."

That was a significant slip, that quick segue from second-person plural to third-person singular. I glanced at Dillon. The marshal remained impassive. But it wasn't my lead and I didn't pursue it. I let Benedetto continue.

"The next day he'd get an email back from a different address instructing him to place the merchandise in a sealed body bag along with a smaller bag containing a certain 'consideration,' as the money was called. The exact sum would be specified in another email from still another address. None of those addresses was traceable."

"Can you give me any of these addresses?" I asked.

"Sure," Benedetto said, and wrote down several on a yellow pad Dillon put in front of him. "But these may not be good anymore. They may have changed."

I took the sheet and nodded.

"There would be one more separate email telling the man who wanted to get rid of the body where to drop off the package," Benedetto said. "Usually that would be a vacant lot or alley somewhere in the city or suburbs at two in the morning or some other awful hour. Sometimes we'd leave somebody to watch and see who came to scoop up the packages. After four or five hours of stakeout he'd have to go take a pee and when he came back the package would be gone. The guy who took the package was very, very careful. We never saw him."

"Did he watch to see who dropped off the package?"

"We didn't think so. We knew, however, that whoever was doing the job didn't belong to us. He didn't want us to know who he was and maybe he didn't want to know who we were, either. No names were ever exchanged. Everything was done in the dark. If buyer and seller don't know each other, they can't tell the cops, can they? Safer that way."

"One thing I don't understand," I said. "Emails remain forever on the Internet. The NSA or the Feds could scoop them up and trace their recipients, if not the senders."

"True," Benedetto said. "But the language was coded, typical business terms. Bodies would be 'freight' or something like that, and there would be 'handling fees' and the like. The drop-off points would be called 'piers' and the street numbers of the exact addresses would be disguised as columns of expenses and the like. We'd know what to look for, because there'd be still another email with the keys to the code. Besides, the email addresses both sides used were one-time Yahoo or Gmail or AOL addresses, and we'd send and receive them from a public computer, like one in a public library somewhere. The users were untraceable. None of this stuff would stand out in a fishing expedition by data gatherers."

"This has been very helpful," I said. "Now, how do you suppose the bodies were ultimately disposed of?"

"We never knew," Benedetto said. "We didn't want to. Again, not knowing helped give us deniability. It didn't matter anyway.

A disappeared stiff is a disappeared stiff, and who cares where?"

"But surely you must have guessed among yourselves?" I said. "Didn't you wonder?"

"Sure we did. Maybe they swam with the fishes, weighted down by concrete blocks and chains and tossed into Lake Ontario. That was the classic way, you know, in the old days. We guessed some may have been burned in pet crematories. Some might have ended up in landfills or in concrete piers."

"What about railroad cars?"

Benedetto stared directly into my eyes. "Now I know why you're here," he said with a slow nod. "Those too."

It was not surprising that the mobster had heard about the discoveries of the bodies dumped into freight cars. There had been plenty of media interest, and an obnoxious cable television personality who specialized in covering juicy crimes involving pretty suburban blond women had spent many indignant prime-time hours accusing the authorities of incompetence.

"Anything in particular?"

"About thirty years ago, a rich old guy tried to hire one of us to go to a luxury nursing home in Grosse Pointe Woods and put his sick wife out of her misery. She had terminal cancer and was in terrible pain. We didn't want to get involved in mercy killing. It's not what we do.

"But we heard later that the guy had taken her for an outing in his car and did the job himself, smothering her with a pillow. He wanted to disappear her body rather than face the music. Somehow he found someone to take the corpse away. One of our boys knew somebody who saw it happen. Supposedly it was dumped into an old hopper car."

"Remember where?"

"Somewhere on the Baltimore & Ohio Railroad, in Pennsylvania."

"Any idea who the person was who did the dumping?" I asked.

"Some railroad guy, our boy heard. That was all."

"What kind of railroader? Brakeman? Trackman, something like that?" I asked.

"Don't know," Benedetto said. "All our guy said was that the dumper worked for the railroad."

I sat back and contemplated this bit of information. It was not exactly the smoking gun we needed, but all the same it was a definite break. We still didn't know where to look, but we now had a very good idea what to look for. Maybe my hunch was beginning to pan out.

"By the way," I said, "why did members of your organization want to use a third party? Wouldn't it have been safer to do the job themselves?"

"It's easy to kill somebody," Benedetto said. "All you do is point a gun and pull the trigger. But in many cases you can't just leave the body there in a pool of blood for the cops to find, or it might get traced to you somehow. You've got to get rid of it so that the law doesn't find out about the hit for a long time, if ever. Corpses are bulky and heavy, and you have to carry them somewhere and dispose of them where they're not going to turn up for a long time. That's easier said than done. There's always a good chance of being spotted. That's why we used an outside specialist. If the job were done right and done quickly, nothing could be traced."

"What did a job usually cost?" I asked.

"In the beginning, about twenty or so years ago, ten thousand dollars. Last I heard, a year or so ago, twenty-five thousand."

"How many jobs did the organization have done every year?"

"Not many. One or two."

"Doesn't sound all that lucrative for the disposal specialist."

"No. Although we weren't his only customers, we probably

were the best ones."

"All right, Dom," I said, standing up to leave. "This has been very helpful. Thank you."

"Welcome," said the mobster, struggling wearily to his feet, once again the frail old man. "I hope you catch the guy," he said as we shook hands.

That was an unusual thing for a professional criminal to say, and my surprise must have been etched on my face.

Benedetto chuckled. "Not because he needs to face justice," he said. "Because I'm curious, too. It all sounds very weird, doesn't it?"

Chapter Fourteen

I pushed the Prius all night on the way back to Porcupine City, stopping several times at service stations for coffee and half-hour power naps, and once being jolted wide awake by a near miss of a couple of deer that had strayed onto the road in northern Wisconsin. It was hard to stay alert, even listening to the animated drone of Minnesota Public Radio while the reflected eyes of unknown creatures followed me as my headlights split the night down the black tunnel of the lonely highway. But I wasn't going to spend any of my tiny and hard-earned salary on a motel room whose expense the county board hadn't approved and probably wouldn't.

An unwelcome apparition materialized in the windshield: a memory of the face of an old Porcupine City pastor so crabbed by life the only pleasure he took in it was his devotion to Jesus and his disdain for those who did not follow his hateful reading of the Bible. "I will not vote for you until you make a honest woman of Virginia Fitzgerald," he yelled at a political rally in front of a hundred people. "You are living in sin, blatant sin, and the Lord will deal with you."

"Casting the first stone, are we?" I had responded. Most in the audience cheered and stomped their feet—everybody loves a confrontation, the more dramatic the better—but there were plenty of folks who subscribed to the pastor's brand of religiosity and remained silent, hands in laps. Ginny, seated next to me on the podium, just smiled and shook her head in none-of-your-business dismissal.

As U.S. 45 crossed into Michigan and left Wisconsin behind, the sound from the Prius's wheels changed from a smooth asphaltic hum to a juddering staccato over tarred cracks, reminding me that Michigan spends less money for road maintenance in these parts than Wisconsin does—and reminding me also of my bumpy relationship with Ginny. We've been keeping company for the better part of a decade but haven't yet cemented things at the altar. A couple of years ago she pressed me in that direction, because she wanted to adopt Tommy with me as the official titular head of the household, or whatever the dominant half of a couple is called these days.

Thanks to her late husband, a heavy-duty industrialist, Ginny is immensely wealthy, though she hides it. I could not bear the idea of marrying someone who could afford to keep me and, if she chose, the entire Detroit Lions defensive line as well. Not that she would, of course. She is loyal almost to a fault and even broke off what could have been a promising relationship with a handsome and well-to-do Finnish academic while studying in Helsinki. She chose to return to her impoverished Lakota boyfriend. She understood my pride, foolish as it might be.

But things cooled to a simmer when the Baraga Ojibwa tribal council decided not to make an exception to its rule—common among Native American nations—that its children be adopted only inside the tribe. The council was fine with Ginny's fostering of Tommy, provided he had a thorough schooling in his birth culture. That was no problem, because the boy was fiercely proud of his heritage and probably knew as much about it as the tribal elders.

And now Tommy's hesitation about going to college had put the problem of him in the forefront of her mind, pushing the problem of me into the background. So things were back at square one. But I was afraid there had to be some kind of change in our relationship if it were to last. What that might be was a question that receded into the night as the Prius crossed into Porcupine County and the morning's first light.

At seven a.m. I walked into the sheriff's department just as Alex was arriving. I had called him half an hour earlier, and he had agreed to meet me there to hear about my afternoon with Joey Nails. Gil and Chad were already present, and we took seats around the cracked linoleum table in the jail kitchen.

"Spent yesterday afternoon in Chicago interviewing a turncoat mobster," I said. "I've given Sheila the recorder so she can type up the transcript of the interview and give everybody copies."

Sheila Bowers is the department's highly competent secretary. She once wanted to become a deputy, but a bad knee prevented that. She insists on being called an "administrative assistant," not the no-longer politically correct "secretary" still commonly heard in the conservative backwoods. Like so many independent women in this rural area, she is a thoroughgoing feminist, although she might angrily reject the label. Times change slowly in the Upper Peninsula, but they do change.

"But here's the gist. The guy said the Detroit mob made use of a shadowy specialist in the disposition of bodies, someone whose identity they never knew. They would deliver a wrapped corpse to a specified spot, and the specialist would then pick it up unseen and then dispose of it. The mob never knew who, where, or how, except in one early case when one of them encountered a witness who said he saw the body of an old woman they thought to be a mercy killing by her husband being dumped into an old hopper car. It was somewhere in Pennsylvania about thirty years ago, the mobster said."

"Ah!" said Gil and Chad simultaneously.

"The mobster said the guy who did the dumping was a railroader."

"What do you know?" Chad said in amazement. "This is like manna from heaven."

"Where's that FBI report?" Gil said. "The one on the town meeting?"

Sheila, who knows where everything is, quickly fetched it.

Gil riffled through to the pages about the four employees of the Keweenaw & Brule River who had attended our little party.

"All these damn redactions," he said. "The Feebs probably blacked out the best clues."

"Let's see what we have," I said. "Mike Perlman, Howard Lehtinen, Billy Travers, and Jim Braithwaite."

"Travers has the most convictions," Gil said. "No felonies, all misdemeanors. Mostly disorderlies in Green Bay. Saturday-night bar squabbles. Fines, a couple days in jail, a few days' public service. Looks like his arrest record without convictions has been blacked out. It's quite long."

"We can get that from the Green Bay cops," Chad said.

"Likewise with Braithwaite. One disorderly that was disposed of on the same date as one of Travers'. Probably went out drinking together."

"Lehtinen?"

"Clean. No redactions," Gil said. "About what you'd expect from an accountant." Gil does not admire bean-pushers, probably because as the department's undersheriff and designated bookkeeper he has precious few beans to push and resents having had the thankless job dumped on him.

"Perlman?"

"Just one item, and that's been blacked out."

"Yeah," I said. "That tax thing." Seven years before, the IRS had indicted Perlman for fudging the railroad's taxes and his own, but he had pleaded the charge down to a settlement and never went to court. There had been newspaper stories about the case, but they had been forgotten except among those who had a bone to pick with the railroad president, especially those who believed he had pulled up his tracks in Porcupine County out of spite, not business necessity.

"None of these guys jump out as suspects," Gil said.

"Let's take a closer look at them," I said.

Both Travers and Braithwaite had been born in small towns in Michigan and graduated near the bottoms of their high school classes. Their education was light on the arts and sciences but heavy in vocational courses, especially auto mechanics. Neither was married.

Travers was sixty-two and a veteran of forty years in railroading. He had worked for the old Milwaukee Railroad as a brakeman and the defunct Soo Line as a brakeman and engineer before coming to the Keeweenaw & Brule River when it was formed. Braithwaite, fifty-eight years old, had bounced for almost the same number of years all over Michigan with the Grand Trunk Western, Ann Arbor, Pere Marquette, and Michigan Central. Together they knew about as much as anyone what went on across the state's railroads.

"What about their financial records?" I said. Often unusual sums in a bank account held by someone in modest circumstances could be a tipoff.

"Both always broke," Gil said. "They seem to live from day to day."

"All the same, they're worth looking at a little closer," I said. "They've got the knowledge."

"Lehtinen?" Chad said. "He's just an accountant." Chad, who is still young enough to be affected by the biases voiced by people he admires, is often influenced by Gil's prejudices.

"Yeah," Gil said, "but in his early career he worked two years in Maryland pounding spikes on a track gang on the old

Baltimore & Ohio. So he does have some grease-stained experience. The FBI says he was born in New Jersey and grew up in Kalamazoo, then after graduating from high school moved to Maryland. He went part time to a two-year college in Pennsylvania to study bookkeeping, then hired back on with the B&O as a junior accountant."

"How old is he?" I asked.

"Sixty-three."

"Married?"

"No."

"Bank accounts?"

"Respectable, the FBI says, but not unusual," Gil said. "Accountants know how to save their dough."

"Sometimes they embezzle it, too," I said.

"No evidence of that here." Gil said primly. Cranky and intolerant he may be about some things, but he believes in facts.

"Now what about Perlman?" I said. "Age?"

"Fifty-one."

"Experience?"

"Born and grew up in Escanaba. Married. Railroader all his life," Gil said. "His father formed the Keweenaw & Brule River from bits of the old Milwaukee and Soo Line, and the younger Perlman has worked just about every job there is on that railroad. Trackman, brakeman, conductor, engineer, freight agent, et cetera."

"That's common enough among heirs to businesses," I said. "Daddy has Junior learn the company from the bottom up before handing it over. He probably started at age twelve sweeping out the office."

We sat silent for a while. It was obvious to all of us that these four railroaders were worth a closer look. But was one of them actually the Beast, the person we were looking for? What about the others who had attended that gathering in the church? Was

115

it someone who had not been there?

"All we got to go on are these guys," Alex said, emphasizing what had already been observed.

"What about the FBI?" I asked. Being higher up the totem pole than a simple sheriff, Alex is sometimes treated kindly by the Feebs. Sometimes, and not often.

"Far as I know," Alex said, "they've truly hit a dead-end with the child kidnappings. No clues at all who the killer might be. They compared the DNA of the male corpse we found at Rockville with that of the semen in the body of the girl found with him and with the rubbers we turned up in the old POW camp shack. No matches at all, not even close. Three different males had produced the semen in those condoms. It's still an open case, of course."

"Maybe that's why Marshal Dillon allowed me to interview Benedetto," I said. Gil and Chad looked up sharply at the mention of the marshal's name, and Alex chuckled.

"I did call in a favor," Alex said. "But I'm sure Dillon checked with the Bureau first before giving the okay. Feds are loyal to their bosses."

" 'Checking with the Bureau' probably means 'checking with Jack Adamson,' " I said.

"I'm sure it did," Alex said.

"Why would the FBI let us go off on this chase?" I asked and answered my own question. "Because it's stuck. Because we've got a promising lead on the body-dumper that we've developed ourselves. They're going to let us follow it until it either pans out or peters out, saving time and manpower. Then they'll move in, as they always do."

"One thing for sure," Gil observed. "You probably owe Adamson one now."

"Yeah," I said. "That means we have to keep him informed about every little goddam detail."

"As we should," Alex said. "You know what might happen if we don't."

Quietly we all gave a collective shudder.

"All right," I said. "Time to get back to work. Chad, would you look into Travers and Braithwaite? I don't think either of them is smart enough to be a professional body-stasher, or corpse-cacher, or stiff-whisker, or . . ."

"Stiff-whisker?" said Alex. "Somebody needs a shave?"

"Whatever," I said, sounding like a weary teenager.

Nobody laughed.

CHAPTER FIFTEEN

Ten days later Ginny and I were again cooling off after another happy time in her four-poster. Neither of us smokes, so our afterplay usually consists of spooning and cuddling as well as long reflections about things weighing on our minds. At the moment hers was the annual budget of the Porcupine County Historical Society.

She's the director and the principal secret benefactor. That means she chooses the line items to spend her own money on, then asks the Historical Society's board for approval of each item. Quite irregular, she admits, but not unethical and probably not even illegal. All the same, she has never felt comfortable with the deception. I've told her not to worry, because nobody is being cheated. If anything, it's exactly the opposite.

As for myself, the greatest subject of worry was, of course, the Beast, or the vexing Case of the Railway Corpses, as Sherlock Holmes might have called it.

"Travers and Braithwaite were dead-ends, as we expected," I said after Ginny had outlined a proposed balance sheet for the Historical Society and we had chewed that subject to the nub. "Neither man ever had a dollar that didn't disappear under a bartender's paw on Saturday night. Both were notorious for bumming cigarettes and twenty bucks until payday. They never left Green Bay unless it was in a locomotive cab. They were skilled railroaders but otherwise not terribly bright. Couldn't have had the intelligence to bring this off. And there's no record of sex offenses, except Travers was caught in a prostitution bust once. At that time the Green Bay cops just let the johns go while arresting the hookers. Visiting a hooker, however, is a healthier outlet than murdering a child. I'm not worried about either guy."

"What about Perlman?" Ginny asked.

"Dead-end there, too," I said. "He may be a railroad president but he has a remarkably small savings account. He plows everything, even most of his small salary, back into the railroad to keep it alive. That's why he got caught fudging on his taxes. Really seems to be a nice guy. He keeps people on the payroll even though he can't afford to. To him 'layoffs' is a dirty word."

"Wouldn't that be a motive to do something even more illegal than tax evasion?" Ginny asked. "For the sake of the railroad?"

"We thought of that, too," I said. "Even though he played games once with his taxes, since then there's been absolutely no evidence of chicanery, such as dubious stashes of cash. Nor is there any suggestion in his record of sexual offenses. He's been married for thirty years and has two children. What's more, Perlman is not a healthy man. He's being treated for leukemia. In the last couple of months he's lost most of his hair as well as a lot of weight. He wouldn't have much libido these days."

"I agree," Ginny said. "You can eliminate him as a suspect."

"Put him on the back burner, rather," I said. "Everybody's a suspect until the case is solved."

"You've said that before, I think," Ginny said. "What about Howard Lehtinen?"

"Crooked accountants tend to commit crimes with balance sheets, not with corpses. Anyway, he lives modestly. Nothing in his financial records to suggest he's getting money from anywhere outside his salary. No criminal record anywhere, no gossip to speak of. He's a shy guy and doesn't have much of a social life except at church on Sundays.

"So there we are," I said. "Four railroaders. Four dead-ends."

"Did you say CSX?" Ginny said. "Didn't you say Lehtinen worked for the Baltimore & Ohio at one time?"

"Yeah, early eighties," I said. "Then he went on to the Milwaukee Road and the Soo and the Canadian National. Kind of a journeyman bookkeeper. Maybe moving around made his job more interesting."

Ginny slowly slid out of bed and into a robe. I always love to watch her do that. Gladdens my heart. But I'd never say so. She'd accuse me of objectifying her. "That too," I would say, if the subject ever came up.

She cinched her drawstring and sat down behind her computer. A flurry of keystrokes followed.

"Steve. Just as I thought. In 1987 the Baltimore & Ohio ceased to exist as a separate railroad and became part of the CSX Corporation. Didn't you say the bones of that old woman were found on the CSX? Where that mobster's story happened, too?"

I sat bolt upright. "Where's your phone?"

"On the night table where it has always been, sweetie," Ginny said.

In ten seconds I had Gil on the phone. "Got a job for you," I said.

"Right now, as usual?" he said, but without rancor.

"Can you get hold of the state police in Pennsylvania? Find out the history of the CSX line where the skeleton of an aged female turned up in an old hopper car? What was the original name of the railroad line?"

"Yes, sir," said Gil, pained forbearance in his voice, the old sergeant humoring the officer. "Right away."

Not five minutes later the call came. "The Baltimore & Ohio," he said.

"That's where Lehtinen worked early in his career," I said.

"Lehtinen?" Gil said. "There's no . . ."

The idea of this small, bashful, bespectacled, mild-mannered, and soft-bodied milquetoast, a man so anonymous and featureless that he wouldn't stand out in a crowd of bikini beauties, as an accessory to and abetter of capital murder at the worst and illegal disposition of human remains at the best seemed absurd. Just by looking at him you'd put him at the bottom of a list of possible suspects. He not only wasn't married but also didn't seem to be the kind of man to draw a second glance from a desperate woman. A potential life with him seemed like a very, very dull one. As they say, however, appearances can be deceiving, and perhaps he used his extreme wimpiness to his advantage.

"Well, maybe," I said. "This could be a break."

"It could," Gil said. "And wait, let me check that FBI report again. Yes, here it is. Lehtinen grew up in Kalamazoo. That's not far from the towns where those girls were snatched. He knows central Michigan very well. Detroit, too, probably. He doesn't have any relatives anymore in the Kalamazoo area, but I wouldn't be surprised if he goes to Lansing from time to time on railroad business. After all, though the headquarters is in Wisconsin, part of the road is in Michigan, and he'd have to meet with transportation officials in both states."

"Time to take another run at Lehtinen," I said. "Maybe we've given him the benefit of the doubt for too long."

I called Alex and told him what we'd found.

"Want me to reach out to the Wisconsin State Police? I know a couple of guys at the Green Bay post."

"Do that, please," I said.

"Good boy."

"Good boy?"

"You said please."

"Up yours."

Alex hung up. Half an hour later he called back.

"This won't be easy," he said. "Sergeant Lee Hamilton, my chum in Green Bay, thinks what we've got is just coincidence and he's reluctant to bother an upstanding fellow devout Episcopalian with a spotless record. He points out that the FBI report says Lehtinen doesn't live high on the hog, that there are no unusual sums in his bank accounts, no girlies on the side. There's just no hard evidence, no probable cause to persuade Hamilton to open an investigation."

"Shit."

"But."

"But *what*?" Alex can be so irritating.

"I said fellow Episcopalian," Alex said. "Hamilton knows him personally, goes to the same church every Sunday."

"They're friends?"

"Acquaintances, rather. There's no bond between them."

"And so?" Alex likes to make me work for my information, drawing it out sentence by sentence instead of in complete paragraphs.

"And so Hamilton agreed to keep an eye on him and let me know if he hears anything interesting. Hamilton owes me one, after all."

June passed, then July, and it was nearly the end of August when Hamilton finally encountered something interesting and called Alex to report it.

"Hamilton said he didn't know if it was important, but he heard Lehtinen say at a church supper that he was taking the Lake Superior Circle Tour next week."

The Circle Tour is a favorite hopeful promotion of the tourism bureaus of three states and one Canadian province, as well as booster publications devoted to the Lake Superior area. It consists of encouraging people to drive entirely around the lake from Point A to Point A again, stopping to rubberneck and overnight at scenic spots as well as supporting the local economy by spending lots of money in motels, restaurants, and gift shops full of authentic Chinese-made trinkets. Ginny and I had taken the tour more than once, unlike a surprisingly large minority of people who live around the lake. For them the tour is something to do someday, maybe, but not right away, as taking the elevator to the top of the Empire State Building is for the typical New Yorker.

Too bad for them. The tour is an extraordinarily pretty drive, especially through the deep boreal forests and rolling low mountains along the Trans-Canada Highway on the north shore of the lake. There are spectacular views of high bluffs, waterfalls, and long sand beaches. Tourists often spot moose and black bear on the road. There are very few small towns along the way to slow one's progress. There is so much beauty that sometimes too much of a good thing can get boring to somebody who's just driving through. For campers, canoers, and kayakers, however, the many Ontario provincial parks are well worth the effort to get there. Ginny and I had set up our tent in more than one tree line facing a sandy beach and sat in lawn chairs dining on broiled trout I had caught in a nearby river.

What's more, the Canadian Pacific Railway parallels the Trans-Canada for much of its length, with lots of spots for rail buffs to pull over and watch trains go by. The railroad magazines have been full of photo spreads of long freight trains rumbling past the cliffs on roadbed carved out of the mighty granite Canadian Shield along Lake Superior.

"You don't suppose?" I said.

"Suppose what?" I can play Alex's game, too.

"Suppose that if Lehtinen is the Beast, that he's scouting out another railroad? Maybe to dump another body?"

"That did occur to me, and that also did occur to Sergeant Hamilton," Alex said. "That's why he called."

"Did Lehtinen say when he's going to take that trip?"

"Next week sometime. And he said he's going to start and end in Porcupine City." My hometown is right on the official Circle Tour route and almost due north of Green Bay. It's a logical spot for those who live in central Wisconsin to begin the tour.

"We ought to tail him," I said.

"Who's we?" Alex said.

"Me." In four years as sheriff of Porcupine County I had not taken a real vacation, just a long weekend here and there. It was about time. "And I'll get a warrant from Judge Rantala to bug Lehtinen's car."

"Why not track Lehtinen's cell phone, the way normal modern cops do?" Alex said, answering his own question with "Because he hasn't got one, Hamilton says. We don't know if that's because he uses burn phones, as a smart criminal would, or because he's a complete Luddite."

"We could track his plate," I said. Unknown to most drivers, governments on both the American and Canadian sides of the border maintain networks of sophisticated cameras on major highways that capture license plate numbers of passing cars and store them in massive digital databases for the use of police tracing the movements of suspected wrongdoers. So far the courts have allowed the cops to snoop on people's whereabouts that way without warrants. After all, cops declare, someone driving down a public street has no right to license plate privacy. A highway camera (or one in a squad car) that records a plate is only seeing the same thing that an officer on the road would with his own eyes. Naturally, champions of privacy want new laws that would force the cops to get probable-cause warrants to access saved location data. That would make catching bad guys and solving crimes much harder, the police reply. I can understand both sides.

For now, however, we in law enforcement can go ahead and mine the databases. That would allow us to tell exactly where Lehtinen's car had been for the last six months.

"But that wouldn't tell us what he did, the actions he took, at the spots he passed through," I said. "For that we'd need our own eyes."

"So we'll need a warrant for a bug," Alex said. "You sure we can get one? We haven't got much probable cause."

"Pretty sure."

So far as those legal documents are concerned, General Rantala—that's the full name the judge's parents gave him—is a pushover, a lawman's wet dream. He's an octogenarian officeholder who thinks Porcupine County law enforcement can do no wrong. He signs warrants almost without reading them. For him, just a hunch of mine is enough probable cause. We'd been lucky so far in the few dubious warrants he'd signed. None of them had been challenged in court as leading unlawfully to a conviction. We'd had enough other evidence to put away our bad guys for a long time.

"I doubt that if Lehtinen is our guy, he would be trying to smuggle a body himself into Canada to dump it there," Alex said. "Too easy to get caught."

Canadian customs and immigration is as tough and suspicious as its American counterpart. There is so much pressure on the agents in the Canadian border kiosks to prevent criminals and terrorists from squeezing through the fence that once in a while an officer can drop his official mask of politeness and snarl like his U.S. counterpart. More than once Ginny and I had to stand by helplessly while the customs men took apart our car looking for contraband. And I had shown my ID as a law enforcement officer.

"Nope," I said. "The actual transportation of bodies isn't part of our guy's MO. I think it's almost certain that he hires other people to do that."

"The warrant will be good across Michigan but probably not Wisconsin and Minnesota and certainly not Canada," Alex said. "You'd have to go to the Ontario Provincial Police and ask for their cooperation. But would they give it?"

"Doubt it," I said. "If what we've got isn't good enough probable cause for the Wisconsin and Minnesota state police, it won't be good enough for the OPP."

"So you'll have to go underground."

"Yes."

That evening I told Ginny what we'd discovered and what I was going to do.

To my utter surprise she said immediately, "I'm going along."

"Absolutely not!" I said. "Too dangerous."

"Don't be silly. You said Lehtinen's probably on a reconnaissance trip, and you're just keeping an eye on him. Maybe he's merely taking a vacation and his trip's entirely innocent. That's all, you said. No opportunity for gunplay. After all, you're the sheriff who can't shoot straight."

"Thanks for reminding me," I said. She was, however, right about all of that. "Well . . ." I added.

"Well me no wells," Ginny said. "Look. If you go on a vacation alone, everybody in Porcupine City will notice. They'll think we're splitting up. They'll even think you're going for police reasons, not for pleasure. But if I go, it'll be the most natural thing. Perfect disguise for you. If Lehtinen or anybody else should spot you on the way, we're just tourists and it's a complete coincidence we're there. And we don't have to worry about Tommy."

She had a point. Her foster son had agreed to try the fall

semester at Michigan State before volunteering with the AIM. I suspected Adela Rogers had had something to do with that. Maybe she just wanted her boyfriend around at school. In any case, he was still interested in a police career. I thought the little tête-à-tête in which I asked his opinion about the case had refreshed his old ambition. With teenage lads, however, it's always dangerous to assume that their futures have been etched in stone. They are just too mercurial. All I could do was hope Tommy's first four months at Michigan State would be fruitful.

"As far as Lehtinen is concerned," I said, "I'm sure he does know we're working the case and looking for suspects."

"But does he think he's a suspect?"

I shook my head. "Doubt it. But he might if he spots me."

"He's not likely to see you. We'll stay well behind him." Ginny can think like a cop as well as a historian. "Besides, you can always use another pair of eyes."

I gave in. "All right," I said. "But . . ."

"But me no buts. I'll start packing so we're ready when he starts the tour."

CHAPTER SIXTEEN

Two days later, a week past Labor Day, Lehtinen did. "He's on the way," Sergeant Hamilton said on the phone from Green Bay. Alex had asked him to keep an eagle eye on Lehtinen, and he had. "He'll be in Porcupine City in about four hours, just in time for lunch. He's driving a green 2010 Ford Escape."

I was in my office. I stuck my head out the door and told both Gil and Sheila that Operation Circle Tour, as we grandiosely called it, was beginning. Then I called Ginny at the Historical Society building a few blocks away and gave her the heads-up. We had packed two Rollaboards with a week's clothes and stowed them in the trunk of her Prius, ready to leave on a moment's notice. Ginny had already arranged her absence, saying mysteriously that she was taking a trip and winking lewdly when asked where. Her corps of volunteers stood ready to mind the store.

I then called the county commissioners' office, leaving a message on the administrative assistant's voicemail to the effect that something personal had unexpectedly come up and that I was taking a week's vacation. I added that Gil would run things in my absence. I was glad the assistant hadn't answered the phone personally, for she is conscientious, as are so many public servants in Porcupine County who feel lucky to have their jobs, quite unlike officious state and county bureaucrats elsewhere. Even though I'm an elected official and don't have to account for my time off, she would have pointedly asked why—and passed the reason up to the commissioners, most of whom think I waste the county's scarce money. I wouldn't have used it for this trip anyway. It might not pan out and I'd be submitting an expense account for a failed enterprise. In a county as parsimonious as ours, that can get you fired. Or, rather, defeated at the next election.

Next I called Alex. "On my way," he said. He added that he was bringing one of the Michigan State Police's latest battery-fed GPS bugs to affix to Lehtinen's car. On my iPhone he'd place a clever police app that would listen to the transmission from the bug, bounced off a satellite to the iPhone, and show the exact location of the car on Google Maps. Geolocation tracking is hardly cutting-edge technology. For several years trucking companies and delivery services have been using similar devices to follow their vehicles all over the country. They know exactly where a driver is at any time of the day or night. So far as Ginny and I were concerned, we would be able to follow Lehtinen unseen all the way around Lake Superior and know at every moment precisely where he—or, rather, his car—was.

After that I called Judge Rantala's office. He had presigned the warrant for the bug, leaving the time element open, and all his assistant had to do was ink in the dates the warrant was good: from today for ten days. I sent Chad over to pick up the paperwork.

One more task: to alert the FBI. I hated telling the Feds everything I planned to do, but if I was to keep them at bay, it was necessary. I just hoped they would not suddenly step in and wrench this small part of the case away from me. Many sheriffs and even state policemen would be relieved to have a bigger and better-equipped law enforcement agency take over a difficult job, but this case had become a matter not only of pride but also superior insight from someone who thought he knew his rural jurisdiction far better than the Beltway boys.

To my surprise all Jack Adamson said was "Sounds like a plan. Keep me posted." Maybe the FBI generals truly were stumped and were letting the privates march out on point, hoping they'd shake new clues out of the trees.

An hour later Alex arrived from Wakefield with a brown supermarket paper bag containing the bug. Instead of his self-described "smart country casual" dress of khaki slacks and Lands' End windbreaker, his standard uniform for cool September days, he wore stained jeans, an old forest camo jacket, and a battered Cabela's ball cap. He looked the part of the average Yooper logger or farmer. On the street, nobody would take notice of him. He blended in well.

As for me, all I did was change my ball cap. On duty it's the sheriff's model, off duty it's a blue Cubs cap, although I haven't been a fan in many years, for my heart has been broken once too often. I suppose the red "C" on the blue field means that deep down I'm carrying a torch for the team. I don't want to think about it. Too dispiriting. Anyway, in the winter my official headgear—and that of all my deputies—is a warm woolen Stormy Kromer embroidered with a sheriff's star.

Ginny is a smart dresser but not a flashy one. She likes tailored jeans and form-fitting sweaters for everyday wear, but always accents those with a bright silk scarf. Today she wore a loose blue wickable nylon long-sleeved collared shirt from REI and tan L.L. Bean hiker's zip-off slacks, the picture of a summer tourist eagerly anticipating a ride around Lake Superior.

I did not pack a weapon. In Canada the warrant would be useless, and I doubted that the Ontario Provincial Police would consider an educated hunch good enough to allow me to tail a suspect through their jurisdiction. Hence I wasn't going to declare my profession. Canada is also very ginger about handguns and the first thing a customs agent asks, after "Business or pleasure?" is "Do you have any firearms?" Rather than lie—I am a terrible liar—it'd be better for me to be able to look an agent in the eye and say, truthfully, "No."

We took up our positions, Ginny and I in her Prius, Alex in the seat of a muddy pickup belonging to Joe Koski, our corrections officer. From our lair in the parking lot of a church at the junction of U.S. 45 from the south and state highways from west and east, we'd see Lehtinen coming up from Wisconsin. We'd be able to follow him either west for a clockwise circumnavigation of the lake or east on if he chose to go counterclockwise. Whichever route he chose, I suspected he'd want lunch before starting the trip and would head north into downtown for a bite to eat.

Almost exactly four hours after Hamilton gave us the heads-up, a green Ford Escape passed us from the south on U.S. 45 at precisely the twenty-five miles an hour limit. Out of habit I clocked him with the radar gun. We let the Escape turn the corner a block away, heading northwest on River Street, the main drag, before we followed.

If I were a betting man, I'd have laid a General Grant on the green baize that Lehtinen would go to Merle's for lunch. Out-of-towners tend to prefer that to the other cafe on River Street, frequented mostly by locals. The food at both is good small-town beanery fare, but Merle's service is quicker and that's why I go there most of the time. It's also closer to the sheriff's department, and Merle's caters the meals at the jail. Those are simple but decent. I'm never surprised by a lousy dish, and neither are the inmates. A good meal, as well as a drag on a vape, helps keep them as content as prisoners ever can be.

Sure enough, at precisely noon Lehtinen parked half a block south of Merle's, walked up the hill and casually stepped inside the cafe without shooting a glance in either direction. He either had ice in his blood or absolutely no idea we were watching him. I felt confident of the latter. Hoped it, too.

Alex parked several cars behind the Escape and stepped onto the sidewalk carrying what appeared to be a small flashlight. Slowly he ambled up the block until he was abreast of the Escape's rear wheel. Then he suddenly stopped as if he had just remembered something important. Slowly he turned and gazed back down the street. Then he turned his glance in the other direction. Absolutely no one was out and about.

If I hadn't been watching Alex, I'd never have seen him suddenly bend down, thrust the cylindrical object under the rear bumper, and stand straight again. The entire procedure took less than a second. The bug was affixed to the frame with a magnet so powerful that the package couldn't be shaken loose, unless the vehicle rolled over an improvised explosive device of the kind that blew up Hummers in Iraq. The bug also was small enough to escape a cursory inspection if the car were raised on a lift. You'd almost have to be looking for it to find it.

Alex didn't leave Lehtinen's car immediately. After shooting another quick look up and down the street, he bent and inserted a dealer's skeleton key into the trunk lock and popped it. After a swift survey he looked back at us and shook his head. Nothing inside. Lehtinen wasn't transporting another corpse. We hadn't thought he would, but we needed to be sure.

Thirty minutes passed before Lehtinen emerged from Merle's, stretching his arms over his head, the picture of well-fed contentedness. I jotted a note in my shirt-pocket pad. *Went to lunch at exactly noon. Took exactly half an hour to eat.* This was a homely detail, maybe not so important in the greater scheme of things, but worth remembering.

Again without a backward or forward glance, Lehtinen got into the Escape, did a quick U-turn, and headed back south on still-deserted River Street. One-eighties over the double stripe on the main street are not exactly legal in Porcupine City, though they are in other Michigan towns, but we don't have the money for "NO U-TURN" signs and therefore don't bother to cite those who break that ordinance, especially if there's no oncoming traffic to endanger. Judge Rantala would just throw out the case. I doubted that Lehtinen was aware of the Porcupine City custom. Nobody else seems to be, even many who live in town. But I thought it worth making a note of the infraction. Just in case.

At the junction of River Street and U.S. 45, Lehtinen turned south, drove one block, then as Ginny watched the bug on my iPhone, turned right and headed west down the state highway on the bridge over the Porcupine River. "He's going clockwise, Steve," she said.

We waited until the Escape had proceeded a mile down the highway before following. Either Lehtinen had a steady foot on the accelerator or made use of the Ford's cruise control, for the bug reported the vehicle doing precisely fifty-five miles an hour.

For the next two and a half hours through Upper Michigan scrub, meadow, and second-growth forest Lehtinen cruised, leaving the state route at U.S. 2, the nation's northernmost national highway, and passing through Ironwood into Wisconsin toward Ashland. It was such a boring, featureless drive that I had to ask Ginny to keep talking about anything that came into her head to keep me from dozing off at the wheel. Nothing on the radio in Upper Michigan, either AM or FM, ever is stirring enough to keep me alert on long drives, except National Public Radio, and that not always.

Fortunately, Ginny's conversation is always pertinent and interesting. "Where do you suppose Lehtinen will stop for the night?" she asked. "Maybe it'll be on the waterfront in Duluth. That has great views, very good upscale motels, and lots of excellent restaurants. I hope so, anyway. That's where I want to stop."

"Me, too," I said. "But I have a feeling he won't. I don't think he's on a joyride."

Otherwise Ginny kept me rapt with her tale of research into a political murder committed in Porcupine County in 1935. An immigrant Finnish churchman had hired a gunman to murder a Communist recruiter trying to entice first-generation Finnish-Americans, impoverished by the Depression, to emigrate to Soviet Karelia. Just as Ginny's hit man was about to pull the trigger, the bug on the iPhone veered off the road and stopped at the little crossroads of Brule. It was almost exactly three p.m. Eastern time in Porcupine City, or two p.m. Central time in Wisconsin. I made a note of that.

Nobody would ever give Brule, a hamlet of fewer than six hundred people on the Bois Brule River, a second thought—except for fly-fishing enthusiasts. The Bois Brule is so famous for its trout that four presidents of the United States—Coolidge, Hoover, Truman, and Eisenhower—fished there. One of the homeowners on the river was the famously paranoid CIA counterspy James Jesus Angleton. He was so obsessed with Soviet moles, his critics said, that he saw one under every rock in Washington. He even denounced two Canadian prime ministers as agents of Moscow.

I thought about Angleton's profession as Ginny and I pulled off U.S. 2 at a filling station across the highway from the restaurant where Lehtinen had parked his Escape. Tailing a criminal suspect isn't much different from following an enemy agent. Except I wasn't paranoid. Or so I hoped as I peered with binoculars through the Prius's windshield at the restaurant's big front window fifty yards away. Lehtinen lounged at a table in plain view, his attention on a cup of coffee and what seemed to be a pastry.

"Whatever he's doing," I said, "he doesn't seem to be hiding."

"Maybe he's keeping an eye out for tails," Ginny said.

Fortunately, I had lowered the binoculars when Lehtinen suddenly turned his head and looked out the window, seemingly straight at us. Quickly I grabbed Ginny, turned her face to mine, and planted a moist kiss right on her lips.

"Whah—" she whispered, startled.

"I don't think he noticed us," I said as I slowly released her. "Saw this trick in the movies."

She looked down at my hand, still cupping her breast. "Did you see that in the movies, too?" she asked. "Well, that was nice. I wish you'd do that more often."

"Which?" I said. "This? Or that?"

"That," she said. "Both."

After I complied, taking my time, I started up the Prius and pulled back onto U.S. 2, heading west. Lehtinen had returned his gaze to his coffee and pastry. I didn't look as we passed the restaurant, but Ginny stole a sideward glance. "He's not watching us," she said.

"Close call," I said. "From here on we'd better stay out of sight. All the time."

Ginny turned on the iPhone and in a few minutes said, "He's moving again."

Lehtinen had stopped for precisely fifteen minutes.

"Let's stay ahead of him for awhile," I said, "at least until we get to Superior."

Tailing from in front with an electronic bug is a good way to proceed, but we needed to stay at least a mile ahead and out of sight. We didn't want the Prius to become familiar to Lehtinen. I set the cruise control to fifty-six miles an hour while Lehtinen stayed at fifty-five, according to the iPhone. We slowly opened the gap, and I had to brake when the Prius crept more than a mile and a half ahead of the Escape.

At Superior, half an hour west of Brule, I pulled off U.S. 2

and hid in the parking lot of the Richard Bong Veterans Historical Center so that we could get back on Lehtinen's tail again. There were just too many possible routes Lehtinen could take through the area.

The Bong museum honors a renowned World War II ace fighter pilot. It sports a beautifully restored P-38 aircraft like the one Bong flew for the Army Air Forces in the Pacific, and lies a quarter of a mile from the SS Meteor Maritime Museum with its original 1896 whaleback lake freighter. Any legitimate tourist on the Lake Superior tour would very likely stop at both sites for at least two hours. Ginny and I had, more than once.

But the bug sped past the intersection, headed for the short Interstate 535 over a bridge across the wide St. Louis River and entered Minnesota at the neighboring city of Duluth. We turned back on the highway and followed a mile behind, watching as Lehtinen pointed the Escape northeast across the north shore of Lake Superior.

Most tourists would also pull off to watch oceangoing vessels stand in and out under the huge aerial lift bridge of Duluth Harbor, 2,300 miles from the Atlantic Ocean. The best views of the photogenic bridge, Ginny and I had discovered on an earlier visit, are from balconies at the harborside Great Lakes Aquarium, another grail of local sightseers. Lehtinen didn't bother. He kept going.

As the highway dwindled from four lanes into two, he passed the resort complexes at Brighton Beach without stopping. Nor did he pause to gaze at the roaring falls under the bridges over the Cross and Temperance Rivers, let alone pull off on the scenic shoreline drive that parallels the highway. Only at Two Harbors did he pull over, and it was not at Betty's Pies, the internationally famous cafe and bakery that no self-respecting tourist could possibly pass up. Rather, Lehtinen headed for the old rail yards on the waterfront.

"This is not going well at all," I said. I had been hoping for a slice of Betty's banana cream pie. So had Ginny.

Lehtinen did not even park his Escape as he drove past long strings of open iron ore pellet cars waiting to offload their treasure onto lake freighters, but quickly resumed his journey. Grumpily we followed in the Prius.

Lehtinen ignored the spectacular Split Rock Lighthouse, a holy destination for lighthouse freaks everywhere, and drove on past the long sand beaches, favorites of traveling campers and sunbathers. Past the gorgeous coves of Silver Bay, Chicago Bay, Horseshoe Bay, Big Bay, and Cannonball Bay he motored without slowing. Nor did he appear to waste a sideways glance at the picturesque resort communities of Schroeder, Tofte, and Lutsen, where Ginny and I had once spent a glorious weekend.

"He's walking the walk," I said, "but he's not watching the watch."

"Come again?" Ginny said.

"I meant he's following a famous tourist route, but he isn't rubbernecking like a vacationer," I said. "He's not stopping to look at anything. Except railroad yards."

"Not even Chad would commit such an awkward metaphor," Ginny said. "I thought you were referring to the clock."

"He does seem to be watching *that* watch," I said. "The one on his wrist."

That was because it was now exactly five p.m. Central time and Lehtinen had stopped in Grand Marais, a small city three hours from Brule and five and a half from Porcupine City. We watched the iPhone as the bug entered the parking lot of a big chain motel on the highway. Five minutes later we checked into a similar motel a mile up the road. Whether Lehtinen had had reservations at his hostelry we didn't know, but luckily it was midweek in early September and there was plenty of room at the inns. I made another note. Lehtinen had followed the clock in the actual time zone where he was, not the duration from Porcupine City. Did that mean anything? It might.

There were plenty of eateries in Grand Marais, some of them celebrated as far away as Minneapolis, Milwaukee, and Chicago. At five forty-five p.m. Lehtinen pulled out of his motel and headed back down Minnesota 61, stopping at a place called the Angry Trout, a roadside seafood restaurant that was a favorite of Ginny's and mine. We chose to stay out of sight and instead picked a cheap and nondescript pizza parlor in town. That was a reasonable decision so far as my wallet was concerned, but my taste buds did not agree. Nor, emphatically, did Ginny's. She had had the grace and understanding not to embarrass me by offering to pick up the check at a fancier place. But her forbearance had its limits.

"I have never had a crappier meal," she said.

At seven p.m. Lehtinen returned to his motel and we to ours. That was it for the night, although I kept getting up to check the bug on the iPhone. It didn't move. Ginny slept on, her slumber unbroken.

CHAPTER SEVENTEEN

The sun streaming through Venetian blinds awakened me at five-thirty. Quickly I checked the iPhone. The bug hadn't shifted. I climbed out of bed and fumbled with the clumsy four-cup coffeemaker so typical of cheap motels and tried not to make a clatter. Ginny looked so angelic with her long, loose red hair spread out on the pillow that I let her sleep. I was glad she had insisted on coming along. She makes a very good co-pilot. She's alert. Helpful. Entertaining. And good-looking.

Quietly I padded down to the lobby for a doughnut just to stave off the morning growls. This huge motel chain is known for its low rates and equally low standards of service, including a free "breakfast" of quick carbs, cheap orange juice, and terrible coffee. I am an impoverished male peace officer with no culinary standards at all. Except when Ginny is cooking, bad food—heavily processed, sugared, and salted—is my typical diet.

"You're looking good for your age, Steve," someone will say.

"It's all those preservatives," I reply.

Ginny, who has a better sense of self-preservation than I do, refuses to eat motel breakfasts. On the road she'll grab half a cup of coffee upon awakening and then demand we stop at a promising full-service roadside cafe. I knew she'd insist on that. Every time she takes a road trip she brings along a little notebook full of jottings about countryside restaurants highly ranked on TripAdvisor.

At seven a.m. the bug still hadn't moved. Was Lehtinen up and going for breakfast? I didn't know, but the day before he'd arrived in Porcupine City at noon. That meant he'd left Green Bay at eight and presumably had awakened at seven. If he was as much a slave to the clock as he was beginning to seem, he'd be up at the same hour today. I thanked my stars again for the bug. It gave us lots of wiggle room. If Lehtinen got a head start, it wouldn't be difficult to catch up.

"Up 'n at 'em," I said as I nudged Ginny awake. She emerged from under the covers and wrinkled her nose at the remnants of the doughnut on the nightstand. As always, her morning toilette took less than ten minutes and she presented herself with suitcase at the door. "Let's go find a bite to eat," she said.

We did, at a cafe just down the street, at a table in the front window. "Mom's," the sign said, bringing to mind the novelist Nelson Algren's celebrated warning about eating at a place called Mom's. But the food at this small-town Mom's belied that gritty urban wisdom. Ginny tucked into her crisp bacon and perfectly done over-easy eggs and snatched a piece of my whole wheat toast. She has a good appetite. In every way, I might add. Lucky for me.

At eight, after our second cup of coffee, I checked the iPhone. The bug was on the move. "Here he comes," I said. In ninety seconds, as I concealed my face behind a *Minneapolis Star-Tribune,* the green Escape drove by at a stately twenty-five miles an hour, right at the speed limit. We settled up and saddled up. At her insistence Ginny drove. She won't let me do the male thing and monopolize the steering wheel. We followed the usual mile behind as Lehtinen proceeded northeast up the highway.

So far as we knew, he had ignored the many attractions of Grand Marais. Its pretty harbor is full of sailboats. On the waterfront sits an internationally known folk school where one can, among other things, learn the arts of boatbuilding and blacksmithing. Well-to-do Minneapolitans flock there in herds every summer. Ginny and I have often talked about vacationing at Grand Marais just to take a few classes. But Lehtinen appeared to be a man on a mission that did not seem to involve such yuppie-duppie fripperies.

Other than the overnight stay, he spent no time at all in Grand Marais, probably because there are no tracks in town or nearby, the only railroad there having gone belly-up in 1912. He headed northeast, and in a little less than an hour arrived in Grand Portage, the last town before the Canadian border. Again he did not stop. I wished he would do just one touristy thing. There's so much of that in the place. There's the Grand Portage National Monument commemorating the long fur trade voyageurs' trek up the rapids of the Pigeon River in the eighteenth century. That waterway forms the border between the United States and Canada. There's also Isle Royale National Park just offshore in Lake Superior, a splendid day trip by ferry from town that Ginny and I had taken a few years before.

But no. Lehtinen blew right through Grand Portage and past the national monument turnoffs. Just after nine a.m. his Escape crossed the low bridge over the Pigeon River and stopped at Canadian customs and immigration. Within sixty seconds the agent waved him through, and we could see Lehtinen's car fading up the road as we pulled up to the customs window.

To my surprise—Ginny's sexuality is unobtrusive and understated, like her hidden wealth—she had undone the top two buttons of her blouse and shrugged out a little cleavage, not blatant but mildly enticing to any red-blooded male. This is a time-honored distraction that customs agents experience every day and are inured against, but a little flash of boob never hurts. Ginny *is* a resourceful person. I suddenly remembered an incident years before in which we had been transporting—quite illegally—an orphaned bear cub to an Indian reservation and were flagged down by a Minnesota state cop. Before the trip, Ginny had had the foresight to dip the envelope supposedly containing the transport permit into a puddle of highly aromatic pig poop. Presented with the envelope, the horrified trooper just waved us on.

At the customs window Ginny offered a cheery "Good morning!"

"Good morning rightbackatcha!" sang the almost equally pretty female customs agent. "Passports, please."

I stifled a grin. But I was glad Ginny was in the driver's seat. She knows how to hide what's going on in her head.

"Business or pleasure?" the agent said as she slid the passports through her scanner. I watched her expression carefully. It did not change when the scanner reported no criminal information, not that there was any to report.

"Pleasure," Ginny responded with the same cheeriness. "We're driving around Lake Superior." That was no lie, except maybe by a little omission. Or perhaps not. On this trip Ginny was having a good time. She always does.

"Now that's a lovely drive," the agent said. "Did it myself once."

The agent lowered her head, cocked it, and peered at me across the front seat. "Sir, where were you born?" she said.

"Pine Ridge, South Dakota," I responded. She glanced at my passport and nodded. She was probably thinking *Stephen Two Crow Martinez. Two Crow. That's Native American, not Al Qaeda or Taliban.* My brown face often gets such scrutiny, at the U.S. border as well as the Canadian one. I am always ready for a little border snark—or a lot—but this time it did not happen.

"Welcome to Canada," she said sincerely and waved us through.

As we pulled away I released a deep sigh. We'd gotten away with it. Not that there was much to get away with. But I had been antsy as we approached the border. Being in pursuit of a criminal suspect without letting the Canadians know about it probably broke half a dozen of their laws.

Past the Pigeon River the countryside suddenly changes from thick scrub to green, rolling meadows full of cows and sheep, red barns, and farm homesteads, with thick forests deep in the background. That scenery always reminds me of Nova Scotia. I doubted that Howard Lehtinen had given it even a cursory glance as he headed for Thunder Bay an hour northeast of Grand Portage.

Thunder Bay used to be two adjacent boom towns, Fort William and Port Arthur, a twin center of grain shipping via rail and lake freighter to the East Coast. During Prohibition a vast fleet of small boats sped bootleg liquor across Lake Superior to shady beaches on the Wisconsin and Michigan shores. Today the city is struggling. Industries have left town and the grain from Canada's breadbasket in the west is moving to the Pacific Coast for shipment overseas. Trucks have largely taken over the rest and grain elevators have closed. Immigration from foreign lands has ebbed. A couple of years ago Thunder Bay was granted the unwanted crown of "Murder Capital of Canada." To put that in perspective, the city had all of seven homicides that entire year. (Flint, Michigan, also with a population of about 100,000, had sixty-six.)

Still the town tries. There's a renovated waterfront park still under construction near the marina downtown, and Fort William Historical Park on the city's outskirts, a palisaded living-history panorama of the fur trade in 1815. Ginny and I greatly enjoyed visiting with the Canadian college students dressed like colonial women and British soldiers of the time. Their knowledge of their own history shamed that of American collegians. We also loved Kakabeka Falls on the Kaministiquia River twenty miles outside town, wild, fast-flowing, and full of rainbows, both in the air and on the hook.

Howard Lehtinen ignored both, preferring instead to drive into the city itself. I was not surprised, for Thunder Bay plays host to two huge rail complexes. One is the Canadian Pacific's yards, where grain trains as well as container trains are coupled together and sent to ports on both Atlantic and Pacific Oceans. The same thing goes on in the Canadian National's marshaling yard just west of Thunder Bay.

We watched as the bug headed for the CPR yards on the Kaministiquia River estuary and followed slowly behind through a warren of streets, taking care to stay two or so blocks behind, well out of sight. We were now all but certain that Lehtinen was unaware he was being followed, and we wanted to keep it that way.

The bug stopped and inched over to the side of a street. We waited three minutes, then drove past the Escape. It was parked off the street on a small dirt verge fifty feet from the closest track in the yard. Strings of stored grain hoppers choked several tracks for half a mile in either direction. They were new, old, pristine, rusted, many of their lower halves covered with elaborate graffiti, some of them seemingly fresh out of the paint shop. Huge lamp arrays atop tall standards towered over the yard. No fence separated the yard from the street. Only "NO TRESPASSING" signs protected the rails from interlopers. Lehtinen was nowhere in sight.

Ginny parked the Prius among several cars across the street from the Escape and half a block away. We had a clear view of the outside track but not the ones within the yard. Frequently a yard worker in signal orange safety vest and hard hat strode by along the rails. One of them stopped to rap the trucks and wheels of each car in a cut of a dozen hoppers with a small hammer and listen to the sound it made. "Car knocker," I told

Ginny. "He's listening for flaws in the metal that might be from a cracked wheel or frame. I suspect the cars he's checking are going out on the road soon."

An Ontario Provincial Police squad car slowed as it passed us on the street. The lone uniformed officer inside looked me in the eye, then glanced away and proceeded on.

"He's wondering what we're up to," I said. "There aren't a lot of people around here and our presence is unusual. But he didn't stop. We look like a normal couple, not thieves casing the joint. But we'd better not be here if he comes back. He's probably on regular patrol."

"Let's get out of the car," Ginny said, reaching into the back of the Prius and pulling out her camera, equipped with a short telephoto lens. "We're going to be foamers."

"Good idea," I said, fishing the binoculars from the glove box. Ginny is full of good ideas.

We got out of the car, walked up the street away from the Prius, and stopped on the sidewalk with a good view of the yard, but on the public way, not the private property of the Canadian Pacific Railway. I scanned the cars with the binoculars and Ginny snapped photographs of a nearby switch locomotive banging cars together to form a train.

"Am I foaming enough?" I said.

"You're not doing too badly," Ginny said.

Within ten minutes of its departure the OPP prowl car returned from the opposite direction and stopped across from us.

This time the lone officer rolled down his window and looked us both up and down. "Sir and madam," he said with grave courtesy, "are you lost? Can I be of assistance?"

"Oh, nope," Ginny said with a winning smile. "We're rail buffs. Just taking pictures. Look at that." She pointed across at the switcher at work. I knew just enough about railroading to know that it was a very old diesel locomotive.

"That's a GP7," I said. "Dates back to the early 1950s. You don't see yard goats that old very often." I hoped I sounded like a real foamer. Ginny thinks I am. She has taken amused notice of what she calls the "choo-choo magazines" on my night table.

"Think it's gonna be a rebuild?" said the officer. The question suggested he was a foamer, too, or maybe he was just testing me. Fortunately, I'd recently read about the railroad's refurbishment plans for the locomotives. They were all to get new and more powerful engines as well as new sheet metal. This one hadn't yet gone through its rebuilding.

"Oh, yeah," I said. "Three hundred more horsepower's going to make a difference."

"Very good," said the officer, now apparently satisfied that I was what I looked like and sounded like. "Please be sure to stay off the railroad property. It's dangerous there."

"We know," Ginny said. "We'll be careful."

With a smile the cop rolled up his window and drove away. I could have sworn he had lifted a skeptical eyebrow at me.

"Whe-e-ew!" I said. "That was close."

"You pulled it off perfectly, Steve," Ginny said. "You can talk the talk. I'm proud of you."

For two hours we stood and watched the yard before Lehtinen finally emerged from the forest of cars. I spotted him through the binoculars as he stepped from between two uncoupled hopper cars two hundred yards away. He was wearing a yellow hard hat and signal orange vest with "CPR" emblazoned on the back. He walked directly toward us.

"Bogie at nine o'clock," I said, like a fighter pilot. "Break right."

Quickly, but not too quickly, we turned in the other direction and slowly walked out of sight to the Prius.

"He didn't spot us," I said. "But what was he doing?"

"Casing the joint, maybe," Ginny said.

"If he's looking for someplace to stash bodies," I said, "I don't think this is the place. Too much activity. Too easy to be seen. And I think those cars come and go quite frequently. He'd know about that before he got here. He's in the business, after all."

"Then what?"

"I don't know," I said. "Maybe he's looking for a particular car. But that would be like hunting a needle in a haystack."

In a few minutes we watched on the iPhone as Lehtinen pulled away, heading north.

Just north of Thunder Bay Lehtinen stopped at a roadside restaurant. It was precisely noon.

"We could set our watches by him," Ginny observed.

"There's something pathological about this," I said. "He seems to be an obsessive–compulsive."

"Yes."

"Do you think he's looking for suitable places to get rid of bodies?"

"Maybe," Ginny said.

"What else could this behavior be?"

"Perhaps a sexual fetish having to do with hopper cars," she said.

"Does a fetish have to be sexual?" I said.

"I think it could be religious or mystical. You ought to ask Sue Hemb."

"When this is over I will."

"Let's go feed my food fetish."

And so we did, at a diner up the road from Lehtinen, until the bug started up and the Escape swept by us.

"He's doing eighty," I said. "The limit."

"Eighty kilometers an hour?" Ginny said. "How much is that

in real money?"

"Forty-nine point seven miles an hour," I said, checking the Prius's speedometer. The Canadians are more conservative than the Americans about speed limits. They allow one hundred kilometers per hour on rural four-lane highways, or a tad below sixty-three miles an hour. As in the States, driver groups are lobbying for an increase in the top limit to one hundred and thirty kilometers per hour, or eighty miles an hour. I think that's a lousy idea, but then I'm one of those who has to clean up after a high-speed highway accident. Of course I'm biased.

"Either Lehtinen has a fetish about the posted speed limit," I said, "or he's being very careful not to get busted while driving and start a personal history with the police."

In late afternoon Lehtinen arrived in Nipigon, the northernmost town on the shore of Lake Superior, seventy-five miles northeast of Thunder Bay on the Trans-Canada Highway. The Canadian Pacific Railway roughly parallels the Trans-Canada, with sidings spotted at irregular intervals. Twice Lehtinen stopped on the verge of the road to reconnoiter the sidings, but did not climb down through the rocky scree below the highway for a closer look. Few cars seemed to be stored there anyway, and what we saw were mostly battered boxcars and gondolas.

In Nipigon itself there was a mile-long siding and a short industrial spur, but the only cars there were boxcars, tank cars, and a long work train. Lehtinen's Escape slowed on the parallel street as it passed the siding, as if he were giving the railroad a cursory onceover, but he did not stop. Rather, he did a wide U-turn on the deserted street and headed back to the Trans-Canada, pulling into a mom-and-pop motel across the highway from us at the pumps of a filling station. It was five p.m.

"Coulda told you," I said.

We found lodgings at a similar small hostelry three-quarters of a mile farther along the highway, and watched as the bug retraced the route in the other direction a short way to a spot Google Maps identified as a Tim Horton's. For Canadians, the Tim Horton's chain is as familiar as McDonald's is to Americans. Whenever we are in an unfamiliar town in Canada, Ginny and I will search for a Horton's rather than take a chance with an unknown restaurant. For the most part, its Canadian highway cuisine is far tastier and more healthful than the deep-fried grub of just about any American fast-food joint.

Not wishing to run into Lehtinen, Ginny and I headed for a nondescript truck-stop beanery a mile away. That was another mistake, as Ginny kept reminding me between rumbles, growls, and belches that evening. I hoped that the ensuing gastric typhoon would not keep me up all night.

I did awaken frequently to check the bug. It didn't move.

CHAPTER EIGHTEEN

Just after we had finished breakfast at the counter of a reasonably acceptable diner on the eastern side of Nipigon, my iPhone started warbling. "Eight in the morning again," I said. "He's on the road."

Before Ginny could respond, two men in rumpled dark suits suddenly shouldered through the doorway, strode over to the counter, and commandeered two stools next to ours, one to my left and one to Ginny's right. Both intruders were tall, broad-shouldered, lean, and unsmiling.

They were cops. I can always tell. These had that typical cop's beetling and swiveling gaze of suspicion and mistrust. They also had bulges under their left armpits and mirrored aviator sunglasses in their breast pockets. Those last often are dead giveaways, like the absence of wheel covers and the presence of buggy-whip antennas on unmarked police vehicles. But cops often wear such shades because they hide their eyes, and not being able to look an officer in the eye is often unsettling to someone who has busted a stop sign or worse. Puts them at a disadvantage. I counsel my deputies to remove their sunglasses when confronting traffic offenders at the driver's window. That simple action, I argue, often puts the offenders off balance, for they're not expecting a friendly face-to-face encounter, and they're less apt to quarrel about the violation. It seems to work.

"Superintendent Ian MacAllan, Ontario Provincial Police," said the first, shoving a warrant card under my nose and getting right down to business. "This is Detective Sergeant John Ferguson. Stephen Martinez, would you and Ms. Fitzgerald please come down to the detachment with us? We would like to talk to you, if we may. Leave your car here." He spoke in the form of a request, but he was not asking.

Busted. They even knew our names. I should have known. Ginny glanced at me and I nodded slightly. Best to go along. Any way you looked at it, they had the drop on us.

"Mind your heads," MacAllan said as we stepped into the back of a nearly brand-new cherry-red Cadillac Escalade, but he did not clap a meaty palm on our pates to guide them through the doors, as American cops do during arrests. We rode on tooled leather seats the few blocks across town to the Nipigon Detachment, as the OPP calls its police stations.

"Who pimped your ride?" I said, just to make conversation. Inside, the Escalade was loaded. Leather trimmings, huge navigation console, elaborate rear-seat entertainment system, backup and side view cameras. Outside, styled wheels and an elegant touch of chrome. I'd never been inside a police vehicle that luxurious.

The two OPP officers stared ahead stonily and did not respond. I shrugged. The Escalade probably had been seized from a wealthy repeat DUI offender. MacAllan may have had dibs on the province's pool of confiscated vehicles. In the States we also had those, usually cars and trucks seized during drug busts. The Canadians sold most of theirs at auctions, sometimes after using them on the road for a few months as "Q-ships"—the term came from the heavily armed merchant ships of both world wars that lured submarines to their doom with concealed weaponry. We did the same, running down startled speeders with high-end sports cars and SUVs equipped with grille flashers.

Our favorite trophy car in Porcupine County was a 2012

Ford Mustang Shelby GT 500, a 550-horsepower brute with the speed to catch anything on the road but unfortunately neither the heavy-duty suspension to survive our rough highways nor the interior room to transport arrestees. We used it as our Drug Abuse Resistance Education car to attract young people to anti-drug meetings. Not that we had the budget or manpower for that anymore. Or that D.A.R.E. ever worked in the first place, for teenagers never listen to authority. Half the time they greeted the car with an expression I can describe only as "If I deal drugs, can I get me one of those?"

But the battleship-sized Escalade, I could see, had lots of room for ferrying perpetrators. Even Ginny leaned back luxuriously on the leather seat. I refrained from making a remark about transporting white-collar criminals in style.

When we arrived at the detachment, MacAllan preceded and Ferguson followed us into the building and directly to an interrogation room, ten by twelve feet. The room was painted in standard institutional green and was furnished with a standard steel table and four standard steel chairs, with a standard one-way mirror on one wall and a standard bright ceiling light. A standard video camera and standard recorder were mounted on one wall. Police standard the world over. A standard the dirt-poor Porcupine County Sheriff's Department could never aspire to. Our interrogation room was the jail's kitchen and our video camera an early digital handheld model acquired on eBay.

"Please sit down," MacAllan said in a flat tone. He said "Please." Maybe that was a good sign. Or maybe, I thought, the stereotype is true and Canadians are excessively polite, even when making an arrest.

As he took a chair on the other side of the table from us, the superintendent's stern features suddenly relaxed into a sad hound-dog smile. "Sheriff. Martinez. What. Were. You. Thinking?" he said, slowly enunciating each word like a weary school principal to an incorrigible truant. Detective Sergeant Ferguson relaxed against the wall, casually examining his nails.

"How did you—" I said.

"Sheriff," MacAllan said, "we in Canada are not stupid. We not only have running water and flush toilets, but also we picked up the signal from the transmitter you were following almost as soon as you crossed the Pigeon River bridge. We use the same technology ourselves. Within a few hours we noticed that you were slowing and stopping behind your target automobile at the same places he did. We then ran your license plate and his and had almost all we needed to know."

"Almost?" I said.

"That's why we followed you for a day before making contact," MacAllan said.

"Making contact." That was good. That was better than "arrested."

"We needed to find out why you were tailing Howard Lehtinen. And why in the beginning you did not make your presence as a law enforcement officer known to us, let alone ask us for assistance."

"How much do you know?"

"Some. Detective Sergeant Kolehmainen, who is well known to us, told us a little. He said you were working the case of the skeletons in the freight cars. We've heard all about that. We have newspapers and television up here in the Great White North, too. But not all the details. Sergeant Kolehmainen said you would provide them if we asked nicely. 'Asked nicely' were the words he used."

"Sounds like Alex all right," I said. "How long have you got?"

"All day, if necessary," MacAllan said. Ferguson pulled a chair up to the table and settled himself comfortably.

For more than an hour I unloaded on the two Canadians, telling them everything we knew, from the discovery of the bones in Omaha to our suspicions of Lehtinen. Now and then Ginny cut in and corrected me if I misquoted a finding or stretched a point. I am lucky to have a trained historian for a girlfriend. Historians believe in precision and accuracy in a narrative, right down to the footnotes and bibliography. The superintendent and his sergeant leaned back in their chairs and listened attentively.

"And so Lehtinen worked for the Baltimore & Ohio, which became the CSX, probably had access to information about the storage of freight cars, and certainly had hands-on experience as a track gang member and brakeman," I said. "That makes him the best suspect we've got, and that's why I decided to tail him around Lake Superior. He told his coworkers he was taking a vacation, but I strongly think he may be casing the Canadian Pacific Railway for good places to stash bodies. Or have them stashed."

"That is all the evidence you have?" MacAllan said.

I nodded.

"Pretty thin," Ferguson said. "Surprised you got that judge to issue a warrant for the transmitter. Not that it's good in Canada anyway."

I threw up my hands. "Howard Lehtinen is all we have to go on," I said. "Maybe we haven't nailed him down yet, but I'll swear on a regiment of Mounties that he's the Beast."

"The Beast?" Ferguson said.

I explained. "Until we eliminate him conclusively as a suspect, we'll just have to follow his trail."

"We?" MacAllan said.

I took a deep sigh. "Superintendent," I said, "I need your help."

MacAllan sat up. "Thought you'd never ask," he said with a broad smile. "What can we do for you?"

"For starters, you could let me get back to tailing Lehtinen.

He's got at least a three-hour head start."

"We know that you know exactly where he is," MacAllan said. "We're not stupid, remember? As for your tail, we can't let you do that. Against the law."

"But—"

"Don't worry. We'll go along and lead from the rear, so to speak. We'll follow you in the Escalade. It may be as big as a tank but it's not uncommon even in Ontario, you know. We'll keep in touch with our cells. You tell us what you see and we'll advise."

"You won't watch on your smartphones?" I said.

"We can, have been, and will, but not officially. We don't have a warrant. We don't have time to get one, and no Canadian justice would issue one anyway, on the evidence you have. What we will say we're doing, if we ever have to say anything, is following you while you apparently do something illegal, and waiting for you to do something even more illegal before we arrest you."

"Very clever way to cover your ass."

"Of course. And if something should happen, we'll provide backup. By the way, you're not carrying, are you?"

"Nope."

"Pity. I was hoping to see a real live Smith & Wesson .357."

"You know about that?" I said incredulously. For my entire law enforcement career outside the army I've carried a heavy .357 Combat Magnum revolver, ancient technology so far as handguns are concerned, because I can't shoot a modern automatic pistol worth a damn. I can't shoot a revolver worth a damn, either, but occasionally manage to hit the target. This failing is well known to my North Woods brothers in arms and I hope the bad guys never learn about it.

"Of course we know about that," MacAllan said. "We're detectives. We know everything."

Because of Alex, I thought.

"No rifles?" Ferguson asked. Canada allows most ordinary hunting weapons and shotguns over the border, but they have to be declared at customs and immigration.

"Nope. Didn't want to attract attention. Not that I succeeded. And I wouldn't have tried to smuggle any kind of firearm over the border. Say, you guys really dug out lots of detail about me, didn't you?"

"Sergeant Kolehmainen likes to talk," said Ferguson with a grin. "He does tell a good story."

"But he thinks you're all right," said MacAllan. "Especially your taste in women."

Suddenly, remembering that Ginny was present, the superintendent colored. Another stereotype confirmed. In mixed company, it's said, many Canadians tend to be shy about sex, at least as a subject for conversation. Ginny raised one eyebrow, shook her head slightly, and gave MacAllan a small, tolerant smile. When she does that to me I am completely undone.

"Okay, let's hit the road," the superintendent said, partly to cover his growing embarrassment and partly because it was almost ten in the morning and Lehtinen's car was now far ahead down the Trans-Canada Highway.

We mounted up and just outside Nipigon reached the junction where Ontario 11, the northern branch of the Trans-Canada, splits from the southern leg, Ontario 17. We kept going straight east on Route 17 and followed the bug on the Ford for some forty miles until it pulled off the road and stopped. Slowly we crept up until we found ourselves at a small settlement, a little more than a bump in the road. If it had a name the sign had fallen down or blown away, probably long ago. We pulled off on the verge of the highway and the Ontario Provincial Police did the same a hundred yards behind us.

The lonely place had a school, according to the crudely hand-lettered banner above the door to a rusty steel Quonset hut: NIPIGON BAY ELEMENTARY SCHOOL. The building, evidently not yet open for the school year, squatted on a weedy lot not twenty-five yards from the Canadian Pacific's main line on a ledge paralleling the lake several yards below the highway grade. A seemingly brand-new chain-link fence, eight feet high, separated school and tracks. Next to the fence, a dozen boys and girls crawled over crude playground equipment made from old tractor tires.

Lehtinen's Ford was parked on a gravel path fifty yards down from the highway with a clear view of the school, the playground, and the main line behind it directly ahead through his windshield. With binoculars we could see inside the car, with what appeared to be a scanner radio with rubber-ducky antenna clapped to one ear.

"What's he doing?" Ginny said.

"I think he's listening to the railroad frequencies," I said. "Waiting on a train, maybe."

Just then we heard the lonely wail of a diesel horn.

"Here comes that train," Ginny said unnecessarily.

Within two minutes the snout of a straining, slowly moving diesel locomotive crossed our view of school and playground below, followed by another locomotive and a long string of freight cars, mostly empty coal hoppers sandwiched between cuts of boxcars and tank cars. Suddenly, the locomotives' diesel engines shifted to a deep roar as the train began to ascend a gentle uphill grade, their exhaust and the rumble of steel wheels assaulting our ears. The children stopped playing and watched the train go by, as youngsters always do. Lehtinen raised a point-and-shoot camera to his eye and held it there.

Ginny's cell phone buzzed.

"What's he doing?" Ferguson said from the SUV behind us.

"Railfanning, it looks like," Ginny shouted over the din.

That was no surprise.

When the train had gone and we could at last hear ourselves, I said, "I can't believe anybody would put a school so close to main-line tracks. Can you imagine what it must be like inside when a train roars by? Ask MacAllan if he knows why."

"It's a temporary building," Ginny said a moment later. "MacAllan says the regular school burned down during the winter and that hut was the only available space within miles. A new one's going up, but it won't be done for a year, so this one will have to do. School starts in a couple of days."

Just then the Ford moved back to the highway and headed east as Ginny and I ducked out of sight in the Prius. We waited a few minutes, then pulled out ourselves, as did MacAllan and Ferguson in the Escalade behind us, and proceeded east, following the bug on the Ford.

Sixty miles and an hour later, the glowing symbol on Google Maps suddenly slowed at the entrance to Neys Provincial Park on Lake Superior. It proceeded half a mile south and stopped where the entry road crosses the Canadian Pacific main line.

"There's a pair of sidings just west of that point," MacAllan said on his cell phone a mile behind our Prius. "Quite a few rail cars are stored there."

"What kind?" I answered.

"Grain hoppers," MacAllan said.

"We may be on to something."

MacAllan grunted. "Maybe," he said, but his tone was not dismissive. He was keeping an open mind.

As we closed the gap, the bug on Lehtinen's car did not move.

"When you get there, wait for us," MacAllan said.

We parked in a small byway hidden from the entry road. "PARK STAFF ONLY," the sign said. Ginny and I got out of the Prius and crept to the edge of a bluff overlooking the tracks. We spotted Lehtinen's Ford parked in the open just off the rail crossing, but we couldn't see the man himself.

Presently MacAllan and Ferguson arrived and parked beside the Prius. Both men emerged from the car, Ferguson with a short-barreled riot shotgun. I looked at MacAllan.

"Insurance," he said. "Just in case."

"I don't think we'll need it," I said. "I don't think Lehtinen's armed."

"Be that as it may," Ferguson said, "we're taking no chances."

Just the same, he hauled out a thick cylindrical map case and slipped the shotgun into it.

"Okay," I said. "But stay out of sight, will you both? He'll make you as cops right away, and that may blow the tail."

"We weren't born yesterday," said MacAllan, opening the tailgate of the Escalade and reaching into a trunk. "Didn't I tell you that already?"

In sixty seconds the Canadians—and I—were clad in brown coveralls and bright orange vests, completing the ensemble with bright orange hard hats. We looked just like generic telephone line workers.

"What can I do to help?" Ginny said.

"Stay here," MacAllan said. "Keep an eye on that Ford and let us know if Lehtinen blows this pop stand."

He reached back into the Escalade and brought out two empty plastic toolboxes.

"We'll tote these as we walk down the tracks," MacAllan said. "Make us look good."

"You're the boss," I said.

"You're learning," Ferguson said, ducking an arm into the strap of the map case containing the shotgun. But he grinned.

"You sound like Sergeant Kohlemainen," I said.

"Huh?"

"Never mind."

We walked westward down the CPR main line on the hard, dusty path paralleling the roadbed. Track workers long have used such paths because the footing is more solid than that on rough gravel ballast. These days they use four-wheeled all-terrain vehicles as well as trucks equipped with flanged railcar wheels to extend their range and save on sweat.

"Look down on the ground every so often and stop for a moment," MacAllan said. "That'll make us appear like we're hunting for something."

"Aren't we?" Ferguson said.

MacAllan grunted. I almost felt at home.

In a few minutes we reached the sidings. They held two long strings of grain hoppers, some old, some new, that stretched far into the distance.

"Let's stay on this side of the main line," I said. "If we get too close to the cars Lehtinen might suspect we're looking for him."

"Good idea," MacAllan said.

A rumble began in the distance far to the west, and grew in intensity second by second.

"Train's coming," I said.

"Let's stop here and step aside and let it go by," MacAllan said.

In less than two minutes bright headlights appeared around a curve half a mile down the tracks. The world started to tremble, and the oncoming earthquake grew closer and closer. Suddenly, a quartet of massive diesel locomotives thundered past in an apocalyptic dust storm, followed by a mile-long string of double-stacked container cars that rattled and roared, assaulting our ears with an ungodly racket. Then the train disappeared to the east, dust devils swirling up from the rails.

"Hey, over there," Ferguson said.

Under the closest string of cars fifty yards away, we could see two legs striding slowly along the shaded roadbed between the two sidings. Car by car the legs sauntered. Then the owner of the legs popped into the sun between two cuts of cars. It was Howard Lehtinen, clad in jeans, cotton work gloves, heavy work boots, and the same signal orange vest and hard hat he had worn at Thunder Bay. He looked the picture of the railroad trackman he once had been. From one hand, on a thin strap, dangled a small camera.

I turned swiftly and ducked my head. "He knows who I am," I told the Canadians. "Don't want him to see my face."

MacAllan took two steps forward, partly to block Lehtinen's view of me and partly to hail him.

"Yo, man!" the superintendent called, in an expression I never heard a Canadian use before or since. "We're tracing an electrical break. See any wires down, cables parted, anything like that?"

As MacAllan spoke, I fished my own point-and-shoot from a pants pocket, held it straight downward and aimed it behind me without looking, and tripped the shutter several times. Evidence of Lehtinen's presence. Better than mere testimony. Just in case.

"Naw," Lehtinen said casually. "Everything looks good back there. Just a couple of rotten ties at a turnout." I glanced at him through the crack between the two Canadians. He did not look at us directly, but slightly down and to the side. His expression was plain and emotionless, like that of a department store mannequin. His manner was not furtive, but there still was something odd about it. He seemed to be both present and unaccounted for, visible but not connected to the rest of the world. There was no menace, just shapeless mystery. I think I'm a pretty good judge of character just by looking at someone, but I could not read this man at all.

"Thanks," MacAllan said. "You take care."

"Yeah," Lehtinen said a little too quickly, and strode down the tracks to his Ford.

"He's on the move, Ginny," MacAllan said into his cell phone. "Keep your head down."

"Sure will."

In a few moments we saw a rising cloud of dust over the low spruce and pine as Lehtinen drove out of the park and back onto the highway, heading east.

"We coulda arrested him," Ferguson said to no one in particular.

MacAllan nodded. "Trespassing on railroad property. That's a misdemeanor in Canada but can be a felony if anything's damaged or disturbed. Let's keep that in mind if we need it."

"Got proof of that," I said, showing my camera.

"Good thinking," Ferguson said.

"Before we go on," I said, "let's take a quick look at those cars."

Lehtinen's tracks were easy to follow in the thick undisturbed dust between the sidings. He had walked more than half a mile down the railroad, and it was clear where he had stopped at the side of several cars, right at the iron stirrups that anchored the ladders affixed to the sides. I climbed up a couple. Trails of footprints showed clearly along the tops of the cars and ended at hatches used to fill them. He had opened and closed a few, as I could see from disturbed patterns in the dust. I opened the hatch covers and peered inside with a Maglite. The hoppers were empty. MacAllan photographed everything with his own digital camera. Ferguson dusted the hatch handles with a fingerprint kit and patted them with sticky tape.

"He was wearing gloves," I said.

"Yeah, but sometimes subjects take off their gloves without thinking to get better grips, and that will leave prints," the Canadian said. "Cotton gloves often leave behind telltale threads. Even if they have rubber palms, the distinctive pattern marks can be evidence. We have nothing to lose doing this."

"Doesn't seem that he dumped anything here," I said. "Looks like he's just reconnoitering."

"Casing the joint," Ferguson said. Canadians evidently read low-rent cop fiction, too, but I knew better than to say so.

"Not really railfanning," I said. "Normal rail buffs don't climb up cars and open their hatches. I think he's up to no good."

"Looks that way," Ferguson said with a nod.

In a few minutes we had mounted up and were back on the Trans-Canada, Ginny driving as I watched the glowing bug slowly moving across the screen of my iPhone. Lehtinen was just six miles ahead of us, MacAllan and Ferguson half a mile behind.

CHAPTER NINETEEN

On the Trans-Canada there was very little traffic, and what there was consisted mostly of eighteen-wheelers. By early September, Canadian summer tourists have gone back to work and the students who staff the provincial parks have returned to college. For nearly ninety leisurely miles we followed the bug on my iPhone, staying well behind Lehtinen's Ford and taking in the rolling low mountain scenery of the eastern Lake Superior basin. The Canadian Shield, the ancient geological core of North America, is at its most gorgeous in these parts. Bald eagles are common in the skies and bears often wander down highway verges, and Ginny oohed and ahed every time we spotted one. From time to time I had to stop woolgathering and remind myself why we were there.

Suddenly, rounding a blind curve underneath a beetling cliff that concealed the highway ahead, I spotted several cars and a couple of eighteen-wheelers jumbled willy-nilly across the eastbound lane. I slowed, pulled up behind them, and peered through the windshield, wary of being seen if Lehtinen's car was part of the mess. Then I looked at the iPhone. The bug was receding rapidly to the east.

The Escalade pulled past me and into the center of the scrum of vehicles. MacAllan and Ferguson got out and strode to the side of the road where three people sat on the verge. Ginny and I followed, staying out of the way. The Ontario Provincial Police was on the job, and we weren't going to hinder them.

It had been an eleven-way fenderbender. No one seemed hurt and all the cars, plus one jackknifed eighteen-wheeler, looked drivable.

"What happened?" MacAllan said. One of the drivers pointed up the highway. A moose and her calf were slowly proceeding along the verge.

"I saw those moose cross the road in front of that Cobalt up yonder. The driver hit his brakes hard and the car fishtailed and spun. The Beemer over there banged into it and then that Impala hit the Beemer and . . ."

"Yes, I understand, sir," MacAllan said. "Was anyone injured?"

"Not that I can see," the driver said. "But there was an odd . . ."

"Yes?"

"We were all standing around catching our breath when a green Ford Escape drove past, going the wrong way in the oncoming lane. It almost hit the moose as it went by them. It didn't slow down at all."

For a moment MacAllan just stared. Then he said simply, "Yes, that was odd."

Just then two OPP prowl cars, their lights flashing, pulled up into the melee. Three blue-clad officers emerged, and Ferguson quickly filled them in.

"Let's go," MacAllan said. "The uniforms will sort things out."

We drove off, and I kept my eyes peeled for stray moose as we pushed along at a steady seven miles over the limit in order to catch up with Lehtinen. On this part of the Trans-Canada Highway, moose warning signs blink by the roadside every few miles, but I had not paid much attention. I have never seen a moose in the wild, although I have searched far and wide, high and low. You never spot them when you are looking for them.

They always surprise you at the most inopportune moments. It is a natural law.

Forty minutes east from Neys Provincial Park, the southern leg of the Trans-Canada Highway leaves behind Lake Superior and plunges eastward into the thick forests of interior Ontario. Finally, fifty-five miles later, Lehtinen turned off Route 17 at White River at almost exactly five p.m., as he had at Nipigon and Thunder Bay, pulling into a motel. Clearly a man of habit and routine, I told myself once more. Maybe even an obsessive–compulsive. I'd have to run that past Sue Hemb when we got back.

Ginny and I chose another motel half a mile west of the one Lehtinen had picked, followed a moment later by MacAllan and Ferguson. Lehtinen knew me and had seen the faces of the two OPP officers. We needed to keep out of sight, and the best way was to stay behind. Lehtinen would be looking ahead.

After checking in and cleaning up, we mounted the Escalade and drove to a sprawling roadside Italian restaurant we had spotted a couple of miles outside White River. I carried the iPhone in with me, planning to consult the Google Maps app frequently to make sure Lehtinen hadn't decided to break his routine, save some time, and keep driving.

As the waitress brought steaming plates of spaghetti and meatballs, I turned on the iPhone. The glowing bug was moving. Toward us.

"Shit," I said. "Here he comes!"

We peered out the window. Lehtinen's Ford was pulling into the parking lot.

"Quick, to the men's!" MacAllan said. We quickly got up and headed for the tiny single-toilet cubicle just off the dining room, leaving Ginny at the table. We opened the door and stuffed ourselves inside just as Lehtinen walked through the front door thirty feet away.

"He just headed for the bar without a backward glance," Ginny said a few minutes later, after Lehtinen left the restaurant with a six-pack of Molson's and drove away. The bug showed him returning to his motel.

"Close call," I said. Both MacAllan and Ferguson let out long sighs.

"Drinking his dinner?" Ginny said. "Is he an alcoholic?"

"Not that we know of," I said. "The FBI report on him didn't mention that."

"I have to say," Ginny said, "that you guys looked funny coming out of that bathroom. Reminded me of circus clowns pouring out of that tiny little car."

"Just a bit of close Canadian–American amity," I said.

"Maybe too close," Ferguson said.

"Your deodorant didn't fail you," I said.

"Shut up, please," MacAllan said. "I'm eating."

We all laughed, but it had been a tight spot, so to speak.

After a nervous meal during which we all shot peeks out the window into the parking lot, we headed for downtown White River and its freight yard. Three sidings and several industrial spurs made up the center of the town, and a long secondary track followed the Canadian Pacific main line southward for a mile before reconnecting with it. Plenty of freight cars occupied the sidings, and some of them were covered grain hoppers of varying ages. A single street crossed the web of tracks.

"Lehtinen might come here tonight," Ferguson said. "Maybe we should stake out this place."

"We could do that from the motel," I said. "He'll probably need to drive over, and we can see the bug."

"But then we'd need to drive over, too," MacAllan said. "It's going to be overcast tonight, and that means it'll be very dark. He'd see our headlights."

In the end the Canadians drove Ginny and me back to the motel and returned to the freight yard, parking on a rise that gave them a good view of the web of tracks. All night they sat in their Escalade, sleeping in relays, and watched the tracks and, quite unofficially, the glowing bug on their iPhone while Lehtinen's Ford stayed put. No one crossed into the deserted yard all night. The only sound, MacAllan said, came from an idling switch locomotive in the center of the tracks.

After breakfast the next morning—Ginny drove out to the local Tim Horton's and brought back plastic bowls of oatmeal, cranberry muffins, and enough coffee to float a small boat—we watched as the bug on the iPhone came to life at eight a.m. and started moving. It headed for the rail yard.

MacAllan and Ferguson donned the coveralls, vests, and hard hats we had worn the previous day, and headed for the yard as well. This time MacAllan and Ferguson walked into the warren of tracks while Ginny and I stayed in the Escalade, safely hidden fifty yards away from the yard behind a screen of trees paralleling the siding on which two dozen Canadian Pacific grain hoppers sat.

Soon Lehtinen's Ford appeared, crossed the tracks, and stopped at the hopper siding. As before, he was clad in CPR garb and hard hat. I watched with binoculars behind the trees as he trudged beside the siding, examining each car as he walked past. At two of the cars, both older and covered with rust and graffiti in equal measure, he stopped and gazed both ways for a long minute. Then he mounted the ladders and scrambled quickly atop the roofs to the hatches, opening them and peering inside. I marveled that such a thick-waisted fellow had enough strength and agility to do that. There was more to Howard Lehtinen than at first met the eye.

He seemed to be carrying nothing more lethal than a

flashlight. I doubted that he had tried to smuggle a handgun into Canada. More and more I was convinced that he was simply on a reconnaissance mission and that he believed things were getting too hot in the States for him to continue his corpse disposal business there.

Four times he ascended to the top of chosen cars, four times he opened hatches and peered inside, and four times he descended. Finally, after twenty minutes of the routine, he returned to his car and departed.

Quickly MacAllan and Ferguson, who had been hiding behind cars on an adjacent track, scaled the hoppers Lehtinen had examined and performed the same forensic tasks they had the previous day at Neys Provincial Park.

Then we returned to the Escalade, stripped off the coveralls, and were off in pursuit, Ginny handling the iPhone tasks after we transferred to the Prius.

Sixty miles later, after an hour of driving through green and rocky wilderness unrelieved by civilization, Lehtinen turned off Route 17 at almost noon and headed a mile north to Wawa, an oddly named community whose history reminds me intensely of the heartache of Porcupine City. Once the booming center of the fur trade in this part of Ontario, Wawa thrived for more than a century from its iron mines and sawmills, but with the collapse of those industries at the beginning of the twenty-first century, its economy plummeted—and so did its population. Now, like Porcupine City, it is scrabbling to stave off oblivion by becoming a tourist destination. Downtown is nearly empty and its buildings largely boarded up, I saw as we slowly traversed the main drag.

"This is sad," Ginny said, and I agreed. I doubted that Lehtinen gave a damn.

"There's no railroad here," I said. The abandoned branch line of the Algoma Central Railroad bypassed Wawa and headed for Michipicoten, seven miles southwest on Lake Superior. The rails had been rusting for fifteen years, ever since the iron mines at Wawa had closed, and held no cars in storage.

"He's just having lunch here," Ginny said. "Let's do that, too."

Carefully we drove to the other side of town as far away from Lehtinen's Ford as we could and found a ramshackle cafe with a cracked linoleum floor, rickety kitchenette tables, and rusty steel chairs. The Escalade pulled up behind our Prius. We washed down soggy burgers with ginger ale. At least the soft drinks had a familiar taste. Ginny pulled a face but did not remark upon the quality of the cuisine. I wondered if Lehtinen's lunch was any better than ours.

Then he was off again, with the Prius and Escalade following closely—but not too closely—behind.

For one hundred and forty miles Lehtinen drove south on Route 17 at a leisurely pace without stopping. Several provincial parks and a few small bumps in the road dotted the highway, and we settled back and enjoyed the lush green scenery of the eastern shore of Lake Superior as we passed the tiny tourist towns of Montreal River, Batchawana Bay, and Goulais River. Almost three hours later we arrived on the industrial outskirts of Sault Ste. Marie.

Ginny and I love the Soo, both the Canadian and American sides, and spend a long weekend there every couple of years. It's full of history, being an old crossroads of trade routes, and is economically healthy, thanks to steelmaking, forestry products, and tourism. I never tire of riding tour boats through the St. Mary's River locks on the U.S. side and marveling at the intricate operations of the Soo Canal. What's more, the Algoma Central Railway, now part of the Canadian National Railway, has extensive yards there—and I was certain those would attract Howard Lehtinen. So, increasingly, were the two Ontario

Provincial Police detectives.

MacAllan had called ahead to the yard bulls—the Canadian National railway police—and alerted them to the possible presence of an intruder, telling them not to grab him up but just to watch what he did and let us know his movements. They said they'd keep a lookout.

Lehtinen's Ford did not move out of his waterfront hotel's parking lot until well after dark. The bug headed west across town to the old Algoma Central yards and at precisely nine-thirty p.m. stopped just across the road from the little parking lot for employees and passengers on the three-days-a-week milk run through gorgeous wilderness to Hearst almost three hundred miles north. The railroad's celebrated tourist train to Agawa Canyon, one hundred and fourteen miles north, departs and arrives from a proper railway station in downtown Sault Ste. Marie.

Clad in the darkest clothes we had, MacAllan, Ferguson, and I crept through cloudy moonlight across the entrance to the yards and entered the warren of tracks as quietly as we could. The sidings and spurs were choked with cars of all kinds, seemingly mixed willy-nilly. Short cuts of grain hoppers shared the same tracks with boxcars, gondolas, auto racks, and tank cars. Only ore cars and steel coil cars seemed to be kept together, the better to serve the steel mills nearby. Finding Lehtinen in that mess, I had thought, would be nearly impossible.

"We don't see anybody," the boss yard bull said on his cell.

But MacAllan and Ferguson had brought along night-vision goggles, and handed me a pair. Through them the yard appeared nearly as bright as day, except in glowing green.

"Let's silence our phones and talk by text message," MacAllan said. "It's awfully quiet in here."

For good measure we turned down our phones' screen brightness until they were just visible.

We split up, each of us heading for a different track. For ten minutes we crept and searched like panthers on the prowl through a night so quiet the only sounds came from the wings of owls and scrabbling small animals. Now and then a coyote would slip out from under a car and trot away. But Lehtinen remained elusive.

Suddenly, my phone vibrated. I cradled it close to my chest and opened the Message app. Ferguson had spotted movement atop a car on No. 8 siding. I was on No. 5, according to the yard chart the railroad cops had provided us. Hoping not to make noise on the gravel, I tiptoed three tracks over through gaps between cuts of cars and crouched low. Through the night goggles I could see a glowing green figure climbing up the ladder of a grain hopper.

"Subj opening hatch," I tapped into the iPhone. "Same m.o. as previous." I sent the message to MacAllan and Ferguson.

"Stay put," MacAllan replied.

Lehtinen climbed down and stepped over to another hopper car on an adjacent track. He repeated his actions, and I messaged them to the Canadians.

In this fashion Lehtinen examined only one other car, and within ten minutes he had walked past me up the tracks to the parking lot as I hid under a boxcar. Soon we saw the bug on our iPhones heading back to the Soo waterfront, and in five minutes the Ford had returned to Lehtinen's hotel. It was just after eleven p.m.

"That's it for tonight," MacAllan said when we climbed back into the Escalade. "I don't think he has plans for the cars in this yard. They're too new, and they're used a lot. Yard cops say so. The grain hoppers are parked here in the winter but come the following summer they're moved to the west and held in reserve for harvest season."

"You would think Lehtinen would know that," I said.

"Maybe so, but maybe he had a reason for scoping out this yard."

We returned to our hotel, where Ginny was watching a rerun of *Doc Martin,* and hit the sack. Twice I arose and checked the iPhone. The bug remained in the parking lot of Lehtinen's hotel.

CHAPTER TWENTY

The next morning the bug still hadn't budged. We went to breakfast, keeping our eye on the iPhone all the way through the second cup of coffee.

Finally, at precisely eight a.m. the bug awoke. We watched on Google Maps as Lehtinen's Ford pulled out of his motel lot and headed west. In a few minutes it headed south over the International Bridge spanning the St. Marys River and the Soo Locks to the United States and Interstate 75.

We followed half a mile behind, and at U.S. customs and immigration at Sault Ste. Marie, Michigan, I showed my badge and passport. "Ontario Provincial Police is in an Escalade behind us," I said. "We're working a case together. Please extend them every courtesy you can." The agent nodded without interest and took the time to run our passports through his scanner. When the scanner did not call in a battalion of border guards, he waved us through with a smile and a polite "Welcome home." A bureaucrat, I thought, but a competent one.

As we sped south on I-75 MacAllan called. "I thought your customs guy was going to make us pull over and let the drug dogs have at us," he said. "He took his sweet time."

"Just like yours did with us at the Pigeon River," I said.

"Ours are as good as yours."

"And yours as good as ours."

"Except for one thing."

"What's that?" I said.

174

"The agent didn't ask if we had our guns with us."

Thanks to furious Second Amendmenters, the United States no longer requires Canadians entering the country to declare their firepower at the border and possess U.S. state hunting permits as well. Makes no sense to me, but there it is.

"You're cops," I said. "That goes without saying." MacAllan and Ferguson were perfectly aware of American firearms laws.

MacAllan snorted. "Now what?"

The night before, he and Ferguson had asked—pointedly *asked*—if they could cross the border with us and follow Lehtinen for a while.

"International law enforcement teamwork is a noble thing to behold," Ferguson had said with a straight face as MacAllan stifled a grin. "That's why we're soliciting your cooperation."

"I thought you'd never ask," I had said with an equally straight face.

The Ontario Provincial Police were now persuaded that we were on to something. Lehtinen's behavior in the rail yards across Ontario had put them over the top. For now the provincials could do nothing, but they had good evidence of trespass, and if Lehtinen should return to Ontario—an event that now seemed quite possible—they would open an official investigation and be ready for him. In the meantime, MacAllan and Ferguson wanted to come out to Porcupine County and have a look for themselves at the scene on the Keweenaw & Brule River and go over the documents of the investigation. That was fine with me. It would cement Canadian–American police amity far better than sharing a tiny toilet.

Now, speeding south at seventy miles an hour on the interstate, I said on the iPhone, "You know, I'm in charge now. This is my territory." That was a stretch—Chippewa County is a good two hundred miles east of my jurisdiction in Porcupine County—and I'm sure the Canadians knew it. But it was my country and my state, and my mission was once more legally authorized.

Just then the bug slowed and moved off the interstate at the junction with a state highway nine miles south of the International Bridge. "Heading west on M28," I told the Canadians. We followed, staying a careful mile to two miles behind as Lehtinen drove the long 115-mile stretch to Munising at precisely the legal limit of fifty-five miles an hour, as he had when heading for Duluth a few days ago. Most drivers will do sixty, figuring the cops will spot them five miles an hour before turning on their sirens, and quite a few push sixty-five and even seventy on the two-lane concrete highway, hoping to get away with it. And they mostly do. There aren't enough of us to nail them.

Did Lehtinen think he'd avoid police scrutiny by sticking to fifty-five? That was reasonable. Rural upper Michigan is full of farmers in old pickups and elderly drivers in big sedans who either can't or won't bust the limit. But I was growing ever more convinced that this was part of Lehtinen's obsession with numbers and that he was following old habits.

For most of its course, Highway M28 is an arrow-straight stretch broken by very few curves, and it follows the similarly undeviating former Soo Line Railroad branch across the Upper Peninsula. The Canadian National now owns the line but has not run a train over it for years, and the tops of the tracks are well rusted. No cars are stored there and I knew Lehtinen would not stop to reconnoiter.

At the Newberry crossroads Lehtinen pulled over at a roadside Subway and for fifteen minutes sat inside, nursing a cup of coffee and reading a newspaper, probably a day-old *Detroit Free Press*. These days the boonies get their major metro papers delivered by mail. We kept his Ford in view through binoculars from a filling station just up the road, and when he pulled out, we followed the usual mile behind, keeping out of his sight. For sixty miles to Munising the highway alternated between birch forest and low aspen scrub, much of it swampy, and I whiled away the time hoping a moose would wander across the road—far enough away for me to stop safely—and break the monotony. No such luck.

At Marquette an hour past Munising, the big hand and the little hand both landed on twelve, and at that very moment Lehtinen—surprise!—stopped for lunch at a McDonald's. We chose another nameless filling station–burger joint around a curve out of sight to refuel our vehicles and stomachs. I called Alex.

"He's heading for Porcupine City," I said. "Be there in two and a quarter hours. Five gets you ten he stops at Merle's for a slice of cherry pie."

"You seem awfully sure of that," Alex said.

"It's where he started," I said. "This fellow is a creature of habit in ways you can't even imagine. I would bet my share of the county budget that Merle's is where he'll wind up the trip."

"That's good to know," Alex said. "But I don't know why."

"I have an idea," I said. "Tell you later."

Before we broke off, Alex said he'd be waiting at Porcupine City for Lehtinen's arrival.

"Stay out of sight," I couldn't help saying. In his long career Alex Kolehmainen has tailed and staked out enough suspects to fill ten Porcupine County jails and a state prison or two. But with him I can't help playing the helicopter parent.

"Yes, Mommy," Alex said impudently, and without further comment hung up.

The two Canadians sitting across the table laughed. Ginny just smiled. The exchange was familiar to her.

The route from Marquette to Porcupine City through the middle of a thickly forested nowhere heads northwest up to

L'Anse, a pretty Ojibwa reservation town, rounds the Lake Superior bay of the same name, and turns west at Baraga. Traffic was extremely light, a few pickups and the odd sedan, but Lehtinen kept his speedometer nailed on fifty-five. The Prius and the Escalade trailed the Ford impatiently, often inching up to just a mile behind our quarry, and we had to put on the brakes to avoid being spotted.

As we drove along, I reflected on how the invention of the GPS and the rise of geolocation tracking had revolutionized the art of the police tail. Before it came along, those who did the tailing had to keep their targets in sight on the road, and even when skilled drivers kept two or three cars between them and the ones they were following, there was always a chance they'd be spotted. Bad guys who had spent any time tailing others knew what to look for and how to shake their pursuers.

The GPS bug changed the parameters. Now the cops' biggest concern was affixing the bug to a car where discovery would be unlikely, even if a mechanic had the vehicle on a lift. They not only had to worry about being seen in the act of planting but also of removing the bug.

Alex, fortunately, was more than skilled at that job. When, just after three p.m., Lehtinen parked his car a block south of Merle's and hiked up the hill to the cafe, Alex stopped his vehicle—his own Chrysler sedan—immediately behind the Ford. As Lehtinen stepped into Merle's, the trooper looked both ways, as he had in the beginning. Porcupine City at the busiest time of day is almost deserted, and nobody saw him reach under the rear bumper and wrench away the GPS package. Nobody except Ginny, the two Canadians, and me as we drove up the street. We turned at the corner before Merle's, safely out of sight, and headed for the sheriff's department two blocks away. Alex followed, and Lehtinen was finally on his own after five days of surveillance, freed from his electronic tether to go wherever he wanted. We figured he went home to Green Bay. Where else would he want to go? He had to get back to work if the alarm were not to be raised.

At the sheriff's department I asked Chad to take the two OPP detectives out to Rockville and the old crime scene on the Keweenaw & Brule River tracks. They'd head back to Canada after their inspection, and I shook their hands as they left.

I told Alex about Lehtinen's punctiliousness about timekeeping on the road. "You might have something there," he said. "Why don't you run that past Sue?"

"Yup. I was just about to do that."

"Good work, my boy," Alex said. "We're making progress."

"We?"

"You and I. I planted the bug, remember?"

"But I did all the dirty work for four days."

"Nice dirty work if you can get it," Alex said. "Driving for a thousand miles through some of the most beautiful country in the world."

"I barely noticed. Had my eyes on the prize all the way."

"Like hell." Alex was still chuckling as he departed.

I picked up the phone and within two minutes reached Lieutenant Hemb at her office in Lansing. I had to go through only one desk assistant instead of the two or three it usually took. Clearly Sue's department was also suffering from budgetary short-staffing.

I told her about Lehtinen and his meticulous reliance on the clock.

"Not surprising. Many accountants have slight cases of Asperger's. That's often why they become accountants. Asperger's sufferers are often very, very bright and adept with numbers."

"Could you tell me more about that?" I asked.

Asperger's syndrome, Sue said, used to be thought a mental disorder all by itself, but now is considered a high-functioning form of autism. Some psychiatrists argue that it's just part of the normal human condition, as most in the profession consider same-sex attraction to be, and should be treated as such.

"Those with Asperger's tend to adopt inflexible routines, repetitive patterns of behavior, as Lehtinen apparently has," Sue said. "They have difficulties in social interaction, such as making friends. They tend to be withdrawn. They find it difficult to understand how someone else might be feeling and therefore say the wrong things to them."

"Isn't that lack of empathy characteristic of psychopaths?" I said.

"Oh, there are different kinds of empathy," Sue said. "There's understanding the thoughts and motivations of others. There's sharing the emotions of others. And there's sympathy for those emotions. Asperger's people can be very conscious about their lack of understanding and often are unhappy that they don't know what to do about it. Psychopaths can understand what goes on in the minds of others, but they just don't care. Some shrinks think psychopaths can't, that something's been wrong with their brains from birth, and that therapy won't fix it. In the past Asperger's was often confused with psychopathology, but we've come a long way since."

"Can psychopaths have symptoms of Asperger's?" I asked.

"There's evidence that autism spectrum disorders involve the same brain components and chemistry as psychopathy," Sue said. "So, yes, it would be possible for someone to be a psychopath and have Asperger's at the same time. The shooter who killed all those children in Newtown, Connecticut, had Asperger's, but that's not why he killed all those kids. He killed them most likely because he was a psychopath. Or maybe he suffered from something else, like schizophrenia. We'll probably never know. In any case, psychopaths have no moral compass. We have to remember, however, like those with bipolar disorders who most likely are not homicidal, a person with Asperger's most likely is *not* a psychopath. The two conditions are not the same."

"But there's a possibility Lehtinen *is* a psychopath," I said.

"A strong one," Sue said, "if he is guilty of what you suspect. Look, let me make a few inquiries among my fellow shrink investigators in Wisconsin. Can you send me the FBI report on Lehtinen?"

"Consider it done."

"I'll be back in touch."

Two days later she was. "Detective Lee Hamilton was a busy boy," she said. "Once he was persuaded that Harold Lehtinen was not what he seemed to be, Hamilton went digging by himself. He came up with some interesting material.

"One is that Lehtinen has a reputation for being meek, timid, and unassertive as well as a loner. Neighbors said that he is a respected accountant but seems to have no life outside work. He never goes out for a beer with them, nor with the people in his office. He seems to be a woodworker. For years, his neighbors said, he has brought lumber home on top of his car and stored it in the garage. He gets regular small package deliveries from UPS and Fedex, but nobody knows what's in them. He gets to work every day at the stroke of eight and leaves at five. Eats at his desk. Nobody sees him outside the office.

"Except at church. He goes to communion every Sunday. He helps out in the Episcopal church soup kitchen every Saturday night, sweeping the floors and cleaning up. The people who work with him says he's awkward and shy but pleasant enough and speaks when he's spoken to. Otherwise nobody notices him."

"What do you make of that?" I said.

"Definitely on the autism spectrum. Sure, possibly psychopathic. That church stuff could be perfectly normal for Asperger's, an attraction to the orderliness of ritual. Or it could be consciously manipulative, to get on people's good side and divert their attention from criminality. It could also just be a clumsy attempt to reach out from shyness. I don't think we can draw any conclusions just from a police report. We'd need a thorough psychiatric workup, and I doubt that he's going to come in for one."

"This is not encouraging."

"I haven't got to the really good stuff yet," Sue said.

I groaned. Sue Hemb hangs around Alex Kohlemainen too much. Some of his irritating playfulness seems to have rubbed off on her.

"Well, dammit, let's have it."

"Howard Lehtinen doesn't take vacations the way we do. He saves up all his two weeks' time off and takes it in dribs and drabs, three days here and four days there, five or six times a year. It's always spur of the moment. He suddenly gets up from his desk and tells the boss he's got to take a few days off. Except for that trip around Lake Superior. He announced his intention to go a week before he went."

"How'd Hamilton get all this information?" I said.

"Mike Perlman."

"The railroad president?"

"Yup."

"But . . ."

"Steve, Sergeant Hamilton said he has had Perlman under his sights for years, ever since he settled with the IRS. Perlman has done quite a few legally questionable things to keep his railroad going, and Hamilton knows what they are. After interviewing Perlman, Hamilton leaned hard on him to keep his mouth shut about police interest in Lehtinen."

"I'll be damned. Why hasn't Hamilton let us know all this stuff?"

"Timing. When I called Wisconsin forensics to see what they knew, they said Hamilton had been consulting with them about Lehtinen's psychology. He was about to call Alex and let you guys know what he'd found."

"Sue, this is wonderful," I said with feeling. "We've got means. We've got opportunity. What we haven't got yet is motive."

"Or enough evidence to take to the prosecutor," Sue said.

"No. But I've got an idea how we can get some."

"What's that?"

"Got to work it out first."

"Call me."

"You bet."

"Don't forget to call the FBI. We're keeping them posted, aren't we?"

"Oh shit," I said. "Yes."

As soon as we hung up I called Jack Adamson and brought him up to speed on the trip around Lake Superior as well as Hamilton's material on Howard Lehtinen.

"Good work," Adamson said. That was as complimentary as he ever got, but it was a lot better than nothing, the normal reaction from the FBI. "I'll pass it up the chain of command."

"Is there anything you want us to be doing?" I asked, ashamed of myself for asking, as if I were a serf begging a scrap from the lord of the manor.

"Just continue your investigation," he said. "And keep us posted."

I suddenly realized that Adamson was actually sticking his

neck out for us. Normally headquarters in Washington would not allow us to do anything without its say-so. The old FBI veteran understood bureaucratic inertia and how to deal with it.

"Oh, one thing," he said. "I'm personally curious. What do you plan to do? Off the record."

"As soon as I figure that out," I said, struggling to keep the gratitude out of my voice, "I'll be in touch."

"Good enough for me," Jack said, and we hung up.

CHAPTER TWENTY-ONE

"And how do you propose to nail Howard Lehtinen?" Alex said as he, Gil, Chad, and I sat around the table in the jail's kitchen. Our meetings about the case were becoming so frequent that Gil was calling us the Monday Morning Bridge Club. That was remarkable in itself because Gil has no sense of humor whatsoever.

"A sting," I said.

"Huh?" Chad said.

"With a corpse we ourselves furnish to be spirited away and disposed of."

"That's inhuman!" Chad said. "And probably illegal."

"No, it's not. And it's been done before."

"Explain," Alex said, as a cloud of skepticism settled over the table.

"Very well," I said. "Have you ever heard of The Man Who Never Was?"

Blank looks all around at first, except from Alex, whose raised eyebrows immediately displayed a glimmer of understanding.

"Not even the movie of that title?" I said. "It's on late-night television now and then."

"Who's up late at night?" Gil grumbled. "We cops need our beauty sleep."

I settled back in my chair. "Let me take you back to the year 1943, during the Second World War," I said. "The British called it Operation Mincemeat."

The German army had been defeated in North Africa, I said, and now the Allies planned to invade southern Europe across the Mediterranean, using the island of Sicily just off the toe of Italy as a stepping-stone. The German war machine had suffered a huge setback but was still powerful on the European continent. To ease their invasion, the Allies needed to blunt the Nazi spear.

A British intelligence officer named Ewen Montagu came up with a brilliant plan. Why not hoodwink the enemy into thinking the Allies would invade Greece and Sardinia instead? If that could be done, the Germans would move reinforcements there, leaving a smaller garrison on Sicily to meet the Allies.

Montagu's idea was to dump the body of a British officer carrying false documents of the Allies' battle plans into the sea off the coast of neutral Spain, where it would wash up on shore. The Spanish would retrieve the body, but German spies would quickly find out about it and bribe their way to it and the documents it carried. If all went well, Berlin would believe the ruse and send troops to Greece rather than to Sicily.

To make it work, the British had to come up with a credible corpse, one that could withstand the scrutiny of both Spanish pathologists and enemy intelligence services. Montagu and his men combed London for a body, and a cooperative coroner told them about a fresh one that had turned up on his slab. A thirty-four-year-old homeless Welshman named Glyndwr Michael had died after eating rat poison made with phosphorus. Phosphorus reacts with stomach acids to produce a gas that kills, and the gas is not easily discovered upon autopsy. Moreover, there was no next of kin to persuade to agree to the scheme, so the number of people in on the secret could be kept small.

For the corpse the British created a complete fake identity down to the smallest detail. They called him "Major William

Martin of the Royal Marines" and clad him in loose battle dress rather than the standard fitted officer's naval uniform a courier would ordinarily be wearing. Such uniforms were professionally sewn by a single Savile Row tailor. He would have to be called in to fit the body, dangerously enlarging the circle that knew about the plan.

Into the wallet and pockets of "Major Martin" the schemers stuffed theater ticket stubs, love letters, and even photographs of a fake fiancée. Once the stage had been set, "Major Martin" was placed in a canister lined with dry ice and driven to a waiting British submarine on the English coast.

Two stormy days later the submarine entered the Mediterranean at Gibraltar and soon set "Major Martin" adrift, complete with a dispatch case carrying the false documents. Later the same day he washed up on the Spanish coast, looking as if he had drowned after a plane crash at sea. Soon the "secrets" were on their way to Berlin while the name of the missing "Major Martin" turned up on casualty lists published in the British newspapers, carefully watched by German intelligence. Josef Goebbels, Hitler's propaganda minister, reportedly devoured the *Times* every morning.

A few days later Allied troops stormed the beaches of Sicily and met light resistance. Not for two weeks did the Germans conclude that they had been hoodwinked and send in a parachute division from Greece—too late. Five weeks after beginning the invasion, the Allies had conquered the island, Mussolini had fallen, and Italy was about to surrender.

"Magnificent hoax, wasn't it?" I said.

"Sure was," Alex said in an admiring tone. "How'd you know about it?"

"Don't forget I keep company with a historian," I said. "She reminded me about it and I did a little research. There have been several books about it as well as a movie."

"I remember," Alex said. "I saw the movie."

"Me, too," Gil said. "I'd forgotten until you brought it up."

Memory is funny. Sometimes old knowledge is buried so deeply that it needs to be coaxed out to the forefront of the mind. For a long moment silence settled around the table as the participants riffled through the musty card catalogs of their brains. I half expected puffs of dust to blow out of their ears.

"Well, there you are," I said. "We'll smoke Lehtinen out by dangling a corpse under his nose and getting him to take it out and stuff it into a hopper car while we watch. And then we'll have the evidence to send him away for a good long time."

"You mean the FBI will," Alex reminded us all.

"Yes. But we'll do the work."

Then Chad spoke. "Isn't that entrapment?"

"No," I said. "Entrapment is when the cops entice a subject into doing something illegal that he ordinarily wouldn't do. We're only encouraging Lehtinen to repeat a criminal act he's been committing for years, this time while we're watching. No judge would gainsay that."

"It's a great idea," Chad said. "But how are we going to do this?"

"Watch and learn," I said.

A week later Alex stopped by the sheriff's department. "Got us a line on a body," he said as soon as he pushed open my office door.

"Another one?"

"Slow on the uptake, are we?"

"What body are you talking about?" I said. "Another corpse in a hopper car?"

"No. The Body That Never Was."

"That was The Man Who Never Was."

"Are you in or are you not?"

188

"Oh, God. Tell me."

"I've enlisted a Detroit assistant medical examiner in our enterprise," Alex said. "Dr. Bruce Gibbons is excited about the whole sting idea and has agreed to let us know when a suitable corpse comes into his shop."

"So we don't actually have a body yet?"

"No, but we will very soon." Alex and I had decided that the first problem to overcome would be to find a medical examiner willing to go along with our idea and give us a hand. Alex took on the task because of his extensive contacts, but the Chicago and Minneapolis medical examiners had just hung up on him. Alex struck oil in his own state. He's known and respected in government circles all over Michigan.

"Oh, all right," I said. "Define 'suitable.' "

Dr. Gibbons had suggested that anyone who was disposing of corpses in criminal fashion would be smart enough to open the package, or the body bag if there was one, to see exactly what he was dealing with—a natural death or a homicide, for instance. Man, woman, young girl—he would want to know what kind of a risk he was taking. He would be careful. He might even want to know the identity of the corpse.

"And I realized that Joey Nails probably was either wrong or pulling your leg when he said our guy didn't want to know the sources of the bodies, either," Alex said. "I don't believe that at all. A careful master criminal—and I believe Howard Lehtinen is just that—wants to know every fact, every detail, about what he's doing. He can't afford to leave anything to chance."

"That means he needs to know the identity of the killer who approaches him," I said.

"Yes."

"Somehow I don't think that's going to be a problem."

"No," Alex said. "For quite a few years now I've sat on a couple of snitches of mine, minor players in the Detroit mob.

189

All I have to do is hint to one of them I'll rumble him to the capos if he doesn't do me a certain favor."

"And that favor will be taking on the job of being our front man in this little enterprise."

"Right."

"You know as well as I do that that would be felony police extortion," I said.

"Of course," Alex said. "But sometimes desperate times require desperate measures."

"Oh, bullshit."

"It's what I'd love to do." Alex said. "But I've got a better idea. It's even legal."

"What?"

"Tell you later."

"Alex," I said with an admiring tone, "I know that you not only are an evil genius but also will stay on the sunny side of the law. Now let's get back to what we mean by 'suitable.' "

"If we are going to use a mobster as an, uh, bagman, who would he be trying to get rid of?"

"Another mobster, maybe. Maybe a Russian gangster or a Latino gangbanger."

"Right. Dr. Gibbons says he'll watch for an incoming customer who resembles one of those. Maybe a big, healthy bruiser. Not a wasted cancer victim or someone killed in an auto accident or anything that would leave obvious trauma on the body. Except maybe for a bullet hole."

"The chances of that are slim to none, and you know it," I said.

"Right. But I don't think that will be a problem."

"What about creating a legend, an identity, for our Major Martin?" I said. "Something that will fool Lehtinen. No, wait, we can't do that until we have a body. We have to give him a plausible identity that fits the way he looks."

"Or her," Alex said.

"Or her. But the identity doesn't have to be all that elaborate. Lehtinen's not an *Abwehr* genius."

The reference to the vaunted German military intelligence of World War II didn't escape Alex, who is a remarkably well-read fellow, although he sometimes pretends not to be.

"Nor is he *Sicherheitsdienst*," he replied, just as pedantically. That, I just happened to know, was the greatly feared spy service of the Nazi Party. I had been to college and had studied modern history, just like Alex.

"Whatever," I said. "He's not a trained spook who goes through everything with a fine-toothed comb."

"That's so. All we need is a fake driver's license and a couple of credit cards with the same name and some other lint usually found in people's wallets. That won't be difficult to arrange. We can get things set up ahead of time so we can move quickly."

"Now we wait."

"I'll be in touch," Alex said. "Hopefully sooner rather than later."

I called Jack Adamson and filled him in about our plan.

"If you can bring this off," he said, admiration in his voice, "there'll be a book. Maybe a movie. And you'll be the hero."

"Got to bring it off first," I said. "There's a lot that could go wrong."

It was another ten days before Alex called. "We lucked out," he said as soon as I picked up the receiver. He was phoning from Lansing. We had decided he would run the show there and in nearby Detroit, while I watched the store in the U.P. and consulted with Lee Hamilton in Green Bay. MacAllan and Ferguson were on the job in Canada. Wherever Lehtinen headed, we'd be ready.

"How?"

"The deputy director of the state police."

"Yes?" That would be one of Alex's bosses. "She knows about our plan?"

"Yes."

"And?"

"She has a sister."

"And?" Alex likes to relay news in the form of stories as beginning-to-end narratives, not with the important stuff first and the lesser details later, as a newspaper reporter would. This can be annoying at first, but the technique does enhance understanding of what's going on.

"Her sister's husband just died. Fifty-nine years old. Massive heart attack. He was an orthopedic surgeon."

"We have a body!" I said. Not a Mafioso, as we'd hoped, but we can't have everything.

"Yes, we have a body. At the time of death the deputy director told the sister about our plan, leaving out the important details, and she thought it would be a good way to honor her husband. 'He could make one more contribution to society. Just one of many.' That's what she said. We promised that afterward we'd return the body for a proper funeral. But she wants it donated for medical study. She's a doctor, too, and many doctors do that."

"I'll be damned. There's no problem with security, is there?"

"Don't think so. The deputy director swears the sister'll keep our secret. It's kind of a medical confidence, after all."

"Okay. Let's get moving."

"Roger."

During the next few hours in Lansing Alex arranged for "Dr. William Martin," as he dubbed the doctor's body in honor of the mythical Royal Marine of 1943, to be prepared for his last operation. We prevailed upon Dr. Gibbons to perform no autopsy. We feared Lehtinen might spot the huge Y-shaped stitches of a postmortem examination if he disrobed the body, as we thought he might, and suspect a Trojan horse.

Dr. Gibbons and Alex dressed the surgeon in his own clothes, a dark gray suit of expensive cut the deputy director had obtained from his widow. Into the jacket pocket Alex stuffed a wallet with false identification, credit cards, and business cards. In a masterstroke of irony Alex had had the crime lab inscribe "William Martin, M.D." on the driver's license, and do the same with the other cards. The business cards were profession-ally printed on expensive card stock with engraved lettering, not run off cheaply on a computer. "Dr. Martin," after all, was a man of parts. "PHYSICIAN AND SURGEON," the cards said, bearing the phone number of a Detroit-based state policewoman in the know. If Lehtinen should call the number to check out the owner, the cop would respond as if she were the physician's receptionist. That would also give us some idea how careful Lehtinen was being.

There was more, a lot more. To cement the body's credibility, we needed to give it a personality as well as an identity. Alex provided a wallet-sized portrait of Lieutenant Sue Hemb that she herself had signed "To Bill with tons of love, Audrey" and dated in ink. The surgeon's widow added his university and wedding rings. On his wrist was placed a knockoff Omega watch Alex had liberated from the Detroit Police Department's evidence locker. He had had the back engraved "WILLIAM MARTIN, M.D." and "WAYNE STATE UNIVERSITY SCHOOL OF MEDICINE, 1978."

Gilding the lily, I thought, but Alex argued that the surgeon's new identity had to be thorough. We agreed that Lehtinen would be unlikely to spend much time trying to find out if "Dr. Mar-tin" indeed had attended Wayne State, especially if the name on the obvious objects like the ID, cards, and watch were the same. The presence of the cash, credit cards, and jewelry, he said, would also persuade Lehtinen that the motive for homicide was not robbery, but something much more sinister, something that warranted the expensive and inconvenient hiring of a third party to dispose of the corpse: a professional hit. A smart assassin wouldn't want to be caught with the possessions of his victim.

I had asked who the dead surgeon really was. "His widow wanted that on need-to-know," Alex had said. "If you really think you should have his actual identity, I'll tell you." I declined, out of a vague feeling that I should respect the widow's wishes. That knowledge was not important to the case. Her husband's body was.

We needed to provide a plausible, and preferably visible, cause of death. That needed to be a homicide. Otherwise, why would our purported killer, a mobster, want to get rid of the body? We batted that around for a while, but settled on the most obvious solution after a short but heartfelt debate over whether it was ethical or necessary. We decided that it was necessary.

We debated the method. In some jurisdictions a forensic detective might suggest firing a large-caliber bullet into the dead surgeon's skull, punching a neat entry wound into the forehead and a jagged exit hole in the back of the head. In such a case the medical examiner could aspirate some of the body's own blood to dab around the entry wound and pour onto the collar and jacket of the coat to simulate bleeding, for a postmortem gunshot wound would not bleed by itself. To add verisimilitude, some of the splatter of brain tissue from the shot could be scattered onto the back of the surgeon's suit jacket. But Dr. Gibbons worried that such an act in service of police deception not only might violate medical ethics but also Michigan laws about desecration of human bodies.

"Why not create a fake bullet wound?" Alex said in reply. "A small one would do. After all, hit men almost always use .22

pistols to do their thing. That wouldn't leave a mess. The bullet just bounces around inside the skull."

And so Dr. Gibbons created a .22-caliber entry wound with a suitably sized drill, a little injected collagen to raise the edges of the skin around the hole, and a trickle of the corpse's blood under it. Finally, he dusted the wound with graphite scraped from a pencil to simulate powder residue.

One more task faced the detective and the medical examiner. There needed to be a reliable way to trace the movements of the corpse after it was dropped off and picked up. That was easy. Into the rectum they inserted a GPS transmitter similar to the one that had been on Lehtinen's car, but with a more powerful battery, one that would last three weeks. For that time we'd be able to follow the body on its travels, wherever they might lead. For good measure Dr. Gibbons pushed the device high enough into the descending colon so that if Lehtinen decided to do a quick rectal exam he wouldn't discover it.

Finally, "Dr. Martin" was returned to his drawer in the morgue's refrigerated file cabinet of corpses to await his mission.

One more trick remained up Alex's sleeve. He phoned a cop-friendly gossip columnist at the *Detroit Free Press* and planted a blind item saying that a well-known but unnamed orthopedic surgeon, a favorite with the upper crust, had been missing for forty-eight hours and his family was frantically trying to locate him. It was a long shot that Lehtinen even read the paper, let alone might spot the item, but every little bit helps.

Everything was ready. Now it was up to us.

CHAPTER TWENTY-TWO

As Alex told the story, slathering it with great relish and drama, the next morning—a Friday—he drove into Bloomfield Hills to the sprawling ranch house of Vincent (Vinnie the Fish) Fincantieri, a mob enforcer feared all over Detroit, and pushed his way into the kitchen where the thug was breakfasting with his wife. Mrs. Fincantieri, who had no idea of the hold the detective had over her spouse, snatched up a bread knife and prepared to defend home, hearth, and husband.

"Settle down, Stella," Fincantieri said. "It's all right." He shooed her out of the kitchen and glared at Alex without inviting him to sit. Alex pulled up a chair and sat in it, gazing calmly and knee to knee at the mobster. Fincantieri was short, balding, and broad, like a sawed-off sumo wrestler, and glared back at the detective through heavy-lidded eyes, barely containing his explosive violence.

"I have a job for you to do," Alex said.

"And if I don't do it?"

"Well, Specs and Jackie the Bathrobe could get an interesting message from me."

Peter (Specs) Toccata and Jack (Jackie the Bathrobe) Gionfriddo are top heavies in the Detroit mob. Like all their kind, they are ruthless toward turncoats. Fincantieri had helped Alex with several mob cases during the detective's early police career in lower Michigan, agreeing to provide sensitive information that would help eliminate small-time but annoying rivals on the

196

street in return for the police overlooking his comparatively innocent peccadilloes. The bosses would consider that an act of betrayal if they ever found out about it.

"That's fucking illegal, and you know it," Fincantieri snarled. He had done time and had been a diligent student at jailhouse lawyering.

"You are quite right," Alex said. "I don't propose to rat you out."

"Then what?"

"This case involves the rape and abduction of several little girls," Alex said.

"Son of a bitch," Fincantieri said with feeling. If there's anything Mafiosi hate, it's crimes against children. To a mob enforcer, knocking off someone who won't pay his vigorish is just business, but targeting a kidnapper and murderer of a little girl would be doing the Lord's work.

That was Alex's ace in the hole.

"If I do it," Fincantieri said, "will we be square?"

"Not necessarily," Alex said. "We may never be square. It all depends on what you do in the future—and how well you do it."

"Bastard," Fincantieri said.

"I am that," Alex said. "Yes or no?"

"Yes."

"I'll put in a good word for you with Specs and Jackie."

"Please don't do that," Fincantieri said. "Now what is it you want me to do?"

"We know there's a guy who gets rid of bodies for the Mob," Alex said. "We want you to contact the guy and set it up to get rid of one for us."

Fincantieri betrayed no surprise.

"Us being?" he said.

"Us is enough."

"Who's the stiff?"

"You don't need to know that."

Fincantieri nodded.

"When?"

"Today. Now."

"*Now?* You're asking a lot."

"Yep," Alex said. "But we don't have a lot of time."

"Let me make a few calls."

"You mean send a few emails."

"Yeah, that's right," Fincantieri said slowly. He now knew Alex somehow had unearthed one of the mob's most closely kept secrets.

"Where's your computer?"

"I can't do that from my own house on my own computer!" Fincantieri protested. Now Alex was certain the mobster not only knew how the thing was done but had done it himself.

Separately the two drove to a Starbucks in neighboring Troy. Neither Fincantieri nor Alex was concerned the cop might be noticed. He was not a familiar face in Detroit and had not been for more than twenty years.

They took a table in the back of the store and Fincantieri was soon online on a laptop. It had been stolen, he said. The mobsters had a stock of purloined laptops that they used like burn phones, to be discarded after using a brief time.

"What do you want me to say?" he said.

"You know perfectly well," Alex said. "You've done this before."

"All right."

"package ready for shipment," Fincantieri typed without capitals or punctuation. "send instructions." The mobster hit "Send," and Alex made a note of the email address. It was a nonsensical amalgam of letters and numbers, as was Fincantieri's.

"How long before he replies?" Alex said.

"Sometimes a few minutes, sometimes a few hours. Depends on where he is and what he's doing."

"I've got all day," Alex said.

"I don't."

"Too bad for you."

Luckily for both Fincantieri and Alex, a reply arrived not ten minutes later.

"wrap package with dry ice in reinforced plastic tarp and tie with duct tape. in package enclose fee in separate sealed plastic bag."

"received," Fincantieri responded.

"We'll have to wait for the rest," the mobster said. "He'll send us further orders from another location."

Fifteen minutes later another message arrived: "shipping fee $40."

"That's forty grand," Fincantieri said. "Next message will tell us where to take the package."

This time twenty minutes passed before the final instructions arrived. They were in code, a series of odd letters and numbers that seemingly made no sense. Fincantieri pulled out a little notebook.

"He'll use the same code he did last three jobs," the mobster said.

"Last three jobs?" Alex said.

"Never mind." Fincantieri laboriously compared the letters and numbers in the notebook. They seemed to be a simple substitution code, easy for a cryptanalyst to break. But the apparent randomness of the characters, Alex saw, could be easily mistaken for a simple bank transfer.

"Here it is," the mobster said.

"deliver to warehouse E by piers bay city and leave on loading dock 1 a.m. tonight. do not hang around."

"Yes, that's how it's done," Fincantieri said. "Bay City is a long way away, though. I don't remember the handoff site the other times being that far from here."

"Not a problem," Alex said. "Stay put."

Quickly Alex took the mobster's laptop and forwarded the emails and addresses to forensics in Lansing, asking the resident hackers to trace their source. The answer came back in three minutes. The emails had been sent from three locations in Green Bay, Wisconsin. One was a public computer at a senior center. The other two were public computers at branch libraries in the same city.

Alex called Lee Hamilton on his cell and told him what had happened, asking the Wisconsin detective to show around the libraries and senior center a photograph of Lehtinen obtained from the driver's license office, but to wait a few days until events had run their course. Hamilton agreed, but pointed out reasonably that memories wouldn't be so fresh if the detective waited.

"We'll take that chance," Alex said.

"Now am I finished?" Fincantieri demanded.

"No," Alex said. "We've just begun. You're going to deliver the package. And one of my colleagues is going to ride shotgun."

"Bastard."

"You already said that. Now email a reply."

Fincantieri coded the message and sent it. "ok. will be there at 1."

Ten minutes later Alex called me at my office. "Got the goombah all set to go," he said. "The handoff of 'Dr. Martin' is set for one o'clock tonight at an abandoned warehouse in Bay City. A guy from ESU is going along to make sure it's done."

ESU, or the Emergency Services Unit, is what the Michigan State Police calls its SWAT team, or special weapons and tactics squad. I knew Alex would have preferred to go along himself, but his face was known to Lehtinen and, for all we knew, to others unknown who might be involved in the case.

"What else?"

"The instructions were emailed from three public computers in Green Bay."

"Aha," I said. I could almost hear the ominous snick of a prison lock.

"Aha indeed."

"We're getting closer," I said.

"Think Lehtinen will drive over from Green Bay for the pickup?"

"If he does, it's just over seven hours to Bay City up across the U.P. and downstate via the Mackinac Bridge," I said. "Around the bottom of Lake Michigan, it's eight hours. It's eleven a.m. now. If he leaves Green Bay by noon or so, he could do it. But he'll be awfully tired by the time he gets to Bay City."

"Not likely he'll fly from Milwaukee to Detroit," Alex said. "That would leave a paper trail. Too dangerous."

"I'm betting he's got an accomplice who'll make the pickup. A mule."

"I think you're right. We might be able to tell for sure by what time Lehtinen leaves the office today. If it's anytime between now and, say, two p.m., he might be on his way to Bay City. But if he stays in the office until five this afternoon, we'll know he's not coming here. I'll call Lee Hamilton back and ask him to run a stakeout on Lehtinen."

"One thing," I said. "The instructions said to use dry ice. That suggests there might be a long time between the handoff of the corpse and its disposal. Dry ice will keep the corpse fresh in a loosely wrapped container for, what, two days? Three?"

"Depends on how much dry ice."

"I suggest you ask Dr. Gibbons to use just enough to keep

the decomposition down for no more than a day," I said. "If it takes Lehtinen longer than that to dump 'Dr. Martin,' the smell might cause him to rush it at the end. And that would be to our advantage."

"You are a talented fellow, Sheriff," Alex said. "You might even make a real cop someday."

All the rest of that day the hours ticked by painfully slowly. I sat in my office waiting for Alex's call. From time to time there was a little sheriff business to do, mostly sending a deputy out to serve a subpoena or pick up lunch from Merle's. I watched the phone. Gil watched me watching the phone. Sheila watched Gil watching me watch the phone. Only Chad busied himself productively, rummaging through the files of a couple of cold cases looking for new clues.

All our troops were on alert. Alex led the squad in Detroit. Lee Hamilton was on watch in Green Bay. He had obtained a warrant and was ready to clap a GPS transmitter on Lehtinen's car. The tribal police in Watersmeet were ready for Lehtinen if he came up U.S. 45. Everyone had GPS tracking apps on their iPhones, iPads, and laptops and would be able to track both Lehtinen and "Dr. Martin."

We had arranged that the tribals would not aim to stop Lehtinen, just report his whereabouts to headquarters in Porcupine City, where I was the operations chief in this case. They would follow Lehtinen at a comfortable distance, ready to provide armed backup if needed. Camilo had deputized a couple of retirees, Ojibwas experienced at night tracking, and would bring them along just in case everything went to hell and Lehtinen rabbited into the woods.

MacAllan and Ferguson were on station in Sault Ste. Marie, ready to follow the bug if Lehtinen crossed the bridge over the St. Marys River into Canada. They had arranged with Canadian customs and immigration to wave through the Yankee lawmen on production of their IDs rather than stop and question them. They had also tipped the Pigeon River customs station in case Lehtinen went that way, but we strongly doubted that he would take the long way around Lake Superior to Neys Provincial Park, the likeliest place in Canada where he might dump a corpse. I had a strong hunch he'd return to his old stamping grounds for this one.

One o'clock came and went, then two p.m., then three p.m., then four p.m., then five p.m. At 6:06 p.m. Eastern time—5:06 p.m. in Wisconsin—the phone finally rang. Gil, Sheila, Chad, and I all jumped. It was Lee Hamilton.

"Lehtinen's just left his office," he said.

"Did he tell Perlman he was taking a few days off?" I said.

"No. It's the weekend, you know. He's got two whole days to do his thing and get back to work Monday."

"Where's he going now?"

"Seems to be his house." Lehtinen lived in a small brick bungalow in Ashwaubenon, a Green Bay suburb. "I'll tag along."

"The bug?" I asked.

"Sneaked into the railroad parking lot and got it onto his car. Plenty of cover."

An hour passed.

"I'll bet Lehtinen is just having supper," I told Gil.

"Maybe he's not the Beast after all," the undersheriff said.

"That is possible. Maybe everything we think we know is an incredible coincidence."

"A coincidence created by a cageful of monkeys with smoke and mirrors," Chad said from his desk.

"What?" Gil said.

"What?" Sheila said.

"What?" Joe said.

"What?" I said.

Before Chad could unmix his metaphor, the phone rang. It was Alex.

"We're all ready here at the morgue. 'Dr. Martin' has been shrouded in a tarp and the forty thousand bucks sealed in a supermarket plastic bag inside. It's counterfeit currency, but very well done, hard to tell from the real thing. We borrowed it from the Secret Service. The whole package is wrapped around willy-nilly with duct tape. It looks like a very amateurish job, exactly what we were going for."

"Fincantieri?"

"Sitting in the garage with the ESU officer who's babysitting him." Alex did not name the officer. Tactical people prefer complete anonymity and their brothers-in-arms comply. "Sitting in his own Town Car, in fact. He's going to deliver the goods in it. He's not at all happy about that."

"Tough shit."

"Exactly what I told him. I asked how many bodies he'd transported in the Lincoln's trunk over the years."

"What'd he say?"

" 'Fuck you.' "

"Knowing you," I said, "I would have, too."

"Lee Hamilton calling on line two," Sheila said. It was eight p.m. Eastern time.

I keyed the conference call button so Alex could listen in.

"Lehtinen has just left his house. He's dressed in jeans and a dark brown windbreaker. Looks like he's wearing heavy leather boots. He's carrying a large canvas grip. He's backing out of his driveway now. Stay tuned."

We all sat watching the phone, Alex listening in, and turned on our computers. The bug on Lehtinen's car glowed with purpose.

"He's heading north on U.S. 41," Hamilton said after five

minutes had passed. That highway goes through the west side of Green Bay and meets U.S. 141 at Howard, a northern suburb. From there the combined four-lane highway called U.S. 41/141 proceeds twenty miles north to the small town of Abrams, where 141 splits off and heads due north, and 41 heads northeast along Lake Michigan to Escanaba and further points.

"If he's coming directly here to Porcupine County," I said, "he'll take 141. If he's heading for St. Ignace, he'll take 41." St. Ignace lies just north of the bridge over the Straits of Mackinac separating the Upper Peninsula from lower Michigan. If Lehtinen chose 41, I thought it likely he would meet the package somewhere along U.S. 2 between Escanaba and St. Ignace. If he chose 141, he'd be heading for Iron River, then west on 2 to Watersmeet and ultimately Rockville. In either case, I thought, it wouldn't matter to us. The traveling bugs would reveal all.

We all hung up.

Twenty minutes later Hamilton called back. "He just took 41 to Escanaba. Am following." Michigan State Police already had been tipped that a Wisconsin trooper would be working in the state on a job involving their agency.

The driving time from Green Bay to St. Ignace is four and a half hours. If Lehtinen drove steadily, he'd arrive at St. Ignace at twelve-thirty a.m.

From Bay City in lower Michigan the drive to St. Ignace takes two and three-quarters hours. If the mule picked up Dr. Martin at precisely one a.m. and headed due north, he'd reach St. Ignace at three forty-five a.m. But I doubted that a meeting would happen at that hour. The mule would most likely wait one, maybe two or even three hours before moving in to pick up the package and driving away. At least he would if he were me. I believed in being careful and thorough.

"Sheila, would you call Merle's for an urn of coffee and some sandwiches?" I asked. "It's going to be a long night."

"Done."

"Thanks," I said. "It's getting late. Better go home and we'll see you tomorrow."

Sheila stiffened. "I'm staying," she said. "You might need me for some reason or other."

CHAPTER TWENTY-THREE

"The package is on the way," Alex said when he called at ten p.m. I quickly turned on my iPhone and watched as the geolocation app warmed up. Slowly the bug moved across the Google Maps screen. It had just left the loading dock of the Detroit city morgue on East Warren Avenue. I watched as it turned left, went one block, then turned right and onto Interstate 75 and headed directly for Bay City, one hundred and fifteen miles north.

"It'll take only about an hour and forty-five minutes to make that drive," I said. "They'll arrive before midnight. What are you gonna have them do, just hang around until one a.m.?"

"Murphy's Law," said Alex. "Something might happen, a flat tire maybe. Better to be early than late. They can park outside the warehouse district for a while and arrive at that loading dock right on the dot."

"You like to get to airports two hours before your flight leaves, don't you?" I said. "What a waste of time."

"I've never missed a plane in my life."

"You need time therapy, Alex, you do."

I turned off the iPhone. Why torture myself mile by mile, hoping nothing would go wrong? Alex would call if anything important happened. He was tailing Fincantieri's car a mile behind and well out of sight. He was in constant cell phone contact with the tactical officer in the right front seat. What could go wrong?

At 11:15 p.m. Lee Hamilton called. "Lehtinen's still moving east on U.S. 2," he said. "Just passed Manistique."

"He'll be at St. Ignace in an hour and a half," I said. "Right on schedule."

"We could set our watches by this guy," Hamilton said.

"You're not the first to make that observation," I said.

For an hour the Town Car proceeded on its stately way north on I-75. Fincantieri was nervous and kept trying to speed up, to cut down the travel time. Twice the nameless tac officer, his face shrouded in a hoodie and muffler, threatened to shoot the mobster if he did not lighten up on the accelerator and drive at a more sedate five miles an hour over the limit. There was no point in getting to Bay City any earlier than they had to. It would just mean a longer wait at a curb well outside the warehouse area.

Past Ferndale, Troy, Auburn Hills, and Clarkston the Lincoln sped through the night. Just outside Flint, less than an hour from Bay City, a chopped Chevy sedan veered out of its lane and sideswiped the Town Car, banging a nasty ding into its left front bumper. Fincantieri cursed at the impact and tapped his brakes. So did the driver of the hot rod. The tac officer turned and peered behind. An unmarked state police cruiser had been following the Chevy, waiting to pounce if its driver put the pedal to the metal. The trooper inside had seen the sideswipe and immediately hit siren and flashers.

The three vehicles pulled off the road nose to tail, like a trio of circus elephants.

"Shut up and stay here," the tac officer told Fincantieri. "I'll be back in a minute." The officer got out of the car and met the advancing trooper halfway. Before the trooper could unclip his holster, the tac officer had his shield and ID out in front of him.

"On the job?" the trooper said.

"Yes. Sensitive operation going down."

"Want me to look the other way?"

"No. Do your job. Somebody might be watching."

"Okay."

The tac officer returned to the Lincoln while the trooper went to the front window of the Chevy and began the "License and registration, please, sir" routine.

After a moment the trooper said, "Please remain in your seat, sir," walked back to the Lincoln, and whispered to the tac officer. "Driver's a Latino teenager. Barely speaks English. No license, no registration, no insurance. Alcohol on his breath."

"Shit," said the tac officer.

"Shit," said Fincantieri.

"What do you want me to do?" said the trooper.

"Standard procedure. But try to make it fast."

Standard police procedure when a driver has no license is to arrest him. Standard procedure when there is no registration is to assume that the vehicle might be stolen and impound it until things are straightened out. Standard procedure when there is evidence of alcohol use is to administer a Breathalyzer test on the spot and, if the driver refuses, make an arrest. Standard procedure when making an arrest while alone is to call in a backup vehicle so that two armed cops are on the scene. The trooper did as requested and followed the book.

The tac officer called Alex, who had stopped on the verge a quarter of a mile south, and told him what was going on.

"Shitassratfuck," Alex said. But he kept his head. "Let things play out. There's a lot of slop in the schedule."

In ten minutes a Flint Police Department squad car arrived and pulled up behind the state police cruiser. It took another twenty minutes for the police to follow standard procedure. Soon the driver, who had refused the Breathalyzer, was cuffed and in the Flint squad for a ride to the lockup in that city. All the paperwork had been done and a tow truck had been called to take the Chevy to the impound lot. The trooper walked to the Town Car to hand the driver his copies.

"You look familiar," he told Fincantieri, and checked the paperwork again. "What are you doing up here at this time of night, Vinnie the Fish?"

The tac officer grimaced, got out of the car, and beckoned the trooper to the side of the highway. "Stay quiet about this," he said. The tac officer was a lieutenant and the trooper well below him on the state police food chain. "Don't screw up my operation, you hear?"

"Yessir."

"Good night."

"Good night, sir."

"Fuck you both," Fincantieri whispered. The tac officer heard him but didn't respond.

It was almost midnight when the phone rang again. It was Alex. "We had a fenderbender and the other driver had no documentation of any kind. That took time to sort out, but the tac guy says he thinks it'll all be treated as routine and nobody outside the bubble will find out."

I looked at the clock above my desk. "You've got just one hour left," I said. "Can you make it?"

"It's about fifty-five minutes to the Bay City waterfront," Alex said. "If nothing goes wrong, they'll arrive right on the dot."

"Hope so." If the mobster was even five minutes late for the appointment, whoever was watching the loading dock might decide things were going south and pull out without taking the package. Normally, I thought, such a criminal enterprise would not hinge on such tiny niceties of time, but we were dealing with Howard Lehtinen, who dealt in nanoseconds, not sloppy minutes. Anybody who worked for him would be, too.

At precisely 12:57 in the morning the Town Car, its headlights off, rounded a corner and approached the abandoned warehouse near the docks on the Saginaw River, just upstream from the *USS Edson* museum ship, a destroyer from the Vietnam era. The bright lights of Bay City across the river barely illuminated the deserted warehouse block.

The tac officer, having marked the GPS location of the warehouse on his smartphone before the ferry operation began, knew exactly where it was, and directed Fincantieri toward it. There was just enough light to see the faded "D" above the big sliding door at the loading dock. Not a soul was visible.

Alex stopped his unmarked car six blocks away in front of a dark movie theater in downtown Bay City so that anyone watching the warehouse area would not see him, and waited as the city slept. He hoped no patrolling cop would blunder into the scene and destroy the operation. The Bay City police had not been tipped off to it. We wanted the need-to-know circle as small as possible.

The Town Car sat idling for two minutes as the seconds ticked away. At precisely one a.m. the tac officer opened his door and Fincantieri his. No light spilled out from the car. Its interior lights had been disconnected before the operation began.

The tac officer motioned, and Fincantieri popped the trunk. They reached inside and hoisted out the tarp-shrouded corpse. Its one hundred and sixty-five pounds of bulk was heavy even for two men but Alex and the medical examiner had twisted the edges of the tarpaulin and taped them into impromptu handles. With stifled grunts the two men counted to three, then swung the package atop the four-foot-high concrete loading dock. It landed with a soft plop.

"Let's get out of here," the tac officer whispered.

The two men got back into the Town Car and shut their doors as quietly as they could. The car slowly pulled away from the dock and retraced its route, headlights out. Three-quarters of a mile from the warehouse, the tac officer told Fincantieri to pull into a darkened filling station.

"Drive back to Bloomfield Hills," the officer said. "Go right to your house and go in and go to bed. Do not talk to anyone. Do not breathe a word about tonight to anyone."

Fincantieri said nothing, but nodded. The tac officer stepped out of the car and into the shadows of the gas pumps.

"Go," he said.

The Town Car pulled away. Fincantieri had the sense to accelerate slowly and quietly, not to lay noisy rubber in a show of defiance. Mafiosi may hate child killers, but they also hate helping the cops.

The tac officer called Alex on his cell. "Package delivered," he said. "I'll take up station."

It was a long shot, and a dangerous one, but we wanted to see who picked up the package, if we could, and try to make an identification. The officer padded quietly across the highway and back in the bushes along the dirt road to the warehouse district, staying out of sight and advancing from tree to tree. Once he had turned the corner and had Warehouse D within sight, he crouched behind a screen of birches, pulled out night-vision goggles, and settled down to wait. Before joining the state police he had been a Force Recon sniper with the marines in Afghanistan and had long ago learned the unearthly patience it took to sit motionless for hours until his target came into view.

Alex had had military experience, too, but not that kind. As the minutes ticked by and no word came from the tac officer, he grew antsy, as anybody would. He called me.

★ ★ ★ ★ ★

"It's done," Alex said on the phone. I had been dozing in the old oak swivel chair I had inherited from the previous sheriff. It was 1:07 a.m. Gil and Chad were sleeping in jail cells, but Sheila, bless her heart, sat at her desk knitting the night away.

"Tac officer in place?" I said.

"Yes. Doubt if anything happens for at least an hour." We figured whoever was picking up the package would want to be sure nobody was watching. We hoped he hadn't spotted the tac officer, but we didn't think he had. Force Recon veterans knew how to stay invisible.

"What's Plan B?" I asked, knowing the answer.

"There is no Plan B," Alex said. If this mission failed, we had agreed, we'd be back to Square One. If that happened, Lehtinen would probably realize he was being watched and might never return to his criminal habits. We'd then face the possibility that all we could do was arrest him and try to pump him for as much as we could before he lawyered up. We had circumstantial evidence, but nowhere near enough to go to trial.

"Hang in there," I said. Tension and lack of sleep had reduced me to banalities. The clock ticked on.

At precisely three a.m. a large shadow emerged from stage left into the tac officer's peripheral vision. It was a van with its headlights turned off. Enough moonlight glowed softly over the warehouse lot to show that it was a Ford of indeterminate vintage and color. The license plate was close enough to read through the night-vision goggles, and the tac officer snapped a photo of it with the built-in camera.

The night was soundless, too soundless for the officer to risk calling Alex with the license number. Instead, he tapped out a text message, barely able to see the screen of his smartphone, turned down to the absolute minimum brightness. He watched through the goggles as the van pulled up parallel to the loading dock, its rear aligned with the tarp-wrapped package. For two long minutes there was no movement, no noise except for an almost inaudible click of metal on metal as the engine cooled. Then the rear clamshell doors of the van were opened from inside.

Another long pause, then a lone figure emerged and stepped to the ground. He was clad in ninja black, as was the tac officer, and wore a nylon balaclava that exposed only his eyes and mouth.

The figure stood almost stock-still by the van doors listening and peering in all directions. After a long beat he reached up to the package and sliced it open, lifting out the plastic bag that contained the currency and peering inside it with a shrouded penlight. Apparently satisfied, he thrust the bag back into the shroud and retaped it shut. Then he dragged the package off the loading dock. It thumped softly on the ground.

Then he hoisted one end of the package into the van. As the tac officer watched through the goggles, the other end followed, accompanied by an audible grunt. The figure stopped again for a long minute. Finally, he stepped into the van and carefully closed the doors behind him. The tac officer saw no one else.

The engine started with a soft cough and the van slowly drove away, lights out, retracing its route from town. When the shadow had disappeared into the darkness, the tac officer stepped out of his hidden bivouac and called Alex. The whole series of events had taken less than five minutes.

At 3:10 a.m. the phone on my desk again startled me awake. "The package's been picked up and is on the move," Alex said. "It's heading north on I-75."

Quickly I turned on my iPhone. We were now certain that the glowing bug inside "Dr. Martin" was bound for the Mackinac

Bridge. The bug on Lehtinen's car had stopped just off the access road to the Straits State Park in St. Ignace, just east of the bridge approach on the north side of the Straits of Mackinac.

"They're going to meet at the park," I said. "Either they'll head north to the Soo and Canada or west, maybe to Rockville. Wouldn't be surprised if they stayed at the park most of the day."

"What for?" said Chad, who had been tossing sleeplessly in the cell and had returned to his desk.

"Making sure 'Dr. Martin' is who he's supposed to be," I said. "They'll also want to get some sleep before going on. They've been up all night."

"Like us," Gil said grumpily from the doorway to the cell block.

"Carry on," I said. "I'll let you know if anything important happens."

We all dozed at our desks as the night wore on. As first light peeked into the windows of the sheriff's department, Alex called again.

"Just as you thought. The mule's stopped at the Straits State Park."

I quickly glanced at the iPhone. The two bugs lay together almost as one.

Just then Joe Koski swept through the door, ready to begin his shift as dispatcher and corrections officer. Quickly I explained what was going on. "Somebody's got to watch these bugs and shout if one or both starts to move," I said. "Keep an eye on them yourself, and get Freddie Fitz to watch when you have to be away from the counter."

Freddie Fitzpatrick is a logger with a heart of gold but the worst judgment I have ever encountered in a working Yooper. He is always being hauled in for some stupid misdemeanor or other, usually involving alcohol or marijuana, and spends so much time in jail that we have dubbed Cell Seven "Freddie's House." When sober he is as trustworthy as the day is long, and we leave him alone outside in the yard to mow the lawn and wash the squad cars. Now and then he forgets he's an inmate and wanders off downtown in his bright orange jail jumpsuit. Everybody knows him and nobody minds. Sometimes a shopkeeper reminds Freddie where he's supposed to be and gives us a call that he's on the way back. We're not so trusting, however, that we don't give him a full patdown when he returns. The only contraband we ever seem to find on him is the occasional package of red licorice, for which he has a genuine jones. Sheila makes him share.

Chapter Twenty-Four

We all slept fitfully until noon, when lunch arrived from Merle's. The two bugs had not moved. Freddie Fitz was unhappy that Joe would not tell him why he had to watch them on the dispatcher's computer monitor.

"My eyes hurt," Freddie said.

"You don't have to *stare* at the screen," Joe said. "Once in a while you could look at the ceiling, across the room, at the sheriff, or me. You could look at Sheila."

"Don't you dare," she said calmly. "That is a privilege reserved for my husband."

We all stifled grins. Sheila is not married and has not been for twenty years, ever since she threw the bum out as an incorrigible philanderer.

I called Alex. "What's doing?" I said.

"I'm on a bluff overlooking the park," he said, "and I've got a clear view of the two vehicles through binoculars. They're parked out of sight of the road into the campgrounds. They haven't moved since last night. From time to time Lehtinen and the other guy get out of the van for a pee but they always get back in."

"The other guy?"

"We don't know who he is," Alex said, "but his skin is as brown as yours and his hair is black. Seems to be a big fellow."

"Latino?"

"Most likely."

"What about the van?"

"A dark gray '96 Chevy, probably stolen. Ohio plates, registered to a plumber in Cleveland who's aboard a cruise ship on the way to Hawaii as we speak. Yeah, a plumber. Those guys make good money. We're trying to reach him on satellite phone but the ship's crew is having a hard time finding him. That's a huge ship. Five thousand passengers."

"Any action at the park?" I asked.

"Some. About an hour ago the big guy came out with a tight bundle that looked like the plastic tarp we wrapped 'Dr. Martin' in. It was tied in duct tape. He dumped it in a covered trash barrel at a nearby empty campsite. The garbage people who pick up that stuff wouldn't give it a second look."

"I think that means they not only went over the body carefully but also wrapped it in newspaper or gunny sacks or something equally biodegradable, and tied it with either sisal or clothesline. A plastic tarp wouldn't deteriorate over the years."

"Yeah," Alex said. "They've probably caught up on their sleep, too. We saw the big guy conked out in the back seat of Lehtinen's Escape."

"Lehtinen?"

"We think he slept in the van."

"With 'Dr. Martin'?"

"Yup. Hard guy."

"Where's Hamilton?"

"Right here," said the Wisconsin trooper.

"How do you like the U.P.?" I asked.

"It's all right, but Alex needs a shower."

The Michigan trooper chuckled. "The sun's getting high," he said. "It's almost eighty degrees in the shade out here. It's got to be boiling inside that dark gray van. I bet it smells to high heaven in there. The dry ice has to be evaporated by now."

While warm days in April are rare but not unheard of,

Septembers in Upper Michigan often bring daytime temperatures in the high eighties, even nineties, although the nights are cool. At Rockville, I thought, we were going to have a reprise of that April day, complete with biting bugs.

I clicked open Mapquest on my computer. "If Lehtinen heads for Neys Provincial Park, that's six hours and eight minutes' driving time. Add forty-five minutes for supper and fifteen for coffee and gas, and that's a bit over seven hours. It's twelve-thirty now. Let's say Lehtinen wants to arrive late at night, perhaps midnight, to avoid attracting attention. If he wants to get to Neys at midnight, he'd leave St. Ignace at about five p.m."

"And if he heads for Rockville?" Alex said.

"That's five hours and eight minutes from St. Ignace. Add an hour for supper and gas, and that's a little over six hours. He'd leave St. Ignace at six p.m."

"That sounds about right," Alex said. "But he might leave earlier, or later. We don't know the exact time he'd want to arrive in either place."

"That's right," I said. "But once he leaves, we can tell pretty much what time he's likely to arrive."

"If he goes to Canada, will he have any trouble getting through the border?"

"No. MacAllan has tipped Customs and Immigration and they'll just wave him through. The OPP will tail him all the way. And we'll assist."

"So we have five hours or so to wait," Hamilton said. "Why don't we just grab them up now?"

"We could," Alex said, "but with the evidence we have so far, all we can charge them with is trespass, conspiracy, possession of a stolen vehicle, and illegal transportation of human remains. We've got only circumstantial evidence for the rest. If we see him in the act of dumping the body in a hopper car, we'll have a much better case. We'll be able to connect the dots."

This time I took up station on a cot in the empty cell next to Freddie's after telling him to stay quiet or he would lose trusty privileges for the rest of his sentence, and slept for six solid hours until Joe clanged his keys on the cell door. "The bug's moving!" he said.

"Which direction? North or west?"

"West on U.S. 2."

"He's heading for Rockville," I said.

The phone rang. "He's on the way to Rockville," Alex echoed. "They left Lehtinen's car in the state park and are using the van."

"What time is it?"

"Seven p.m. They ate at five p.m. out of a cooler Lehtinen brought."

"With that stink?"

"They used the picnic table of the adjacent campsite."

"If they already ate, they won't stop for long if at all. Probably they'll arrive at half past midnight."

"Or thereabouts," Alex said.

"Or thereabouts. But Lehtinen sticks to schedules the way you don't." For all his neediness about the clock, Alex is notoriously late for social events and always has an excuse nobody believes.

"I'll call the OPP and let them know," I said, and did, while Alex stayed on the other line.

"All right, Sheriff," MacAllan said from his cell. He and Ferguson were at dinner on the Soo waterfront. "We'd love to come down and help but OPP headquarters isn't likely to approve expenses for the trip. It's not our case, after all. Good luck. Catch the bastard."

He hung up and I clicked Alex back on. "Time to muster the troops," I said.

Our plan was to pack the woods around the sidings at Rockville with deputies from three counties, half a dozen tribals from Watersmeet, as many troopers as we could get from Wakefield, and, most of all, the Emergency Services Unit. Nine of the tac troopers were on the way from Lansing in two state police helicopters and would arrive at Porcupine County Airport before nightfall. They and their equipment would be driven out to Rockville in a county transit bus and they'd be on the scene by ten-thirty p.m. The transit department would send a modest bill to the sheriff's department, and I knew the county commissioners would complain over the unauthorized expense. Screw 'em. But we hoped to have everyone emplaced and all vehicles hidden in the bushes an hour before midnight.

We had an inexact idea of where Lehtinen would go at Rockville. Four dirt roads, each approximately half a mile from another, cross the two sidings where the cars are stored. Two tracks lie at either end of the sidings and two roughly divide the middle. The plan was to split the troops more or less evenly at the roads, so that at least half a dozen officers covered every inch of the sidings as far as their eyes could see. Everyone carried night-vision goggles. Two tactical troopers would bivouac inside the tree line at each of the four points, ready for instant deployment. If shooting started, we hoped a tac trooper would lead the response, because they're the best trained for returning fire. They carry highly lethal M-16 military rifles equipped with night-vision sights.

As for me, I would carry not only my next to useless .357 but also the 12-gauge riot shotgun clipped to the dash in just about all police cars in the United States. Unlike the high-velocity M16s, the riot gun is considered a defensive weapon. Mine is a pump-action with an 18-inch barrel and carries eight buckshot shells in its magazine, each shell packing nine "double-ought" sized lead balls about a third of an inch in diameter. At thirty yards one 00 ball can cripple a human target and the full load of nine can almost blow it in two. The weapon is most suitable for quick aiming at close targets, and the conical scatter of shot increases the chances of hitting something. With the .357 I am not a lethal weapon. With the riot gun I am.

"Let's try to capture Lehtinen if we can," I had said during the conference call with the participating law enforcement agencies the day before in my role as the local incident commander. We expected him and his collaborator to arrive on the site, locate a suitable hopper car, hoist "Dr. Martin" to its roof, and push him through the hatch. Then they'd button up and return to the van, intending to drive away. The best action, we decided, would be to swarm them suddenly as they reached to open the van doors and take them down to the ground under our combined piled-on weight, like the entire Michigan State defensive line atop a running back.

"But we have to assume Lehtinen is armed and dangerous and possibly the other guy as well. We think he's killed two people already, maybe more. For your own safety, do what you have to do."

That always means "Shoot to kill."

As the evening wore on into night, Alex reported the van's progress across Upper Michigan at Engadine, Newberry, Munising, Marquette, Negaunee, L'Anse, and Baraga. From time to time I checked the bug on my iPhone, but not for long, because I wanted to conserve the battery. Shortly after eleven p.m. we were all bivouacked well out of sight in the trees and brush on both sides of the tracks, communicating with each other mostly by radio because cell phone coverage in this part of the Upper Peninsula is spotty. Each of us was dressed in dark clothes, the tactical squad in customary ninja black.

All of us had smartphones, but I'd instructed the troops to keep theirs on vibrate-only, at the lowest possible screen brightness, and in their pockets. They were to be used only to check Lehtinen's location if absolutely necessary. I'd keep everyone posted by radio. Otherwise we stayed silent.

The only sounds were the wind sighing through tall grass, a few bird calls, and from time to time the scrabbling of a small animal. Owls hooted. Once a sharp scream broke the silence as a predator captured its prey. From time to time each of us shifted on the ground and groaned softly as our muscles began to clench. I stretched out on my back but quickly sat back up as a beetle dove into my collar looking for something to bite. The tension grew as time stood still.

In the cloudless sky, starshine outlined the roofs and hatches of the long rows of hopper cars. The moon rose, its brilliant light overwhelming the stars. It was a full moon, the kind Allied airmen in World War II called a bomber's moon. The scene had become so bright that we'd need the night scopes only to see what was in shadow. I spotted a fox trotting down the line of cars. I hoped a cougar wouldn't decide to make an entrance. As the human population has dwindled, the big cats have returned to the Upper Peninsula, as have wolves and the occasional moose. The wilderness country around Rockville is perfect cover for cougars, and the presence of one is occasionally reported to the sheriff's department. We don't yet know if they've actually taken up residence or are only passing through. Soon, I was sure, they'd set down roots and raise their young, and when that happened we might have a large and tawny problem.

Midnight came and went. Suddenly, the sky to the north lightened even more, green tendrils of flame shooting high up from the horizon as radiation from the sun behind the earth collided with gas in the earth's atmosphere. The aurora borealis.

For long minutes we all watched the spectacular aerial display. It was one of the year's best.

Shortly before one a.m. our radios crackled softly. "This is Kolehmainen. The van's just left Greenland. Four miles from you." Quickly I checked my iPhone.

"Understood," I said. "We're ready."

My ball cap shrouded the iPhone's glow as the bug slowly traversed the Google Maps display. Southwestward it rolled on the blacktop of a county road just fifty yards away and paralleling the tracks, and I watched closely as it passed first one, then a second dirt road that crossed the rails, heading into the interior. At the third—just twenty yards from the spot behind the tree line where a tac trooper and I crouched—it turned south and bounced across the double tracks. Then I saw the van, its headlights off, slowly rolling westward down the narrow path between the rails and the overhanging forest. Toward us. Its engine chugged softly and I could barely hear the tires crunching gravel and branches. It must have a brand-new muffler, I thought, apropos of nothing.

The van stopped directly in front of me and I shrank back into the shadows. The tac trooper gently gripped my arm. "Steady, boss," he whispered. "Stay still."

He didn't have to tell me twice.

The van's rear doors slowly opened.

Lehtinen stepped out first, then his helper. They peered up and down the tracks, Lehtinen with a foot-long night-vision scope, the kind usually seen affixed to a rifle. I could see no weapon. He whispered something I couldn't hear, and then the two set off eastward down the line of cars. At the third car, just two up from the dirt road, I could hear Lehtinen hiss, "This one."

In the bright moonlight, unaided by the night-vision goggles, I could see "WISCONSIN CENTRAL" painted on the flat side of the hopper. Squinting, I saw "BLT 8-79" on its side. It had been built in August 1979, not that that made any difference to me. I had no idea if Lehtinen cared. But it was one we had inspected back in April. I wondered if Lehtinen knew that, but then realized he probably assumed we had looked into all the cars—as we had. Not that that made any difference to anybody.

The two men walked back to the van. They got in and closed the doors. The van backed sixty yards down the tracks until it stopped right at the car's ladder. Made sense to me. They wouldn't have to carry-drag "Dr. Martin" for much of a distance. But now the van blocked my view. I tapped the tac guy on the shoulder and motioned. He nodded and the two of us crept through the woods, the trooper confident in wilderness footing but I nervous that I would snap a twig or stumble over a small animal, causing it to shriek in protest. Slowly we closed the short distance until we reached a point ten yards away from the two men, right across from the hopper car and the van.

Just then Lehtinen emerged, followed by the mule with coiled ropes and two large double-ended pulleys in his hands. Block and tackle. With that apparatus they were going to lift the package to the roof of the car.

As Lehtinen stood by, peering in both directions every few seconds, the mule scrambled up the ladder to the roof with his equipment. At the first hatch, closest to the end, he wrapped two loops of rope around the structure jutting from the roof and snugged them tight. Then he clipped one pulley to the loops and fed another rope through it, then through the other pulley. That tackle would double his pulling power on the main rope, enabling him to lift a heavy weight with ease.

He waved to Lehtinen standing below, then descended the ladder. He had made no noise going up, and he made no noise coming down, not even a slight scrape of soles on the steel rungs.

The two men stood silently for two minutes, listening and looking, Lehtinen peering through the riflescope. The bright moonlight probably made them nervous. If they could see almost everything, then almost everything could see them, too.

Finally, Lehtinen tapped the other man on the arm and said, "It's time." I could hear his whisper distinctly, and doubled the grip on my shotgun until my knuckles hurt.

The confederate reached into the van and dragged out the package, letting it thump softly on the ground. I could see that it was wrapped with a soft heavy paper shroud of some kind. I could not see the string that bound the package, but it was thin enough to be either sisal or clothesline.

Even at a distance I could smell the miasma of decay through the aroma of a cheap and cloying industrial-strength air freshener, and almost gagged. Lehtinen and his accomplice must have emptied an entire spray can of the stuff on the corpse. It did no good. The place smelled like a combination of brothel and charnel house.

Swiftly the confederate attached the rope from the block and tackle with a carabiner clip and pulled the line taut. He nodded to Lehtinen. Together they put their backs into it, and the package first dragged a few feet across the ground until it was directly below the pulleys, then lifted upward. Slowly the package progressed at half the speed the two men pulled on the rope. When it reached the lip of the roof and stopped, the mule then scrambled silently up the ladder and dragged it onto and across the roof with a slight scraping sound as Lehtinen pulled from below. Clearly the pair had had practice. Their movements were swift, coordinated, and almost completely silent.

Finally, "Dr. Martin" lay before his intended fate, a yawning hatch at the near end of the car. Lehtinen ascended the ladder and crouched beside his helper and the package. For a full minute the two men sat quietly, taking slow deep inhalations, catching their breath.

Lehtinen moved forward to one side of the head end of the package, the confederate to the other side. Together they lifted the head eight inches or so to clear the top of the hatch, then with a coordinated heave slid the rest of the package through the opening. It landed at the bottom of the hopper with a muffled boom loud enough to be heard a hundred yards away.

"They've done it," I whispered into the radio as quietly as I could. "All hands into position." Eight men—two deputies, two troopers, and four from the tactical squad—moved silently through the woods toward the van, ready to rush the subjects and crush them to the ground. The tac guy with me and another trained their rifles at the roof, prepared to fire on command.

But the confederate still knelt at the hatch as Lehtinen stood and whispered. I could not hear what he said. But I saw clearly as Lehtinen fished an automatic pistol from his jacket and pointed it at the back of the mule's head.

"Drop it!" I bellowed automatically, quickly standing up and taking a step into view without thinking.

Lehtinen spun and fired. At me. The bullet slammed into a tree, the sharp report of the pistol echoing through the woods.

In the next hundredth of a second I raised the shotgun and without taking aim yanked the trigger. An enormous "BOOM!" and muzzle flash exploded into the night.

At least two double-ought pellets caught Lehtinen in the left thigh. He staggered for a moment and fired again, blindly.

Then a barrage of automatic fire from the tactical troopers' M-16s lifted Lehtinen, spun him around, shredded his jacket, and sent gouts of fabric and blood flying into the air. Swiftly he collapsed and tumbled off the roof, falling twelve feet and landing squarely on his head with a sickening crunch. I could hear his neck snap.

Hands in the air, Lehtinen's accomplice screamed in a

language I had never heard.

"Kneel down!" a tac trooper shouted. "Hands behind your head and lock your fingers!"

As four rifles trained on the man, another trooper climbed the ladder and swiftly patted him down. "Unarmed," the trooper called, one hand gripping the man's collar and the other pressing a pistol into his spine.

Both men slowly climbed down the ladder. The mule was pushed face down on the gravel ballast, a black-clad knee in the small of his back, and handcuffed. Then a trooper roughly yanked him to his feet and shove-marched him to the nearest squad car. He'd be driven to the Porcupine County jail, the nearest lockup, before being transferred to a more secure location.

"Shooter down," I said into the radio, this time in a normal voice. "Scene clear."

I stood staring down at what was left of Lehtinen, and wondered if we would ever be able to find out how many corpses he had ferried across the River Styx, and for whom. Dead men, as they say, tell no tales. I doubted that the mule would be able to add much to the story.

Slowly I became aware that Alex was standing next to me in the darkness, a flashlight in his hand.

"Jack Adamson just called," he said. "Washington has ordered us to stand down and leave Lehtinen alone. They're taking over the operation."

"A little late for that," I said.

CHAPTER TWENTY-FIVE

It was a beautiful and cloudless first of October, "CAVU," as pilots say—"Ceiling and Visibility Unlimited" in a sky of deep, deep blue. The fall colors still had a couple of weeks to go before their peak, but in the intense sunlight the trees still glowed with Technicolor-spectacular finery. The only downer of the day was that the FBI was tearing me a new one. Or trying to.

An ensemble of a neat blue suit, a pristine white shirt, a blood-red tie and a fat blond head stood quivering in fury before me as I gazed out the window and leaned back in my chair, feet on the desk. He was the quasi-Aryan who had glowered at the town meeting we had held in Rockville all those months ago.

"We were getting close to solving the murders of those young girls before you decided to screw off into the woods and kill our best witness!" the agent said.

I didn't believe that at all, but had been going along with the tirade, just to watch the clown wind up and then wind down. But now I was fed up.

"You were close to solving those murders?" I said, keeping my voice infuriatingly calm. "What evidence did you have for that?"

The agent chose not to answer directly, but to hide behind the universal weaseling of officialdom. "I can't answer that. That's sensitive information in an ongoing investigation."

"Ongoing?" I snapped. "It's all over, and you know it."

I took my feet off the desk, sat forward, and sighed.

"Look," I said gently. "I know how this must be for you in Washington. You've needed some new scalps in your belt, right?"

The agent blinked. Whether he was pinked by the truth or was simply surprised I'd use such a crude Native American metaphor, I don't know.

"Maybe you just went down the wrong rabbit hole and the rubes in the sticks somehow found the right one," I said. "Now your bosses are chewing your ass. It happens. But it's over now and you'll solve other cases. Bygones?" I offered my hand.

Doubt began to flicker in the agent's eyes. I definitely had struck home. For a fleeting moment I thought he was going to cave, to accept my olive branch. I was wrong. He had worn his protective carapace of arrogance for too long.

"You're going to prison," he spluttered. "We know all about you."

"I thought that crap went out with J. Edgar," I said, and swiftly stood up. At six-three I am tall for an Indian, and big enough so that the agent all but vanished into my shadow. I gave him the stink eye of menace and suppressed violence that I have practiced on bad guys for so many years that it's all but second nature. It works, too.

"You are full of shit from your muddy feet to your brown eyes," I said. "Now get out of my office and get out of my county."

"You haven't heard the last of this!" Fat Head all but shouted as he quickly turned on his heel and performed a well-practiced stage exit. As the outer door slammed, Joe gave him the finger and Sheila giggled.

Two days before, the FBI had performed its usual press-conference circus after the solving of a major case. Instead of a tiny courtroom in the County Building, the arena was the three-hundred-and-fifty-seat theater in the Porcupine Township Hall. Every seat was packed, if not by reporters and TV crews, then by townspeople and hangers-on from all over the Upper Peninsula. Judge Rantala later said he was surprised that the usual elderly trial buffs who lounged in his courtroom had gone across town to the Township Hall instead. In these parts, one finds one's entertainment where one can.

Jack Adamson, as the titular head of the investigation, presided. At one side of the stage, in folding chairs, sat the sheriffs of three counties—including me—as well as Alex and Camilo. A large movie screen had been pulled down in the front of the stage. A digital projector glowed ready for use from the ceiling of the auditorium.

Jack began by proclaiming the usual lofty "The Federal Bureau of Investigation is pleased to announce that the case that occupied our attention in Upper Michigan for the last five months has been closed. One suspect is now deceased, and another suspect is awaiting trial.

"The FBI is also pleased to acknowledge the valuable aid of the Michigan State Police, the Wisconsin State Police, the sheriff's department of Porcupine County, Gogebic County, Houghton County, and the tribal police of the Lac Vieux Desert Band of Lake Superior Chippewa. In addition, conservation officers from the Michigan Department of Natural Resources and detectives from the Ontario Provincial Police . . ." He continued down a laundry list of institutions and individuals that had anything to do with the case, leaving out only my wastebasket. He even had the grace to include Ginny. After all, she had ridden shotgun for me all through three states and one Canadian province.

As his audience's eyes slowly began to glaze over from the opening boilerplate, he said, "Now the FBI will take you step-by-step through the solving of the case." He said "FBI," not "I."

That wasn't necessarily unusual, but use of the first-person singular is not uncommon with leading agents in public presentations. They have egoes, too, as Fat Head had proven. Jack was up to something.

To my surprise, Jack told the audience in great detail almost day by day, week by week what had happened in the investigation, while illustrating on the screen each bullet point with a new photograph or diagram. He began with the discovery of the bones in Omaha and segued into the initial search at Rockville, even showing a video of our drone in action over the roofs of the hopper cars.

Jack told all about our Lake Superior Circle Tour following the bug on Lehtinen's car. With considerable relish he related the World War II story of "Major William Martin" and the present-day tale of deception involving "Dr. William Martin." By the time he got to the end with the demise of Howard Lehtinen atop the hopper car in Rockville, the entire audience was riveted to its seats, except for the reporters, scribbling furiously. Jack Haygood, the novelist and true-crime artisan, sat with his eyes closed and a beatific smile on his face, no doubt dreaming of a national bestseller.

Halfway through Adamson's narrative I realized that he was actually giving full credit to the actual law enforcement officers who did the work, not the FBI. He did not say the FBI had reached a dead-end in its investigation, but that conclusion was clear from the facts he laid out. Harold Wright seized upon it right away, and jumped to his feet as soon as the lights went up.

"You said the FBI solved the case," Harold said. "But it didn't. Our guys did." Harold has never been shy about interjecting his opinions into his newsgathering, and I chuckled quietly.

Without a pause Jack responded smoothly, "As was said at the beginning, the Federal Bureau of Investigation is pleased to acknowledge the valuable aid of . . . *your guys.*" I had to admire Jack. He was maintaining official institutional loyalty while admitting the facts. The FBI hadn't done jack shit. We all knew it. And now so did the public.

As the press conference broke up, the same lowlife cable news guy who'd offered cash for an on-air exclusive during the town meeting in Rockville materialized before me.

"Twenty grand," he said.

"No," I said.

"But the case is over! You got your man. What's the problem?"

"Talking to you just would make me feel dirty," I said.

In his spiel Jack had detailed the involvement of Lehtinen's mule, one Pedro Guerrero, who has the same name as the former Los Angeles Dodger with the prodigious bat. Jack had delicately skirted the twenty-four hours Guerrero spent in Porcupine County custody, letting his audience assume the FBI had squeezed him of every drop of intelligence. It had, but Guerrero had also given it all to us, in a gusher.

Shortly before noon after the showdown at Rockville, Joe Koski came into my office.

"Steve, Guerrero wants to talk," he said. "I told him he didn't have to talk to us, that the FBI wanted to hear him. I said he can have a lawyer present. He doesn't care about that. He wants to get something off his chest. All of it, I think."

"Why not?" I said. "The FBI's not likely to give us everything. Might as well listen to him."

I called Camilo Hernandez at the tribal police station in Watersmeet and told him Guerrero wanted to talk. Having grown up on the border in Texas, Camilo speaks Spanish and, having dealt with many undocumented Maya immigrants from southern Mexico and Guatemala, he also knows quite a bit of the Yucatec Maya language. Guerrero, we had learned, originally was from Guatemala and his first language was Maya. His Spanish was shaky and his English even shakier.

"Be there in an hour," Camilo said.

He was as good as his word and almost as soon as he arrived, he, Joe, Gil, Chad, and I stood in front of Guerrero's cell door. Sheila dragged a chair over, but Joe said, "Somebody has to be at the dispatcher's desk. Would you cover it?"

"Sure, if you tell me everything," she said.

"No problem," we all said.

After I had Mirandized Guerrero and he waived his rights, I said, "Okay, let's hear your story." I did not turn on the video camera or the recorder.

Pedro Guerrero was forty-one years old, he said, as Camilo translated his Maya-accented Spanglish. He said he knew that he worked for an evil man and had done evil things, but he did not have much choice.

"I looking at death penalty," he said.

There is no death penalty in Michigan, and I doubted that he would be charged with a capital crime anywhere. So far as we could figure out, he was guilty mostly of illegal disposal of human remains, conspiracy, and obstruction of justice, but we had nothing to link him to murder. We did not tell him that. That was the province of the FBI. It was not our job to ask questions. We just wanted to listen to what he had to say.

Guerrero had been born in a dirt-poor barrio just outside Antigua, the old capital of Guatemala, to Maya parents who had the surname Canul, as common as Smith is in America. They named him Huehuelotl, after the Mayan god of fire. His family lived in grinding poverty, as do so many Maya who stubbornly refuse to be assimilated into Spanish culture. He had had little schooling and at age fourteen had begun laboring as a stevedore on the docks of Puntarenas on the Pacific coast, barely earning enough to keep over his head the leaky tin roof he shared with four other Guatemalans. When he could, he begged dollars from cruise-ship tourists and salted them away in a ceramic urn he buried behind an outhouse. Finally, having heard about the land of plenty far to the north, he paid a man a few *quetzal* to take him up through Mexico and to the U.S. border along with a dozen other Maya.

On the long ride he decided that it might help if he took a Spanish name, and he picked the one on an old baseball card he found on the floor of the bus. And so Huehuelotl Canul became Pedro Guerrero.

With the others he squirted through a hole a Mexican coyote had found in the border fence at Piedras Negras and entered Texas at Eagle Pass. The group scattered, and Guerrero used some of his dwindling dockyard dollars to take a bus north, as far away from the prowling *La Migra* as he could get. Over the next two years he drifted through San Antonio, Dallas, Little Rock, St. Louis, and Indianapolis, picking up a little money at day labor, mostly with Mexican lawn services. It was a hard, isolated life because he could not speak Spanish well and had to communicate with his fellow workers largely by gestures. But he learned to drive and picked up enough English to get by. Finally, he ended up in Detroit.

He was living out of a packing box in a camp for the homeless and had just finished supper at a church rescue mission when a gringo in a new car across the street beckoned him over.

"You look like you're willing to work," the gringo said in bad Spanish. "If you are, I have a job for you, and if you do it well, there will be other jobs."

"What is the job?" Guerrero asked.

"Helping me carry things," the gringo said. "Once in a while."

"What things? How often?"

"It doesn't matter."

The decision was easy. Either you worked and ate, or you didn't.

"What do I call you?"

"*Jefe.*" Boss.

Drugs, Guerrero assumed. He was familiar with the drug trade in Guatemala—the whole country was a four-lane highway for contraband from Colombia to the States—and knew that people didn't talk about it, not if they wanted to live to see the next day.

The first job was simple and straightforward. The *jefe* provided him with an old van. With it Guerrero picked up a large and heavy bale-shaped package at a deserted street corner in Detroit, then drove it all night upstate over the Mackinac Bridge and then west to a railroad siding. There he met the *jefe,* and the two men dumped the package into a hopper car. Then the *jefe* gave Guerrero $1,000 in cash—more money than he ever imagined in his life—as well as a cheap cell phone and a number to memorize. Afterward, they dumped the van in a deserted pond deep in the woods. At the end of the day they arranged a place in Detroit to meet when Guerrero next would be needed. The *jefe* did not tell Guerrero where he lived, nor did the Guatemalan ask.

Twice more in the span of a year they did the same thing, always with a different van Guerrero assumed was stolen. The *jefe* himself provided all but the last one, for time was short. On a previous disposal he had left a wad of cash with a Detroit fence who specialized in hot vehicles, and sent Guerrero to him. No questions asked, and Guerrero drove away in a battered old Chevy van, the most common on the road and the least noticeable.

His last job, the one during which the police surprised them, was the fourth he had performed for the *jefe.* When the *jefe* cut the plastic shroud from the package, Guerrero saw for the first time what he had been carrying.

"Help me strip him," the *jefe* demanded. Nervously Guerrero complied. They removed the clothes, the *jefe* carefully examining the contents of the corpse's pockets and wallet before throwing them into a paper bag. Then the *jefe* inserted a finger into the anus and probed deeply. Guerrero said he could not watch that and wondered why it was done. Perhaps it was a cavity search for drugs. Finally, they wrapped the naked body in a shroud that Guerrero recognized from his lawn service work as biodegradable weed barrier paper, and tied the bundle with clothesline.

At Rockville they thrust the bundle into the hopper car, and Guerrero's old world came to an end in a shower of gunfire.

"Dios mio," he groaned at the end of his story. "Will God ever forgive me?"

It was striking how similar to—and yet how different from—Guerrero's story was to the portrait we had drawn of Diego Guzman, whose decaying body we had found with that of a child in the bottom of a hopper car at Rockville. Both had been semiliterate and destitute, isolated from society, and easily manipulated. That made me wonder how many other desperate men from south of the border Lehtinen had killed after inveigling them into becoming accessories to his sick enterprise. I also wondered if any of the packages Guerrero had carried were small ones, child-sized perhaps, but decided not to ask questions.

The FBI would do that. Jack Adamson was to arrive in the evening to pick up Guerrero and transport him by air to Detroit. Right at that moment he and the FBI agent-in-charge at Green Bay were executing a search warrant on Lehtinen's home in Ashwaubenon.

★ ★ ★ ★ ★

"Here's the custody paperwork for Guerrero," Jack said when shortly after eight p.m. he walked into the sheriff's department, having arrived from Green Bay in a FBI Learjet. "Got a few, Steve?"

"Sure."

"I'll tell you what we found in Green Bay this afternoon. Unofficially."

"I'd sure like to hear that," I said. "Have a seat."

When the agents picked the lock of Lehtinen's front door and entered his home, they were immediately struck by the pristine tidiness of the house. The windows were sparkling, the carpets freshly vacuumed, the pillows on the sofas placed just so, the kitchen spotless, a place for everything and everything in its place.

"It was as if a photographer had staged the place for *House and Garden* magazine," Jack said. "It didn't really look as if anyone actually lived there. No socks in the hamper, nothing in the wastebaskets. The magazines were lined up on the coffee table with micrometer precision."

Lehtinen's office, in a small den off the kitchen, told an astonishing story. It was full of model train cars in every size imaginable, from a tiny two-inch-long Z scale example to a three-foot custom job on a pedestal in the corner.

"Scores of them, Steve. Every last one a covered hopper car. No boxcars, no cabooses, no locomotives. Only covered hopper cars of all kinds. We even found a model of a car that must have been used in the Civil War. There were paintings and photographs of hopper cars on all four walls."

In a closet the agents found dozens of rolled railroad maps and charts standing neatly on edge in a long wooden rack. One was a fairly new surveyor's map of the Canadian Pacific Railway in Ontario that displayed every siding and yard on the route.

"Big black crosses were scrawled over some of them," Jack said. "The yards at Thunder Bay and the Soo, for instance. But the sidings west of Neys Provincial Park were circled in bold red ink."

And yes, Jack said, there was a route map of the Keweenaw & Brule River. Underneath the tracks at Rockville stood eleven neat check marks in blue ink.

"Victims?" I said.

"That's what we think, too," Jack said. "We're still looking at the maps of the other railroads. They cover the whole country, from the West Coast to the East."

"Let me know if you find anything on the CSX, specifically the old B&O."

In the desk, Jack said, a locked drawer held three revolvers of cheap generic manufacture, two .32 and one .38 caliber, with the serial numbers ground off, plus two boxes of commercial ammunition.

"We won't be able to trace the guns," Jack said, "but it'll be easy to find out who sold Lehtinen the cartridges. Not that it's going to make any difference now, but you know how forensics people are—they want all their questions answered even if the answers are unimportant."

"Did he have a computer?" I asked.

"Yep. On his laptop we found Excel spreadsheets showing a cash deposit account in a bank in the Bahamas. Six hundred thousand dollars. A pretty good sum, but each individual deposit was not really large enough to catch the immediate attention of Internet snooper software. If a deposit was in six figures or more, it would have been spotted as soon as the wire transfers had gone through. We can probably work backward and find out when the deposits were made."

"Can you also find where the deposits came from? If he were paid in cash, he'd have had to launder the money somewhere."

"Probably," Jack said. "Our hackers are pretty good at tracking down that kind of stuff."

"Hey, what was the name of the file folder where the spreadsheets were?" I said.

" 'Retirement.' "

"That figures."

And now, for the *piece de resistance*," Jack said.

"What's that?"

"A huge model train layout in the basement. HO scale. About ten feet by sixteen. Just tracks and trains over wooden benchwork, no scenery. But the layout must have taken years to build. The carpentry is exquisite, the wiring impeccable."

"The cars?" I knew the answer.

"Hoppers, hoppers, hoppers," Jack said. "And more hoppers. There are locomotives, of course, but every single freight car is a covered hopper. We counted two hundred and thirty-two of them. They had the logos of every railroad I could think of and some I never heard of.

"What's more, about sixty of them were arranged on two siding tracks next to each other. There were pencil markings on the wooden benchwork across the tracks that looked like roads. Just like Rockville."

"He planned everything very carefully," I said, "down to making models of his own crime scenes. But why?"

"We'll have to leave that to the shrinks," Jack said. "I just cannot imagine."

"There's something else I've been wondering about," I said.

"What's that?"

"Why they wrapped the body of 'Dr. Martin' in weed mulch paper rather than newspaper, as all the other bodies had been. That was a major departure from the MO."

"We thought about that, too, and asked Guerrero why," Jack said. "He said all the other packages he had helped Lehtinen with were done up with newspaper. When they took the tarp off Dr. Martin, he asked Lehtinen why they were using a big roll of mulch paper. Lehtinen just said in so many words that he wanted to make things easier for his loyal helper. Can you believe that? Making things easier just before putting a bullet into his brain?"

"I think he was just making things easier for himself, not for Guerrero," I said. "I don't think he gave a shit about him."

Five days later there was a memorial service in Detroit for "Dr. Martin," whose body had been shipped to an unnamed research center. We still had not heard a word from Washington. Either the FBI profilers were still trying to figure out what had gone through Howard Lehtinen's head or they just weren't sharing. But Lieutenant Sue Hemb had come up with a working hypothesis, one she thought might, with further evidence, become a persuasive theory of the case.

"I do think Howard Lehtinen was a full-fledged psychopath," she said on the speakerphone in my office as Alex and I listened. "A psychopath who also happened to have Asperger's. The one condition fed on the other. The obsession with detail so common to people with Asperger's helped him plan that whole scheme of acquiring, transporting, and disposing bodies.

"All those model hopper cars suggest he was an extreme collector, a hoarder even. That's another characteristic of the condition. People with Asperger's often collect things just to possess them, not to admire and enjoy them as other collectors do. Possession of objects can be a kind of power. That's why some forensic shrinks think that being a collector is often a marker for psychopaths as well."

"What about that trip around Lake Superior, when he looked over and inside all those hopper cars?" I asked.

"That could have been part of his collecting habit," Sue said.

"Maybe he liked to collect experiences as well as objects. He possessed them not as things, but as memories."

"That sounds logical," I said. "Could he also have dumped bodies because he was collecting memories?"

"I wouldn't say no," Sue said. "But I wouldn't necessarily say yes, either. Maybe he just wanted to make some money. Dumping bodies might have just been a sideline to his day job as an accountant. That Excel folder with the name 'Retirement' suggests that he thought of corpse disposal as part-time work, the salting-away of extra money in a nest egg, not the product of an insatiable compulsion that had to be fed constantly."

"What about Lehtinen being a member of a church?"

"At first I was puzzled by that. People with Asperger's usually aren't religious, partly because they have difficulty belonging socially, and partly because they have a hard time with faith-based thinking rather than the rigorous logic of reproducible science. But there are exceptions. Sometimes churchgoing is a way of reaching out. But it is also quite possible that Lehtinen's volunteering in his church was simply an act of deception, part of the manipulativeness of true psychopaths, to induce his neighbors to think of him as an ordinary human being. What we don't yet know—and may never know—is just what all these things meant and precisely how and why they were connected."

"There's one big difference in the MO," I said. "The earlier bodies were wrapped in newspaper. But 'Dr. Martin' was wrapped in black weed mulch paper. Why the difference?"

"I suspect Lehtinen was just modernizing his method as he went along. Psychopaths are perfectly capable of that."

"Yes. And he wrapped the packages to make them easier to carry up the cars, or drag them up with block and tackle. That way they wouldn't leave wet streaks on the sides of the cars."

"Correct."

"But the old lady in Connellsville, Pennsylvania, apparently went into the hopper naked," I said.

"If Lehtinen actually did that one, it could have been his first disposal," Sue said. "He could have done it alone when he was younger and stronger. And maybe putting her in unclad got him wet and dirty, so he decided to wrap the next bodies."

"One thing I've wondered about," I said, "was why Lehtinen went back to Rockville to dump that last body. True, six months had passed since we first discovered the remains in those hopper cars. Maybe he thought that was long enough for us to stop watching the place. If that's so, he was right. There just aren't enough of us cops to be everywhere all the time."

"Maybe Lehtinen felt relaxed about that for another reason," Sue said. "People with Asperger's often seek out familiar things and places, because they know them and are comfortable with them. It's habit, routine, even obsession. Think of Canada geese returning to the same breeding grounds every year. Those places are imprinted in their brains."

After a few moments I said, "There's still one mystery. Did Lehtinen rape and kill those little girls, or did he just transport their bodies? Did he do both?"

"If his DNA is the same as that in the semen found in the victim at Rockville, I think that'll close the case," Sue said.

"Even if the DNA is the same," I said, "what if Lehtinen was a necrophile, that he had sex with the bodies of victims other people had killed?"

"I've thought of that," Sue said, "and I'm sure FBI forensics has, too. But necrophilia is very, very rare statistically, and Lehtinen most likely had so much else going on in his disturbed mind that I doubt there was room for that practice. Besides, he grew up in the area where those little girls disappeared, and that gives him both knowledge and opportunity, which counts for a lot in assessing the truth about the commission of a crime."

"I guess we'll just have to wait for the FBI report," I said.

The waiting ended the very next day when Jack called from Detroit.

"Got two pieces of news," he said.

"Shoot."

"Washington finished the DNA test on Lehtinen," he said. "His DNA matches that of the semen found last April in the body of that little girl who was discovered with the deceased male at Rockville."

"So much for my theory," I said with feeling. "The killer of the little girl *was* the disposer of her body. One and the same. Not two separate people. How could I have been so wrong?"

"But you were half right," Jack said. "Chasing down how the bodies were dumped was the key to the case. That's how we broke it."

"We?" I said. Jack was a creature of habit, but he was honest.

"You, of course. You and your merry men—and women." Jack laughed.

"There's one thing, though," I said. "I should've known, back when we were driving around Lake Superior."

"What?" Jack said.

I reminded him about the school forty miles east of Nipigon, the one unusually close to the railroad tracks, where Lehtinen had stopped and Ginny and I had watched him as a train went by.

"Lehtinen wasn't photographing that train," I said. "He was photographing the children."

"He was scouting for another victim?" Jack said.

"I think so."

"That explains it," Jack all but shouted. "We found his camera."

"And?"

"Lehtinen wasn't very skilled with the thing. Many of the pictures of the hopper cars were soft and fuzzy. So was the train he photographed behind that school. But the kids in front of it were in sharp focus. We thought he'd just screwed up the shot. Maybe not. You think he was contemplating a snatch there sometime in the future?"

"I think it's very possible," I said. "Or maybe he was just collecting memories."

I told Jack what Sue Hemb had said about the psychology of possession.

"We'll probably never know the truth," I said. "Anyway, what about the other juvenile victims?"

"Washington is applying the MO to those—the details are almost identical, you know—and is declaring those cases solved."

"Sounds like the sensible thing to do," I said. We left unspoken the truth that few criminal cases ever are 100 percent solved. There are always facts that don't quite fit, dim possibilities that something else might have gone on that we may never know the truth about. But if justice ever is to be done, prosecutors and juries alike must subscribe to the rough wisdom of "If it walks like a duck and talks like a duck and looks like a duck, then it's a duck." That's essentially what "guilty beyond a reasonable doubt" means.

"Now what's the second piece of news?" I asked.

"I've been—I'm retired. As of next Friday."

"Congratulations," I said, not quite sure if congratulations or condolences were in order. Repeatedly Jack had stuck his neck out for us, and now his bosses were handing out payback.

"For a while I've had my eye on a little piece of property out Norwich Road," Jack said. Norwich Road runs from the western edge of Porcupine Township several miles through thick wilderness to a highway near Bruce Crossing. That rugged country is packed with hunting cabins and old mine diggings. "Got a two-bedroom cabin on it, nice woods, a stream running through. Put down an offer on it this morning."

"Well, well, well," I said. "When trout season starts next spring, give me a call."

"Sure will." For the first time in all the years I had known him, Jack sounded relaxed and contented. I suspected that under pressure he had agreed to retire early, but also had negotiated the terms to his considerable advantage. He was, after all, a trained lawyer as well as a law enforcement officer. And I suspected he knew plenty of dirt on his superiors, having been a Washington bigfoot for so long.

I hung up and dialed Tommy in East Lansing. He answered immediately.

"Steve!" he shouted.

"How're things going?"

"Okay, I guess. I like my classes but they're tough. The workload is huge. There's a lot of reading. The profs think we know a lot more than we actually do. But I think I've got it figured out."

Here was a kid well on the way to making the big adjustment from home to college. He'd discovered the yawning chasm in educational standards between small rural high schools, even the one in Houghton, and Michigan State University. He was having to learn daunting new study habits as well as fill all the gaps in his secondary education.

I chose that moment to say quickly, "I'm calling to tell you that you were right."

"Right about what?"

"The killer and the body-dumper."

"Huh?" Tommy said.

"As you thought, they're one and the same."

"Oh yes. I remember. I've been reading about the case online. Split personality, huh?"

"Not really. Something more complicated. A *lot* more complicated."

"How?" Tommy asked.

"I'm still not quite sure. I'm still processing the facts in my head."

"Did you talk to Lieutenant Hemb?"

"I did. She's working on a theory."

"Good." A brief pause, then "Gotta go. Dorm meeting in five. Say hi to Mom for me, will you? Give Hogan a hug."

"Oh, wait," I said. "How's Adela?"

"Good," he said. "We went to a rock concert last night."

"I'd like to meet her someday."

"You'd like her," Tommy said. "She's just great. She wants me to go to law school."

"I'm *sure* I'd like her," I said. "So would Ginny."

"Yep." And Tommy hung up.

I phoned Ginny.

"Could you call back?" she said. "I'm just out of the shower and dripping all over the rug." For a long moment I contemplated that happy image. She looks very good in a towel as well as out of one—not that I'd ever tell her that, of course.

"Coming home now," I said.

ABOUT THE AUTHOR

Henry Kisor is the author of four previous Steve Martinez mysteries, *Season's Revenge, A Venture into Murder, Cache of Corpses* and *Hang Fire*. He and his wife Debby spend half the year in Evanston, Illinois, and the other half in a log cabin on the shore of Lake Superior in Ontonagon County, Michigan, the prototype of Porcupine County. He is also the author of three nonfiction books, *What's That Pig Outdoors: A Memoir of Deafness, Zephyr: Tracking a Dream Across America,* and *Flight of the Gin Fizz: Midlife at 4,500 Feet.* He retired in 2006 after thirty-three years as an editor and critic for the old *Chicago Daily News* and the *Chicago Sun-Times.* In 1981 he was a nominated finalist for the Pulitzer Prize in criticism.